DEATH TWITCH

Carter Pugh

1

Cover design by Donato Pizzuti

Edited by Melisa Graham

Published by Carter Pugh Writes LLC

ISBN: 9798998807718

ISBN: 97989988552048

ISBN: 97989988552031

ISBN: 9798998807725

To Gram, who read Death Rattle seven times
and called me with questions and notes.
Love you, Gram!
(btw you might want to skip Chapter 41)

A *death twitch*, or *cadaveric spasm*, is a rare form of muscular stiffening that occurs at the moment of death and persists into the period of rigor mortis. This instantaneous rigor mainly involves the hands and sometimes other muscles used before the person's death, making them seem to move after death. The death twitch makes the dead appear to come back to life.

Perhaps death is not final after all.

TELERAN

PROLOGUE

Alison

"Ugh, come on!" I wailed, rattling the black cell bars, certain that someone nearby could help me out of this fucking dungeon.

That stupid wraith lady had tricked me. All because she wanted something from *Clarke.* The wounds that marred my immaculate face stung when I remembered how the wraith had gouged her talons into my chin.

I itched my arms; they felt like something was living underneath them. I didn't know how long I had been in this dank cell, but someone better get me out soon. I couldn't remember the last time I had been so bored and dirty.

Most people would've been scared if they were knocked unconscious and locked up in an underground dungeon, but not me. I knew it was just a big mistake. The only thing scary down here was the smell.

And seriously *fuck* Clarke. Why was everyone so obsessed with her? Sure, she was sweet and friendly, really beautiful, super helpful, and really fun, but she wasn't *me.* I had better clothes, a better apartment, a flawless face, and a flawless body. Had Daddy paid for most of it? Yes, but what did that matter?

Unfortunately, with the bad lighting and subpar accommodations, I feared some of the things I loved most about myself were fading.

My Botox would be good for a couple of months. My hair had been freshly dyed, but I'm sure it looked awful since my cell didn't have a shower. Not to mention, I'd been peeing in a rusty old bucket. *Gross.*

I was pretty sure blood was still caked in my hair from where that brute had pushed me into that rock. Ugh, what if it stained my hair? I shuddered at the thought—I would make a hideous redhead.

How could this have happened? I refused to accept it. I just needed to charm some sexy guard and then get out of here. Or speak to the warden. Clearly, someone had made a mistake and was about to be in big trouble.

The fumes in here had given me some weird dreams too. Like the other night when I had dreamed of Clarke—come to think of it, she was in a jail cell again. Maybe my plan had worked, and she was in jail for good this time, or maybe I was projecting. My therapist said I did that a lot. Anyways, I dreamed that Clarke had found me, and I tried to tell her where I was, and that dumb bitch woke up before I could. If that was real, like my other dreams of Teleran, then maybe she could save me. It's not like she knew I had set her up … *twice.* And there was no reason she needed to know. Sure, I had killed her roommate, but even if she found that out, I'm sure if I told her that Heather was Cody's ex, she'd understand why I jumped at the chance to end her. After all, she knew more than anyone how much I loved him.

And if I explained that I was supposed to reap all these fantastic benefits, she'd get it. It's not like she was friends with Heather anyway, and Clarke knew how much I loved Cody. He was my soulmate. She also knew I was always worried I was going to lose him somehow. I mean, it's why I was okay with framing Clarke in the first place.

Cody had flirted with her on more than one occasion. I mean, ew, right? But, like, she was beautiful or whatever, and he was hot, powerful, and successful, but he required so much attention. That's why I had planned on dazzling him with the allure of Teleran and all we could have here. Sure, we had plenty of money back home, but I could offer him power and a whole world here. Let's see Clarke or any other girl do that.

I just needed to get out of this damn dungeon so we could get on with it. Someone would be giving me what I was due, and I would ensure that.

It was hot and humid, and I was sweaty. My clothes were sticking to me, and I smelled. Something had to be seeping up from the steam on the floor; my skin felt atrocious.

Deep down, if Clarke knew I wasn't dead, she'd try to find me. She was like that. Constantly worrying about me, checking in. Bitch was a good friend; I had to give her that. But so was I. I had rescued her from her horrible jail cell, so the least she could do was repay the favor.

How long could it take them to realize that the dead body behind the salon wasn't me? I didn't do that great of a job of planting my DNA on her. If they did an autopsy or more extensive DNA testing, they'd find out it wasn't me, and then someone would be looking for me.

The problem was that no one knew Teleran existed, so, unfortunately, it would be impossible to find me. Damn it. I just had to keep hoping my dream was real. Clarke would find me, and everything would be okay.

Footsteps echoed off the walls of the cave prison I was in, and someone from the shadows shoved bread through the bars of my cell.

"Um, excuse me, I'm *sorry*, I don't eat carbs," I whined.

When no one answered me, I moved toward the bread that had fallen to the floor, right into a puddle of liquid that I would not even think about. My stomach grumbled—I was hungry, and if I didn't eat something, I might die in here, and that so wasn't an option. I had to get out of here and find out if that lady was telling the truth about Cody or not. He couldn't be dead. I would not accept that. They were just trying to scare me. Well, they could just keep trying. They had no idea who they were messing with, but they'd soon find out.

My stomach made an embarrassing sound, and I looked back down at the bread on the floor. I carefully picked at it, ensuring only to eat the parts that weren't touching the ground. Although stale and gross, it made my stomach feel less nauseous.

After eating a few bites, I went back to the farthest corner of my cell and leaned against the wall. I fell aslecp in seconds, letting exhaustion take over as I dreamed of Clarke rescuing me.

PART ONE

The Awakening

CHAPTER 1

Luck

No one had seen me or would suspect the quiet tech girl. I had cut the power to the entire police station, rendering the alarms temporarily inert and automatically opening all power locks.

Chaos erupted as the building went dark. Shouts and slamming doors echoed through the building as I scrambled into the shadows of the hallway. For the first time, I was thankful for the way Earth dulled my senses.

When I'd let them out the back door, Haywood had sped Clarke away from the police station. I hoped all was well.

We'd detected a strange and unidentifiable magical signature surrounding Clarke's home, which had expedited our plans. We needed to get Clarke to Teleran immediately. Further delays could be disastrous.

Haywood and I had argued about it for days. Finally, he'd agreed with me. His plan to gain Clarke's trust before disrupting everything she'd ever known was a luxury we could no longer afford. Perhaps she did trust him after all.

However, in the interrogation room, all I'd felt was fear as I attempted to convey that we wouldn't abandon her and that she could trust Haywood. I could tell she wanted to believe me, but fear still shone through her green eyes.

When the lights turned back on, I returned to my office to carry out my final orders from Haywood: Erase Clarke's file and all the evidence against her to make prosecution impossible should Clarke ever return to the human realm. I would make it appear like a computer glitch, and they'd be none the wiser.

The office was cold and empty, perfect for tying up loose ends. I moved the mouse back and forth to wake up the computer as I sat in the creaky wooden office chair, adjusted my decoy glasses, and began my task. I reached for my coffee cup and reluctantly took a sip, hoping it would still be drinkable. Remarkably, it was still warm, courtesy of the thermal mug craftsmanship, one of few human inventions that had impressed me in my time on Earth.

After double and triple checking that I'd erased all necessary files, my task was done. I stood from my desk and moved toward the door. I paused at the sound of boots pounding down the hallway. It seemed everyone in the station was scurrying around, trying to ascertain what had occurred during the power outage. By now, they'd have discovered Clarke's empty cell, but Haywood would have her far away, so for our purposes, whatever action the police took now didn't matter.

I opened the door to my office, exited, and headed toward evidence storage. One piece of physical evidence still tied Clarke to Heather's death.

Among the many skills I'd learned from the Guild of Shadows were how to hide in plain sight and how to pick locks, any locks. They taught me how to become unremarkable and completely forgettable, which came in handy. No one would notice I was missing or suspect that the red shoes caked in a dead girl's blood left with me. It was almost too easy.

I approached the caged room at the end of a long hallway. The evidence technician, Alexa, sat at her usual perch cataloguing bags of evidence and seized property, unbothered by the chaos in the rest of the building. Her domain, several floors below the main level, was quiet.

Her normal supervisor was noticeably absent, which worked well for me.

Alexa hardly looked up from the small TV on her desk before buzzing me in.

I walked through the heavy metal door of the storage room, which housed shelves full of various cataloged evidence. I knew exactly where to go to retrieve the bag I needed.

I exited just as quickly as I entered, muttering a goodbye and silent apology to Alexa as I briskly walked toward the elevator at the end of the hall. Hopefully, she wouldn't get into too much trouble for the missing evidence after I had wiped Clarke's case files from the computer.

After ascending to the main floor, the elevator doors opened to disarray. The energy had shifted from the chaos and confusion of finding Clarke's empty cell to … something else. I moved back into the shadows, bending them around my petite frame and carefully concealing the bag of shoes I was carrying. I made my way through the main floor to my office, when I overheard two officers speaking.

419…male…Caucasian….it's confirmed…Cody Mason…neck appear to be snapped…

The last I knew, Cody was in police custody. Had he escaped somehow when Clarke did? How long had it taken me to erase those computer files? I had never gotten used to the way time moved on Earth, so precise and linear. My magic was already so dim that I found it difficult to draw a full breath, and then Earth time tried to smother me. Time was more fluid in Teleran. Of course, there was an ordained time and place for certain pivotal moments, but we had more wiggle room with everyday tasks. Here, the rigidity was so stifling that I often wondered how the humans weren't crushed by its weight.

419? 419? I was trying to remember what that code meant when I felt a tug on the bond Haywood and I shared.

I was happily duty-bound to him, which was effective in situations like this where communication was difficult, especially now that I sensed he'd crossed through a portal into Teleran. I needed to hurry and leave the police station to see what was happening. His emotions and those of the humans around me were like a whirlwind, making it increasingly difficult to ascertain their sources.

I was already packed. I had not brought much from Teleran, just a few changes of clothes. I made my way back to my office to collect my things while avoiding anyone of note. After grabbing my duffle and shoving the shoes in, I followed the shadows to the back of the station and walked out into the alley.

A pale moon amplified the eeriness that filled the air. My hand shook, and I held it close to my body to calm myself down. Something was wrong; the atmosphere felt off.

It couldn't have been more than a couple hours since Haywood had gotten Clarke out, but something had happened. My mind was racing through scenario after scenario as I approached my car. I drove quickly to Clarke's condo, where the nearest door to Teleran lay hidden in the nearby park just outside the city.

I pulled up to the alley behind the condo to check and make sure everything was in order. I smelled Haywood, Clarke, and a scent I recognized but couldn't place. I also spied a black and blue duffle bag adorned with a snarling panther lying next to Clarke's ajar back door. I parked, turned the car off, and approached cautiously, palming the beretta at my hip. Without the full use of my magic, I had adapted to the humans' preferred means of protection. I hated to admit how much I loved its power and sleekness. I still preferred the dagger I had been gifted after I finished my training with the Guild, but there was no harm in adding a new weapon to my arsenal.

The alley was empty, and as I peered into the condo, I noticed all the lights were off and detected no signs of life inside. Something had happened here, but what? I picked up the duffle, which smelled like Clarke, and looped it over my shoulder. Haywood would've had Clarke pack some essentials, and if they were okay, she'd need whatever was inside. I darted out of the alleyway and hopped back into my car.

I put the car in gear and sped to my final destination. I pulled up and parked my car on the curb of the sidewalk, not bothering to turn it off, and approached the shrub-shaped doorway cloaked in the darkness of the hour.

The veil between our realms was thinner here allowing me to conserve my energy. I wouldn't need to open up a portal here, just say a phrase in our ancient tongue.

Passing through the threshold, I ventured inside, feeling the movement and warping of the portal as it stretched and yawned at my approach.

I recited the phrase, fates muciparous, and the gateway transformed.

Before I stepped through the portal to Teleran, I removed the glamour of my Earthly disguise. I had studied human stereotypes and chosen a disguise that humans would perceive as intelligent but otherwise unremarkable. Donning the short black hair and glasses had helped me get into character which I had to admit was fun. I shook out my medium-length, pale blonde hair as it fell around my shoulders, tossed my glasses, and stepped through the portal, a surge of power and relief filling me as I finally returned home.

CHAPTER 2

Clarke

I was a stranger in my own body. I was myself but not. I was awake but not. Death had welcomed me, beckoned me to her arms, and viciously spit me out. The rejection stung as the fire burned in my veins. Energy crackled through every cell in my body, and my vision turned white. I was nothing and everything.

I couldn't be contained in my body any longer. Warmth traveled up my arm to the center of me. I felt a tug, and I opened my eyes. My vision was so bright that, at first, I thought I was blind, but then I realized that I was truly seeing. Everything was glaringly vivid—the colors intense and overwhelming.

My ears itched ferociously, and I felt as if I was sinking in and out of water. One moment, the sounds in the room were so loud that I flinched in pain, and the next moment, complete silence.

I inhaled intense waves of various smells as they crested against my senses—lavender, cinnamon, sugar-sweet and warm, nutmeg, flowers, and cedar. Pain surged through my skull as I was overwhelmed with so much at once. The fire that I had felt was now a full-on raging inferno. I almost wished that bullet from Cody's gun had killed me because I was about to burn alive.

I felt weightless and detached from reality. Shouts erupted around me, and I became aware of the presence of Haywood and the jewel-eyed man from the warehouse. They were moving around me, their panic lancing through me. I could feel them, not just their presence, but their emotions, which rippled toward me like a tangible sound wave.

I was engulfed by feelings of agony, fear, bewilderment, and awe. Hands held me tightly as I was propped up against a hot chest; I whimpered because if there was anything I needed right now, it was not more heat. However, the scent of cinnamon and cedar calmed me slightly as Haywood's hands found my skin and tilted my head back.

What felt and tasted like tar hit my tongue and dripped down my throat, causing me to gag. Haywood gently whispered something that I couldn't hear around the roaring in my ears, but his deep brown eyes were so gentle, assuring me that whatever he had just given me would help. I mustered an ember of strength and swallowed. My eyes instantly grew heavy, and my breathing leveled out as my lashes fluttered. Darkness enveloped me, quieting the fury at last.

CHAPTER 3

Lachlan

A shock wave rippled through the room, knocking me backward as I collided with the armoire by the bed. My knees buckled while I struggled to remain upright. Clutching my chest, I felt the air being stolen from my lungs.

I jerked my gaze upward, meeting Haywood's just as his body was hurled against the French doors leading to the balcony. The horror reflected in his expression mirrored my own, indicating he had no idea what was happening either. I glanced at Clarke on the bed and gasped.

Her eyes were wide open, glowing white, but expressionless. The veins in her arms were alight and pulsing like something was trying to escape her body. The whole manor started to shake.

"Clarke? Clarke!" Haywood shouted as he regained his balance and struggled against the force emanating from her. He reached her and tried to shake her from her trance.

"What's going on?" I shouted back. Wind whipped wildly around the room as if a cyclone had taken up residence in Haywood's bedroom. Anything not secured flew through the air or crashed to the floor.

"I should've never brought her here!" he shouted. "She wasn't prepared; her body is reacting to the magic in Teleran."

"What do you mean, reacting?" I had seen fae magic awaken before but had never experienced anything like this. I struggled to regain my own balance and mustered the strength to return to Clarke's bedside. I was slowly regaining my power as the suffocating stench of Earth shucked off me.

"It's too much, too soon. She's too powerful. I did not anticipate this." Haywood said.

"Well, don't just stand there! Help her!" I commanded, desperation coating my words.

"Yes, maybe there is something. Here, come hold her steady."

"She's starting to levitate. Is this normal?" Our kind knew what to expect when awakening; we were prepared and trained for it from an early age. I remembered my training vividly. I had been taught control above all else and that I was to use my magic only when it was necessary, not merely out of desire. Our magic resembled energy: It could be depleted and required time to recharge. If we burned out, we risked permanent damage or, in rare cases, death.

Clearly, Clarke had not received any warning or preparation, and if we didn't calm her soon, her body might succumb to the shock of her awakening powers.

"No, nothing about this is normal. *She* isn't normal. Now, hold her down so I can get something that should help."

I obeyed him only to help her. My heart was beating so wildly that I was becoming dizzy. This was ridiculous. As my hands came to rest on her forearms, I felt a surge of power so strong that I bent slightly at the waist, the air had been knocked out of me. I was practically lying across her when Haywood returned with a mortar and pestle in his hands.

"I didn't say to suffocate her like a brute. What are you doing?" he questioned angrily, jealousy dripping from his words.

"Oh, you know, I just thought I would join the lady in bed. I thought this would be a good time to get to know her better." I gritted my teeth, my response laced with sarcasm and annoyance.

Haywood shot an icy glance my way before he returned to mixing some sort of rank concoction.

"What the fuck is that?" I asked, eyeing the brown liquid Haywood held.

"It'll act as a sedative until we can form a plan and figure out how we can help her."

"We?"

"Yes, unfortunately. You're here, and I need help. Even if I would rather chew glass than share a room with you, Clarke is in trouble. She comes first."

His words filled me with anger and relief. Anger that he seemed to have feelings for her, and relief that he was entrusting me to help her. I should not have felt either emotion, however. Caring for her was a problem. Stupid fucking mate thread.

Clarke let out a groan and moved against the restraint of my hands. Her movement evaporated any other thoughts.

"Prop her up. I'll try to get her to swallow this."

I did as he said. Again, only to help her, not the infuriating Estival.

"Seriously, is it okay for her to ingest that? Isn't it customary for adolescents to wear Vincula bracelets while awakening?" I questioned, turning my nose up at the stench. The oily, burnt amber substance smelled like day-old socks.

"Yes, it is customary, but as mine happen to be downstairs in my workshop, this will suffice for now. I would never do anything that would harm her," he said, sounding appalled and offended. "Besides, it's mostly valerian root and a special indica strain I've been cultivating. It'll make her sleep. The more we can get her to rest, the better her body will adjust to the unfamiliarity of the power."

I just nodded and shifted onto the bed behind Clarke, so she rested upright against my chest.

Haywood coerced the liquid down her throat, cradling her face and whispering something I couldn't hear. She relaxed at his touch, and he gazed at her like she was the fucking savior of Teleran. This guy was intense, and Clarke seemed to welcome his touch; I never hated him more than in that moment. We were natural enemies but something about Haywood had always sent my teeth on edge. He was always so pompous and proper—always looking down on my kind.

Once Clarke is resting, I thought, I have to figure out why he behaves so familiarly with her—wait, no, what? No, I didn't. That was the least of what I need to do.

The stupid mate thread was confusing my thoughts. I shouldn't care about her, her well-being, or her close connection with Haywood. But I couldn't control my feelings. She'd awoken something in me like a livewire. For the first time in my life, I felt unhinged and unpredictable.

This was nothing like the spell Osiria had cast for me to find Clarke on Earth, which had dissolved when we'd entered into Teleran. No, this was something seeping into every pore, every crack and sealing us together. I had to find a way to stop it.

Clarke's breathing took on a soft, rhythmic tune as her body weight leaned into my chest. Her head fell back with a sigh as it rested on my shoulder. Her dark lashes fanned against her full cheeks, highlighting the small peppering of freckles I could see only now that I was so close to her. My throat seized up with emotion I couldn't decipher, and I suddenly needed to be far away from her. We had an audience, for one thing, and I didn't want this feeling anyway. Hell, she wasn't even conscious. I'm sure if she were and understood anything about what was happening, she'd feel the same way. We were strangers, and it needed to stay that way.

I pushed her off me as I abruptly stood and exited the bedroom, stumbling into the washroom nearby. I slammed the door shut, needing a physical barrier between Clarke and me.

Ignoring the banging on the door and Haywood calling my name, I turned on the water and splashed my face, trying to remove the haziness that being so close to her had caused. I leaned against the black marble counter and peered into the baroque mirror. My hair was jutting out everywhere, and a slight shadow of stubble covered my jaw. My eyes had lost their luster, and my skin was pale.

"Get your shit together, idiot, we have a job to do." I chided the image in the mirror.

Amiburro! What had I said to Clarke at first? "It's you?" The words had tumbled past my lips without thinking of the implication. Luckily, Haywood had been too distracted with the situation to have noticed. If he'd sensed what she was to me, he'd said nothing. What would he do if and when he found out?

This was not happening. I couldn't have a mate. I didn't want a *fucking* mate. I thought I was having some pleasant sex dreams about a beautiful woman. These bonds were known to give glimpses of your future with your mate, and it seemed that our bond was giving me visions of her and me having sex.

I loved Osiria, my sovereign. Maybe I wasn't *in love* with her and had no reason to believe she had any romantic affection for me either, but I did love her.

Nevertheless, this would not do. I didn't have time for mates or women past the quick fuck here or there. I was perfectly happy in a pleasant exchange of pleasure between consenting adults.

My ambitions had landed me in the coveted position of Osiria's second and, very briefly, *regent*. I refused to lose everything I had worked hundreds of years to attain; there had to be a way this mate bond could be undone.

The easiest route would be to inform Clarke about the bond. If she rejected it, it would sever the connection. And if something were going on between her and Haywood, I could potentially use that as leverage.

No. I couldn't. I wouldn't do that. She didn't need to know; no one needed to know. There would be another way. Perhaps our elders knew of a way?

That was it. I would consult the Alternae about this when I questioned them about the scroll's meaning. I could deliver to Osiria the answers to the riddle on the scroll everyone was so concerned over and Clarke, and I would be rewarded for my efforts. Two birds. One stone.

A persistent thought crossed my mind again: *You can't seriously be thinking about turning your mate over to whatever fate Osiria has planned for her.*

Why should I care about what Osiria did to her? Mate or not, we were strangers, and I was duty-bound to the sovereign. The caring was just a symptom of the mate thread between myself and Clarke. There was a cure. I just had to find it.

The mystery surrounding her was inconvenient at best. What did this all mean? I needed to prepare her for the journey to Osiria—to Aurantia, the red palace, my home. Then she'd be out of my hands and out of my mind.

Had Osiria known what Clarke was to me? And why the blood magic? There was little that my sovereign didn't know. She had said Clarke was special but revealed little else.

Typically, like many times when she'd surprised me with some knowledge or research or new ability she'd learned, I took what she'd said at face value.

She always knew better, and I had nodded obediently as I had always done. Now, I was growing cautiously suspicious of her. If she'd known, what was her angle?

She often collected intelligence on the fae in Teleran to find their weakness. The purpose was to store this vulnerability until such time when and if she'd need to exploit it. Either to apply pressure to get what she wanted or to make them do something she needed done but didn't want to dirty her hands with. Primarily, this was used on fae from the court of Estival. I had always commended her wisdom in the past.

How could she question my loyalty after so many years, after everything I had sacrificed? She knew I didn't desire a mate. I recalled a rare night of debauchery and flowing alcohol where we'd laughed at the stupidity of it. We agreed: Neither of us wished to have anyone deter us from our ambitions. We fucked when the need called for it but left emotions at the door. That night, we'd found that ache filled with each other's bodies. Afterward, she'd said she would slit my throat if I ever spoke of it and assured me she had no desire to bed me again. The rejection momentarily stung, but she had been right; attachments were messy and obsolete.

CHAPTER 4

Haywood

"Lachlan!" I yelled through the closed bathroom door. After I had successfully administered the sleeping draft for Clarke, he'd unceremoniously thrown her off him and run out of the room like her mere touch burned him.

That potentially answered whether Clarke was Estival, as our two kinds were naturally repellant to one another. She was feasibly the strongest of our kind, rivaling my sovereign, Solana, in power. Maybe that was why Solana desired Clarke? She was in direct competition with Solana's position and would be a strong contender for the crown.

Worry had creased my brows as I'd inspected Clarke, ensuring Lachlan's carelessness had not injured her. Much to my relief, she had collapsed onto the pillows and not hit her head on the sturdy, cedar headboard. If he had harmed her with his haste, I would have broken down the door instead of banging on it like an idiot. Maybe I would still drown him while he was in there, as the mess would be easy to clean off the stone, and there was already a drain.

I pushed my murderous thoughts aside. Lachlan wasn't answering me, so I decided to take this time to check Clarke and her injuries over.

Granted, Lachlan had healed her gunshot wound, but I needed to make sure everything was progressing. Fear had gripped me when her power had nearly exploded all over my house. The intensity of her outburst could've brought the building down and us with it. I shuddered at the thought. I just had to keep her sedated until I could retrieve the Vincula bracelets.

She'd been in her awakening since her thirtieth birthday, but as I had often experienced on Earth, that realm significantly inhibited our abilities. It must have kept her in a manageable state.

And while her incarceration certainly hadn't been ideal, her exposure to so much iron at once in that human prison evidently slowed her awakening to a snail's pace. Our people were extremely allergic to iron. In small doses, it could calm, but in large doses, it could kill.

The snapback her senses experienced—previously dulled by both the earthly realm and iron, then suddenly exposed to both Teleran and healing magic—sent her awakening into hyperdrive. Add that to the growing list of complications, we were out of our depth.

I was convinced that my sovereign, Solana, knew more about Clarke than she'd let on. Or she didn't know at all, and that presented an even bigger problem. Her ignorance, coupled with Lachlan's presence, could mean Osiria knew more than we did. The Obscurus sovereign always did seem to have a leg up on us, and it grated on me to no end.

If Osiria moved to state her claim on Clarke, would I be powerful enough to stop her? It would be a grave offense to abduct Clarke from my manor home, but would Solana even act against Osiria? While powerful and brilliant, my sovereign could be complacent and detached. I couldn't let her reluctance to act blow back on Clarke. I needed to find out what they wanted from Clarke so that I could be prepared.

Clarke, whose existence beggared belief, was here, peacefully sleeping in my bed. Her brown hair cascaded in waves across my pillows. She looked like a goddess, and perhaps that's what she was, some ancient creature reborn. A smile crept to my lips at the thought. Whatever she truly was, she had no idea what awaited her once she opened those captivating green eyes. The fault of that rested squarely on my shoulders, and I would bear the brunt of those consequences when she woke.

I reached down to push a curl back from her face and sighed. I would have to work with Lachlan. For reasons he'd not yet divulged, he had also been sent to retrieve Clarke. No matter what, I would soon get to the root of that situation. I couldn't let him leave to report anything he'd seen here, so he'd just have to stay and help or become my prisoner. I didn't think I possessed the ability to hold him. His power was substantial, potentially a revival to mine. But we couldn't keep Clarke safe and be at odds. I would have to brush aside my hate for him.

I pulled back the blanket I had swaddled Clarke in and exposed her ruined shirt. As I looked at the stiff, bloody shirt, I shuddered. So much of Clarke's blood. I'd almost lost her. I shook the thoughts away and turned to the matter at hand. There was no getting around it: I needed to cut the shirt from her body. I reached down to free the dagger I had sheathed in my boot holster, a gift from Luck, and carefully cut the shirt open, exposing her mother's necklace that lay underneath. I thumbed the chain and rotated it until I found the clasp. I carefully unhooked it and moved it carefully to my bedside table. The red stone in the center glowed in the moonlight that spilled in from the skylight above my bed. The necklace meant so much to Clarke, so much so that she'd delayed our escape to Teleran to retrieve it and walked right into a trap.

It wasn't her fault that she'd never suspected Cody would be lying in wait to grab her. It was mine. At the very least, I should've sensed another presence in the alleyway. I was only in the car, yards away. I should've taken her to safety and told her I would go back for the necklace. Then we could have avoided this: her pain, her grave injury, and the entanglement with the Obscurus in the washroom.

I sensed Lachlan's return and clenched the snarl that threatened to breach my lips. My posturing would help no one, least of all Clarke, so I resumed removing the ruined garment.

"What the fuck are you doing?!" Lachlan hissed. His tone rattled my composure. Unlike him, I was an Estival, a gentleman, and I refused to allow his brute nature to compromise my integrity.

Instead, I spared him a tertiary glance as I tossed the bloody shirt at his face. He caught it effortlessly in mid-air.

"I'm examining Clarke's wounds, which I would think was obvious."

"There are no wounds; I healed her," he scoffed, running his hand casually through his dark waves. "I was questioning the removal of her clothing."

"If you think she'll be calmer waking up in a dirty, bloody, stiff shirt, reminding her of the horrors she experienced, then by all means, let's try to put it back on her," I replied sarcastically.

Stupid Obscurus. Was he implying that I was up to something nefarious with Clarke? He didn't even know her. And even if he did, I had never harmed her or taken advantage of her in any way. Besides, she was wearing a bra, which was mostly just stained; she was hardly nude. I would leave the removal of it to her when she woke. Not that I had not seen every inch of her before, but he didn't need to know that. And our previous intimacy didn't permit me any future liberties.

"Apologies," he said, clearing his throat and moving to adjust his shirt, a gesture that implied nervousness. "You're right; we should get her cleaned up," he said as he reached for the cloth sitting atop my armoire. I blinked; the sincerity of his apology struck me speechless. Was he serious?

Lachlan conjured fire in his hands, effectively disposing of the ruined shirt. He brushed his hands together, letting the ashes carelessly fall to the floor. I rolled my eyes at his brutish behavior and, wordlessly, summoned a breeze to clear my room of the ashes and smoke.

We worked in tandem. I removed the blood from Clarke with a little of my water magic and dried her with a bit of my air magic while Lachlan applied a bit of his fire magic to keep her warm. Working with him like this was strange, to say the least, but I couldn't help but appreciate its efficiency.

Her wounds had indeed been completely healed. Only a pale pink mark remained from where the bullet had entered her chest, and even that was fading. With any luck, no signs of her injuries would remain by the time she gained consciousness.

I could only hope. She'd carry the memory of what happened, but at least the physical scars could be prevented through magic.

"Here," Lachlan said as he pulled off his black shirt. I balked at his offer and the unwanted sight of his tan torso. He was larger than I was and slightly more fit. I felt a sudden urge to try bulk-enhancing spells for my physique.

Offering the literal shirt off his back was an unusual gesture to extend to Clarke, who he didn't even know. The fae in general never offered help without a cost, and the Obscurus fae always collected on those debts.

"Whoa, there. Keep your shirt on. I have extra shirts in my dresser that she can wear for now," I said as I cast a breeze to open a drawer containing my white button-down shirts. A clean one floated over to me, and I carefully adjusted Clarke into it.

After making sure Clarke was clean, clothed, and as comfortable as we could make her, I reluctantly left her with Lachlan and went to clean myself up and retrieve the bracelets before Clarke woke up again.

CHAPTER 5

Clarke

"Cody, no!" I screamed as a bullet pierced my heart. "I'm not ready," I pleaded to anyone who would listen. "I was just starting to live. I'm not ready to die, not yet." Pain flooded my body, and I was dragged under with the weight of regret and sorrow.

A deep scent of eucalyptus, lemon, smoky cedar, and a hint of cinnamon surrounded me. I felt warm and secure. Safe. Loved.

Warm, calloused hands cupped my face, and a thumb caressed my cheek. The hands fell away, and I felt alone and empty until I was suddenly embraced, my body cradled against a firm but warm and inviting chest.

"Shh … I'm here. You're not alone." A deep baritone voice said as I realized I had voiced my feelings aloud.

My eyes felt like lead, and I was too relaxed and too weary to try to open them, so I sluggishly wrapped my arms around my comforter, leaning into the ease of their embrace.

"Your comforter," the voice chuckled. "Why do I like the sound of that?" The rough voice was like a soothing caress

"Hmm …" I hummed my response. My mouth was too dry to speak, and my tongue felt stuck to the roof of my mouth.

"Sleep, Clarke. Rest. I'll be here when you wake up."

And for some reason, I did as they said.

CHAPTER 6

Lachlan

I was in deep shit. So much for keeping my distance.

After my meltdown in the washroom, I had composed myself. I was in charge of my feelings, and I wasn't going to let some little tug overpower me.

But then seeing Haywood remove her shirt sent me into a blinding rage. I forgot all about self-control. Once I realized he was trying to take care of her, I decided that's what I would do too—but better.

I swelled with pride at the way her body responded to my healing powers. Her wounds had closed and healed in record time. For the first time since this whole mate thing happened, I was thankful for the bond, if only in this instance, as it was the reason for her accelerated healing.

The failure I had felt when I couldn't save her from that filthy human had subsided only slightly. I would carry the stain of that guilt for a while.

Since the cracks in Teleran first began to emerge, our powers had been slowly waning, but that was nothing compared to the shock of debilitating weakness I had felt on Earth. It angered me that just being there could render my power and strength so inept.

I was so thankful that my forebears had the good sense to create Teleran. Why Osiria prattled on and on about her time on Earth and how we deserved more than this minuscule place to rule was beyond me—as if Teleran were a paltry trinket to her and not the marvel that it was. She'd become obsessed with the need to reclaim Earth one day. She had delusions that the problems of the atmosphere, gravity, and general climate not being conducive to our kind and magic, could be solved. However, when asked, she became guarded, urging me to continue looking for that ridiculous scroll with the equally ridiculous prophecy written on it.

"It is my birthright, as it is all of Teleran's birthright, to reclaim what was once ours. Why should we accept that this is all we are entitled to? We are better and stronger than humans; Earth should be ours," she'd said.

Well, now that I had been there and felt the weight of it, I couldn't support her mission. The humans could keep their stinking garbage, suffocating air, and filthy Earth. I was content to stay in the haven that was my home.

After Haywood had left to clean himself up, I took a seat on the edge of the bed and stared at Clarke. I was hopeless, falling into the depths of her glowing beauty.

I mentally berated myself for offering to give her my shirt. Luckily, Haywood hadn't read much into it, but I needed to try to calm my innate urges towards her. *Protect. Provide. Please.* The mantra repeated in my head like a crow picking at my skull. It was simple: If Clarke needed anything, I was compelled to give it to her. If she needed a shirt, then, of course, take the one off my back. The hold she had on me was immense and primal, and she wasn't even awake. I couldn't continue to give into those desires, though, or Haywood would realize what she was to me and use it against me.

She shifted on the bed and started to groan and thrash, like she was having a nightmare, mumbling something like. *"Cody, no."* And just like I had with my shirt, I threw caution to the wind and stroked her face, trying to comfort her. I knew touching her could send the bond into hysteria, but I couldn't help myself. She was likely dreaming about that vile excuse of flesh. The way he'd put his hands on her and then tried to kill her. Pride swelled when I remembered I had killed him with my bare hands. No matter that it had taken much of my strength to do so.

As I attempted to comfort her, Clarke leaned into my touch, took a deep breath in, and visibly calmed.

Shit. I removed my hands from her face to drag them down my own and sighed.

"I don't want to be alone," she mumbled, her voice raspy and pained.

"Clarke? Are you awake?" When she didn't answer, I determined she'd only spoken in her sleep. The cavity that held my heart thawed at her words. She wasn't alone; she had me. I was right there, and I wasn't ever going to leave her side.

Fuck, those intrusive thoughts needed to end. But as much as I tried to resist, her pull was too strong.

Like an idiot, I scooped her in my arms and held her. My treacherous lips assured her that she wasn't alone and that I was there.

When she turned her body to face mine, chest to chest, her arms came around my neck, and I melted into her. She murmured something about me being her comforter, and I knew then I was done for. Everything I had ever wanted paled compared to her needing me or taking the comfort I offered her so freely.

It felt *right*. I had always felt like I was searching for something bigger, better than my current station. I had thought it was my secret ambition to rule the Obscurus one day, whether as Osiria's successor or her consort. I had often fantasized about rising to power and becoming the first male to do so.

Now I knew my desire for more was because I had a mate—a mate who had lived on Earth all this time. It was in my nature, however, to continue fighting the pull toward her. A mate bond was a vulnerability, a weakness, and I was not weak. And the thought of giving up all my ambitions for this beautiful stranger in my arms made me feel worse than weak; I feel lost and then oddly found. I had thought I knew exactly who I was, and now I knew nothing.

Clarke hummed something, and it vibrated my chest where she lay her head. A bit of drool was sliding down her chin, and I had the distinct urge to lick it from her face, to taste her.

Yep, I was fucked. Most definitely fucked.

I shifted us so that I could prop myself up against the headboard. Then, whispering to Clarke to rest, I said I would be here when she awakened.

A strange peace came over me, and my eyes suddenly felt heavy. I leaned my head back against the headboard and fell into a deep sleep with Clarke in my arms.

CHAPTER 7

Haywood

Despite the dire situation, getting clean had refreshed me. The events with Clarke had left me weary and depleted. Not only because I had spent so much time on Earth, more prolonged than any other time previously, but also because of the whiplash that was *her*. I hadn't expected to love her. I had no expectations of her feelings toward me; attraction did not equal love.

My life had been calculated, formulaic, and reliable. Right up to the moment Solana commanded me to be Clarke's keeper.

Then came the devastating realization that we could never be together, that Clarke likely didn't even desire such a thing. She had found comfort in me, and I knew she cared for me, but her affection and how I felt for her were different. It could never be the same.

I exited the restroom and descended the front staircase with determined steps. I needed to get the Vincula bracelets from my workshop.

I entered the room at the bottom of the stairs to the right of the entryway. A small smile broke across my face; it'd been months since I had been home, and the familiar smell of the room warmed my heart. The many plants littering my desks, shelves, and floor were miraculously still alive and thriving. The watering spell I had cast before leaving had worked surprisingly well.

An unlit marijuana joint beckoned me as it perched perfectly on my workstation. If any day required calming, it was today. I picked it up, plucked a match from my pocket, and lit the joint. My shoulders relaxed slightly as I inhaled. At ease enough to regain focus, I turned my attention to the task at hand.

I walked across to the large desk; it was as long as the ceilings were high. The bracelets were exactly where I had left them in the bottom right drawer. The energy rippled as I opened the desk, and the front door to my manor swung open.

I wasn't alarmed; I could feel Luck's presence. Our bond should have alerted me of her presence when she crossed into Teleran, but I had been distracted. Luck barreled into my workshop, breathless.

"I got here as soon as possible," she said, gulping down air. I turned to face her and was comforted to see her normal blonde hair.

She walked farther into my workshop and threw two duffle bags onto the floor. "What's happened?" she asked, taking the joint from me without asking and puffing a huge plume. She would've felt glimpses of my emotions through everything that had occurred.

In my haste to save Clake, I had forgotten Luck was still on Earth, fulfilling the last of her duties there.

"We don't have much time, but the short of it is Clarke was gravely injured by Cody, who'd posted bail. He abducted her from her apartment when we went there to retrieve some things for her before we traveled here. He took her to an abandoned warehouse, and I arrived there just as Lachlan did, Osiria's second. Cody shot Clarke, and Lachlan killed Cody in retribution. We brought her here, and Osiria's second healed her. She is awakening, and her power is … substantial. I'm taking these bracelets to her now as she sleeps."

"Haywood, that is … a lot." Luck blinked. "What can I do to help?" she asked. I loved how she didn't mince words and didn't need lengthy explanations.

"I need you to go to Luna Palace and make sure Solana isn't planning to send one of her guards here. She would've detected my entry into Teleran, and I'm not certain that she'll wait much longer for me to fulfill my charge."

"Got it; I will do what I can," Luck said before bowing slightly at the waist and exiting the workroom, her shadows swirling around her feet as they often did when she felt frazzled. It was one of her only tells, and I wagered I was one of the few who knew of it.

After retrieving the Vincula bracelets, I walked around the first floor of my manor to make sure everything was in order. I had time; Clarke should sleep for a while still.

After taking the time to inspect every room, I made my way back to Clarke.

I stopped short when I entered my bedroom, seeing a sleeping Lachlan holding a sleeping Clarke. Peace swirled around them. I gritted my teeth to fight the pang of jealousy I felt; Lachlan was only trying to comfort her. There was nothing inappropriate going on, but the moment seemed intimate, and I felt like I was intruding.

I was grateful to him. He'd saved Clarke's life by healing her. He also seemed to have a weird, erratic response toward her. One minute, he was growling and protective, and the other, he was discarding her like she was repulsive. I could see he was warring with something, but I didn't know what. She was beautiful; perhaps she'd bewitched him too.

Our time was running out, as our arrival in Teleran wouldn't go unnoticed by either of our sovereigns, and the barrier between Earth and Teleran was still deteriorating.

Our sovereigns were expecting us to deliver Clarke imminently.

I knew I certainly was no longer willing to do so, and I sensed Lachlan felt the same. We both had our orders, and soon they'd summon us one way or another. Fighting a summons was as impossible as fighting a siren song, and eventually, our vows to obey them would tear us apart if we tried resisting.

We had to do something. We had to work together. My first idea was to send Luck to the Luna Palace, or Silver Palace, as it was nicknamed, to run interference if need be. Hopefully, this would buy me time to think of our next move.

If Solana did send her guards here, or worse, the head of those guards, I knew Luck would find a way to warn me in time to get Clarke out of my home and somewhere safe.

No sooner was the thought out of my head than I heard my front door slam open and shouts ring out from the first story of my home.

"Stop!" a voice I recognized as Luck shouted.

"You'll unhand me at once, or I'll run you through with my sword," said another voice. "Something is going on, and I will find the source of this rouse!"

Ice ran through my veins as my greatest fears were realized. General Leora, Solana's daughter and commander of her guard, was here, and I had no plan. Lachlan had stirred and was looking back at me with alarm.

"What do we do?" he said in a panic, scooting a still-sleeping Clarke out of his lap and coming to stand by the door with me as if our brute strength could keep Leora out of my bedroom.

"I'll handle this. You stay with Clarke and lock this door," I commanded, hurrying over to Clarke and clasping the bracelets on her.

"And what in the fuck do you think a locked door is going to do against the General, you idiot." He spit back his retort.

"I will calm her down and explain that Clarke fell ill, so we could not transport her right away. I'll essentially tell her the truth but leave you out of it."

"Why is she here, Haywood? What will she do when she feels Clarke's power?" he said through gritted teeth. He looked murderous, and in this instance, I couldn't blame him.

"You know why. Solana knows we are back; she probably felt the power surge from Clarke. Don't you think Osiria felt it too?" Lachlan shrank back with acknowledgment as I continued. "So take your judgmental and accusatory remarks, do something productive, and guard Clarke. I'll handle this and distract her from Clarke and her immense power."

"Fine," he huffed, "but if you do anything to jeopardize her—"

"I would never," I said with conviction. "If she does make it past me, you might want to hide somewhere. The general would sooner separate your head from your shoulders than ask what you are doing here."

We both nodded, and I exited the room, leaving Lachlan to guard the female I loved while I tried to reason with the female to whom I was betrothed.

CHAPTER 8

Lachlan

Fear gripped me and held me in place. I had enough wisdom to admit that General Leora was the source of terror that was coursing through me.

I feared not only for myself but also for Clarke. I feared her discovery, what Solana wanted from her, what Leora would do about it, and the tales whispered around campfires about the general. If only half of them were true, it was enough. To say the least, she was formidable.

Clarke had the Vincula bracelets on now, and I could feel how much they'd stabilized her.

Before Haywood had burst through the door, waking me from the most restful sleep, I could feel Clarke's power gaining strength. With our bond connection, I was able to feel a fraction of what was going on inside her body. My insides felt like they were on fire. I hoped she wasn't in pain, or that as she slept, she didn't feel it.

I heard a scuffle in the hallway and debated abandoning my defensive position in front of Clarke and listening to Haywood's advice. Logic won, and I dropped to the floor and wedged myself under the bed.

If Osiria could see me now, a coward hiding underneath my enemy's bed, she'd probably toss me into the lava that flowed around our castle.

It didn't matter now. The situation with the general needed to be de-escalated, which wouldn't happen if she found me here. I had to trust Haywood to get her to leave peacefully and quickly. I closed my eyes and directed my thoughts toward the tug at the center of my soul. I felt it vibrate and could feel Clarke on the other side.

As the bond flared, I felt the vow I'd made to Osiria disintegrate, an unexpected effect of the mate bond. I felt as though someone had loosened their grip on my throat, which had been controlling my voice. I felt free as a heaviness evaporated from my chest. At the very least, I could speak of Clarke without discomfort or the threat of a terrible death.

My relief was temporary as the General of the Estival burst through the door, breaking the lock.

CHAPTER 9

Haywood

"As I said, Leora, she is in her awakening and is not well enough for travel. And now that you've seen her, would you be good enough to leave her alone and let her rest?" I implored, willing my voice to sound no less desperate than I felt. I followed closely on Leora's heels as she forced herself into my bedroom.

"It smells of Obscurus and human filth in here, Haywood; what in the *cremtnux* is going on here?" Leora cursed.

As she looked at Clarke in disgust, I realized my mistake. The impropriety of the situation was that a female who was not my betrothed lay in my bed, clothed in little more than a shirt covered in my scent.

I didn't see Lachlan, but I knew he hadn't gone far. I had been concerned about Leora sensing Clarke's power, but she appeared to be more subdued with the Vincula bracelets, the overwhelming pulsing gone. That, coupled with the sleeping draft, must be doing its job, keeping her calm and at rest, so her body could acclimate to the changes it was going through.

"Well, Leora, you see—"

"I can already taste the lies on your tongue, Haywood," she interrupted. "I would cease speaking were I you." Her voice was cold and threatening. I feared very few fae, but I had developed a healthy fear of her. She could cut me down before I uttered my next breath, having harnessed the Estival powers of air and water in a way that enhanced her combat abilities. She was rumored to have fashioned a mighty sword of water, *Tidebringer*, that she could summon at will, although I had yet to see it myself.

I held my tongue momentarily as she approached Clarke, her armor and silver hair glinting off the sun pouring in through the skylight above, and assessed her with a snarl. "What happened here? And do not lie; I will know."

I didn't doubt it. As commander of the guard, she had gained certain qualities and skills to extract knowledge, using mental or physical pressure to do so.

"She was injured gravely before I brought her here. A human had taken her prisoner, and there was interference from an Obscurus—"

"What Obscurus?" she said, leveling me with a knee-wobbling glare.

I shuddered at her question, knowing that I had to respond honestly and that Lachlan was somewhere in the room. He was my enemy, but I couldn't alert Leora of his whereabouts. I had to convince her that she merely detected the remnants of his magic.

Why did she have to wear her armor to my home? Seeing her angry and armored struck fear in me down to my toes. Still, I had to persevere. Too much was at risk here—Clarke was more important than my fear.

"It was Solana's second, Lachlan," I answered hurriedly and honestly.

"That villain!" she shouted. *"Why was he near her?* What business had he on Earth?" Leora bellowed her questions. It was a marvel that Clarke remained sleeping with the volume of her screeching.

"That I do not know. However, I aim to find out," I said, grinding my molars at the thought. Every answer rang true.

Luck entered the room and said something under her breath that sounded like an insult. That's all I needed; their childish rivalry could crumble everything I was trying to do.

"Oh, was that you, *Luck*, I mean Felic—" Leora started but stopped when a dagger lodged just past her with a thud, embedding itself in the wall while smoke billowed from it. I hadn't even seen Luck throw it. I gasped. I knew tensions ran high between them, but it was a grave offense to attack the heir apparent to the Estival throne.

"Utter another word, and you'll be missing the tip to one of your ears," Luck warned with a faux saccharine tone, seemingly unbothered by the potential consequences of her actions.

Ever since her training with the Guild of Shadows, Luck refused to let anyone call her by her given name. It seemed she was still a bit sensitive about it.

"You dare attempt to strike me, *worm*?" Leora spat. She was fuming, her hand flexing at her side. If she drew her sword, we were done for.

"Keep my name out of your mouth, or I won't miss next time, *General,"* Luck answered, walking calmly to retrieve her dagger. Leora was taller than Luck, but at that moment, you would not have known it. She stood tall and level as she squared her shoulders and locked eyes with Leora.

The air between the two grew tense, prompting me to bring Leora's attention back to Clarke. Did Luck not understand the danger we were all in?

"As I was saying, I have not yet ascertained the cause of Lachlan being on Earth and with Clarke, but I will."

"Where is he now, Haywood? Why can I still smell him?" Leora questioned while her nostrils flared.

"She was on the brink of death, and I had to act quickly. I'm sure Solana would accept aid from an Obscurus to save the person she's charged me to keep alive all these years. Much energy was expressed to heal her, which is why his scent lingers," I answered, again, honestly.

"So all is in order then? The Obscurus is gone, and she is healed? Then let us proceed to the palace," Leora said while moving toward Clarke.

"No," I said too quickly, too eagerly, stepping into her path.

"No?" Leora quirked a questioning platinum eyebrow that would have cut down a lesser fae. I, however, only slightly quaked inwardly. I'm sure she wasn't used to hearing the word *no* from anyone.

"As I've said, she is not well enough to travel. Her body went into shock when I transported her here. Too much magic at one time. I had to act quickly and sedate her. She must remain here and rest until her body accepts its new power and calms." I said, sturdiness in my voice. I would not let Leora take her, no matter the cost.

Leora seemed to consider this. It was the truth, after all, and I knew she could sense it.

"Fine, I'll return to my mother and explain what has transpired. But you must bring her the moment she is able, Haywood. My mother does not tolerate insubordination," Leora stated dismissively as she moved to exit my bedroom.

"Have I ever not done as she commanded me, Leora?" An unintended bite bled into my tone along with a double meaning. Leora's beautiful purple eyes flashed, hurt for a split second. Likely, she was imagining the day Solana had surprised us both with news of our betrothal.

"I suppose you have not," she replied with an iciness that made me ache for the friendship we'd once shared. That was before time, duty, and circumstances had warped our relationship into something cold, resentful, and full of regret.

With that, she slammed my bedroom door shut and stomped down the stairs, her boots resounding through the manor, signifying her departure. I let out a relieved sigh and slumped against my bed.

Luck had remained quiet, perched on a stool by my armoire while using her dagger to clean underneath her short, chipped fingernails.

"Well, that went swimmingly," she quipped sarcastically, not looking up from her nails.

"Pardon me for having to think on my feet. You were supposed to warn me of her arrival," I said, frustrated.

"Yes, please tell me how I was supposed to delay the general. She got here before I could even step foot out of your manor," Luck answered.

"Well, did you have to antagonize her? It was a miracle that I calmed her enough to leave. Not to mention, you almost struck the heir to the Estival throne. Do you have no care for your own life?" I asked.

Luck's glare mirrored Leora's cutting one. "You know exactly why I must *antagonize* her. She needs to be cut down several pegs, Haywood."

I sighed heavily as a disheveled Lachlan extricated himself from underneath my bed and threw himself unceremoniously into the winged-back chair beside it. The green velvet brought out the color of his eyes, making them appear to glow.

"This is fucking disastrous," he said, wiping the dust from his black slacks. He looked frazzled and exhausted.

Perhaps he'd been as scared as I was when Leora burst into my bedroom.

"An understatement, I assure you. We now have less time to form a plan than we thought originally," I answered.

"Whoa," Luck had tried to stand from her perch on the stool and wobbled back. "Is that coming from her?" she asked as she pointed to Clarke.

"You can still sense it with the bracelets on?" I asked as Luck nodded. "Then you can see why we've delayed. We are in over our heads. I've never felt power like this before. Have either of you?" I was genuinely curious. Clarke was singular in so many ways. I feared what either side of the fae would do if they had her in their clutches. Would she be formed into a weapon? And where would that leave her? Her innocence and naivety, her sense of wonder and optimism, while sometimes misplaced and often used against her, were endearing and rare qualities. I would not see them snuffed out, not by Solana, not by anyone.

"Are you kidding me, Haywood? This is insanity. I can barely stand or get a deep breath. It's suffocatingly strong. How can she endure it?" Luck questioned.

"As you can see, she sleeps," I said. "She does not endure anything. She doesn't even know she's fae."

Luck recoiled from me with a gasp. "You had one job. You were to explain it to her before you brought her here. Instead, you traipsed around bouncing from house to house with your stupid moon eyes like you were on your fucking honeymoon."

"That's enough!" I shouted, exhausted and annoyed. Luck was right, of course, but I didn't have the mental capacity to lay out how I had made a mess of everything.

"It's not nearly enough, Haywood! My life is on the line here, as well as your own, as well as hers. How could you be so remiss in your duties?" Luck chided.

"Luck," I warned.

"Oh, no, Haywood," Luck gasped again. "I knew you acted more than just protective when Leora was here." She laughed then, an unkind and mocking laugh. "You *idiot,*" Luck said with a snicker. "You fucked Clarke, didn't you?"

CHAPTER 10

Haywood

Anger, acute and burning, erupted from Lachlan, and I suddenly felt his hands around my throat. Then my head slammed into the wall so hard that the plaster splintered and dust fell to my sandy blonde hair. Luck ceased her inquisition and jumped on Lachlan's back, attempting to pull him from me, her blond hair whipping into her face.

"Unhand him, Obscurus carrion!" Luck shouted, attempting to bash his skull with her dagger but failing. His unrelenting eyes held my death.

The Obscurus was like a wild animal. Whatever possessed him, I did not know and could not speak to question him. But he would need to control his behavior; I wouldn't allow him to act this way around Clarke.

"You did what?" Lachlan bit out, his words laced with hate.

"He can't answer you, you fucking idiot," Luck answered for me, still astride his back.

When Luck's shadow dagger appeared at his throat, Lachlan released his grip slightly, and I started coughing while gulping in precious air.

"While it's no business of yours," I wheezed, "I did not *fuck* her. I wouldn't degrade what we shared with those words. We had a connection, and she was grieving. She found comfort and solace in a friend in a physical way, and if you say anything in front of her when she wakes, I don't care if it starts a war between our people. I will find a way to kill you, Lachlan. She has been through so much, and who are you to even ask? You don't even know her."

51

Pain and anguish leeched from Lachlan at my words, leaving me even more confused. My theory of him being bewitched by Clarke was starting to look more and more plausible.

"What's going on?" a groggy voice questioned. Lachlan immediately released me as we both turned to the bed.

Clarke was awake.

CHAPTER 11

Clarke

Shouts shook me from the deepest sleep I'd ever had. I still felt tired and sore, but I felt good. I also felt a sense of stillness. Usually, I felt a constant low hum of anxiety, but now, I just felt right. Almost like something in me had been adjusted to the correct setting—*finally*.

My memory was a little hazy. The last thing I remembered was being shot and thinking I was going to die. I shuddered. Wait, how was I not dead?

"Are you cold, Clarke?" Haywood asked, his eyes holding that familiar combination of care and concern.

"No, I'm okay, just … what happened? Where are we?" I said as I found myself in a huge bed in a room I didn't recognize.

"You don't remember?" he asked softly.

"I have a few flashes, but they're faint. Physically, I feel fine, but that doesn't make sense. Cody shot me; I should be dead. I felt my heart stop," I said.

Haywood winced. "You were seriously injured, but we were able to bring you to my home and heal you," he explained.

"We? What do you mean, heal me?" I suddenly became aware that Haywood and I were not alone on the bed. The weight at the foot of the bed shifted—and *holy shit,* a gorgeous god was sitting at my feet. He had dark hair curling around his ears in mussed waves. His exposed bronzed skin was adorned with intricate and beautiful tattoos that disappeared beneath his black shirt. I briefly wondered how far they traveled and where, and weirdly, I wanted to get up close and personal so I could find out. An image of me licking him from his abdomen to his neck popped into my mind, and I felt my cheeks heat. I averted my eyes. What the fuck?

"I'm Lachlan. We met earlier, and there was no *we* in healing you." His voice was deep and gravelly as he flashed a slight grin, one that made me forget I had asked a question.

It came flooding back: his hypnotic jewel eyes peering at me from the darkness before Cody shot me.

Bang. Crack.

The sound of Cody's neck snapping reverberated in my skull as my stomach rolled. Lachlan, the Adonis sitting at my feet, had killed Cody with his bare hands. That was after I had been shot.

I'd never forget what it had felt like for my body to shut down. I'd thought I had died.

I took a deep breath in.

"Lachlan, yes. I'm sorry; I remember now."

"You thought I was named after someplace with a monster," he said, sounding slightly offended.

"I thought that was an inside thought," I replied, embarrassed.

"Nope, you said it loud and clear," Lachlan responded.

"Wait, I'm sorry. I got distracted. Are we in a fancy hospital or something? Are you a doctor?" I asked Lachlan. "How long have I been out? Was I in a coma?" I asked.

"You weren't in a coma, and this isn't a hospital," Haywood answered instead.

"And, no, I'm not a doctor," Lachlan replied.

What the hell was going on? I only felt sore where I should have a hole in my chest. I didn't even feel like I was bandaged. I looked down and realized I was in an

54

unfamiliar white dress shirt. It smelled like Haywood, and then my cheeks heated, realizing someone had removed my shirt while I was sleeping.

Peering down inside the oversized shirt, I could just make out light pink skin from where the bullet had entered my body. I brought my hand up to the spot. That's when I noticed my mother's necklace was missing, and I was wearing strange metal bracelets with markings in a language I didn't recognize. What the …?

"If I wasn't in a coma, how did my wound heal so fast? Seriously, how am I okay? And what the hell are these?" I questioned, attempting to remove the bracelets but unable to find a clasp or anything to unfasten them.

There was no way I had healed that fast from a gunshot wound. My anxiety began to buzz again, the calmness I had briefly felt evaporating. I felt like the gravity in the room had shifted, and I wasn't connected to my body, like I was floating. My hands started to shake, I felt a fluttering in my chest, and I started sweating.

By all accounts, I should be dead. It wasn't adding up. The bracelets on my wrists reminded me of the ones they'd put on me in prison, causing my anxiety to spiral.

Haywood placed his hand on top of mine, the one that wasn't clutching my chest. I opened my eyes, realizing I had squeezed them shut. The fear of being back in that place—that prison, caged in darkness—threatened to unravel me.

He reached over and silently handed me my mother's necklace, which had been resting on the end table next to the bed. The gesture softened my heart. I quickly fastened it around my neck and soon felt a wave of relief.

"I will attempt to answer your questions, Clarke, and I know there are many. I take full responsibility for you being improperly informed. Let me try to remedy that now," Haywood said, his calm demeanor easing my fear.

"Okay, Haywood. I really need you to go into detail about how the hell I healed this fast, why the fuck I have weird-ass bracelets on that kind of hurt, and where the hell we are," I said.

"It may make more sense for me to start at the beginning, but I'll start wherever you'd like. And the bracelets are to keep you calm. They'll make sense, I promise," Haywood said.

"The beginning is good then," I decided, crossing my arms over my chest. I remembered that he had wanted to tell me something before everything went to hell and never got the chance to do so during our time together. And I tried to stop freaking out about the bracelets. They were even a little bit pretty, nothing like the cold metal cuffs I had worn in prison. Haywood had saved me from that hell. I was nowhere near that awful place; I was in a home.

I was wrapped in white cotton linens, the plushest I had ever felt in a bedroom. The room was simply yet tastefully decorated with intricately carved wooden furniture and gray slate floors. Things were scattered around the room as if a strong wind had blown through and knocked everything onto the floor, and I could see French doors that led out to a balcony.

Judging by what I could see from the doors, we weren't on the ground floor. The room smelled like Haywood: fresh and floral, reminiscent of a spring morning, blended with a seductive, masculine scent. Maybe we were in Haywood's home?

Above me was a giant, domed, circular skylight that showed the night sky twinkling with a million stars and not even a hint of light pollution. The vibrancy of the sky made me itch to pick up a paintbrush and create. I hadn't felt that urge for such a long time.

"Okay …" I said warily, wanting so much to have the answers finally but also afraid of how I would handle the truth. I sensed but knew I wasn't seeing a bigger picture here. The three people in this room were looking at me like a ticking time bomb—like I wasn't going to like whatever they were going to tell me.

"Look, I'm not made of glass, guys. I can handle it. Just tell me the truth. You owe me that, Haywood." I said.

"You're right, I do. Before I get to the beginning, I'll start by expounding on where we are. We are in my home, my bedroom, in Teleran," Haywood explained. I had been right when I had guessed this was his home.

"Teleran? Isn't that somewhere in New Jersey?" I asked, vaguely remembering the name.

"No, it's … um … well, Teleran is my realm. We are no longer on Earth," Haywood said timidly.

Wait, what? Were we on a different planet?

"We're in space!?" I screeched, unable to control the volume of my voice.

"No," he chuckled. "We are in a realm connected to your Earth, separated by a protective veil that keeps my kind safe. Are you following?"

I nodded, sort of processing what he was saying to me. His explanation was quickly sounding more like fiction than fact. I had read about pocket realms in my favorite fantasy novels. I decided to oblige his story but stayed wary, feeling more and more like what he was telling me was just another ruse to leave me in the dark.

"So … are you an alien?" I asked, half joking, half not.

He laughed again. I didn't find anything particularly funny, and I felt my temper rising.

"Not exactly. I'm fae, Clarke, an Estival, to be exact," he said as if that explained anything. Wait, did he say fae? Yeah, this was exactly like my books.

"Okay, either I'm having a fever dream while I'm dying in a hospital somewhere, or you just said you were fae," I said, sounding a bit annoyed. He'd promised to tell me the truth.

"I did say that, and you're not dying, and you're not dreaming. You are truly right here, in front of me," Haywood said.

"Be serious, Haywood. I know the fae. I read fae smut books all the time. I love the fae, but they are just fiction," I said pointedly, waiting for the punchline.

"Smut fae books?" Luck questioned, looking amused. I only recognized her from her voice and proximity to Haywood. Since I'd seen her last, she'd grown out her hair, dyed it blonde, and ditched her glasses.

"Luck! I almost didn't recognize you," I told her.

"Oh, yes, this is what I normally look like. I changed my look while on Earth," Luck said, like that was supposed to make sense to me—like I was supposed to take it in stride that we were not on Earth now.

"Okay, I understand that completely," I said sarcastically. "And Haywood, don't act like you don't know what books I'm talking about. You remember: They're the ones I had in my bag while we were together," I said. "When I left with you the first time I had them with me. They were just like the stories from when I was a kid but with lots more sex."

"That's what you were reading while we were together?" Haywood gulped, and his Adam's apple bobbed.

"Don't play dumb, Haywood. They are my favorite books. You obviously saw them, and now you're making

58

fun of me? I really don't think this is a time to be joking around. You just promised you'd tell me the truth."

"I didn't know anything about fae sex books," Haywood said, denial strong in his voice. "I'm not joking or lying. We are in Teleran. Your fiction books were likely based on real stories, Clarke."

"But fae aren't real," I said with disbelief. I had to admit, however, that my resolve was wavering. Haywood spoke with such conviction. In my experience with him, he wasn't that good of a liar. Even when he'd tried, I'd always had a feeling he wasn't telling me the whole truth.

"Do I *look* fake to you?" Lachlan questioned, sporting one of those sexy, wry grins my favorite authors always described. I had never seen one up close, and it was doing many things to my lady bits. What the hell, Clarke? I was having a tough time staying focused.

"Um, no, you don't." I averted my eyes. He was just way too sexy, and so was Haywood; I was basically sitting in a way-too-sexy sandwich.

"I'm fae; I'm real. He's fae; he's real. That one small one in the corner, she's real." Lachlan jerked his head in Luck's direction. She'd perched on a chair playing with … was that smoke swirling around her hands? She was taunting me—magic was real, and it was right in front of me.

My throat became so dry I couldn't speak at first.

"Shut. The. Fuck. Up," I croaked.

"No?" Lachlan said, furrowing his brow in confusion.

"Wait, so you are all fae. And we are where?"

"Teleran." The three of them answered at once.

"Teleran," I repeated.

"Just tell her, you idiot," Luck said to Haywood, sounding exasperated.

"Tell me what?" What else could be as shocking? I was in a fae realm, and I had been hanging out with fae for the last few weeks. Oh. My. God. I had slept with a fae.

"Clarke," Haywood said, breaking my spiraling thoughts. "I'm sorry. I wanted to wait and attempt to find the right time to tell you this. Unfortunately, we have run out of time," Haywood said.

"Okay, now I'm really freaked out. Just rip the Band-Aid off, Haywood. Just tell me," I said.

"You're fae, Clarke," Haywood said with so much conviction that it hammered into my chest like a nail.

I looked pointedly at the three fae in the room and, lastly, at Haywood, the truth shining unquestionably in his eyes; I was *fae*.

CHAPTER 12

Clarke

"I'm fae?" I screeched. Haywood winced. Lachlan rubbed his pointed fae ears. Luck just smirked, seeming happy to let the two men in the room take the brunt of my questioning. She looked like she should be holding a bucket of popcorn, watching this situation unfold.

"Yes, Clarke, it's what I wanted to tell you before. But with everything that was happening, there wasn't a good time," Haywood said.

Luck scoffed in the corner.

"I'm *fae*," I repeated. This was either the best day of my life following the worst day of my life, or I really was dead and had found a warped nirvana in a fae realm. Either way, both options sounded acceptable to me.

"Yes, Clarke, I wanted to tell you so many times," Haywood said, placing his hand atop mine. Luck rolled her eyes while making an exasperated sound.

"Do I have powers?" asked.

"Yes, you do," Haywood answered.

I looked down at my hands and flexed them. When that didn't do anything, I threw my arms out and extended my hands. Still, nothing happened.

"What are you doing?" Haywood asked.

"You just said I have powers. I was trying them out, but nothing happened," I explained.

Haywood smiled warmly, "You will have difficulty using your powers right now, but I was getting to that."

"Right, you were explaining something," I said. "Do you know what kind of powers I have?" I questioned further, my eyes alight with wonder. I didn't feel any different. I still felt like me.

"I only know of two for sure. You can control water and air, like me. Remember when the roof leaked in the safe house in the mountains, and I told you it was from the sudden snowstorm?" Haywood asked.

I nodded as I remembered, urging him to continue. I was eager to learn more about who I was as I slowly started to believe the truth of his words.

"Well, that was all you," he said. "You dropped the temperature to freezing in your sleep. When I found you that night, you were going into hypothermic shock from it."

"That's why you had me bundled up and naked. To get me warm again?" I questioned. A growl sounded from the foot of the bed, and I ignored it, wanting Haywood to tell me more. Could I control the weather?

The fact that I could control anything was amazing to me. I had spent so much of my life feeling like I had no control at all, and now I was a freaking fae with freaking magic powers. This couldn't be real, but I suddenly wanted it to be.

"Yes, Clarke," Haywood continued. "And do you remember when we were in the car, and you had just heard that they'd found a body that they thought at the time was Alison's? You hit your head because the car stopped abruptly? You did that too. That was the first time I witnessed your power. Time froze along with the car and everything around us for a moment."

"I stopped the car?" I whispered.

I looked down at my hands, pulling them from Haywood's as if they held the answers to my questions. They looked the same. Nothing notable had changed about them, but if Haywood was to be believed, they had the potential to wield power over two elements. I looked back up at Haywood as another question stirred in my mind.

"So what was all that about being a third-party investigator and helping me clear my name? Was that another lie?" I accused. My brief excitement turned back into anger at the man who'd lied to me so many times. He had hidden something vital from me; I had to know why.

"Not entirely." I went to interrupt him, but he held up his hand, "Please, let me explain. My sovereign, Solana, sent me to retrieve you, to bring you here to live among your people. Something is wrong with Teleran. The barrier that protects and separates it from Earth is thinning. Do you know all those phenomena that were occurring on the news? Those were parts of Teleran that disappeared here and bleed into your world. We are searching for a way to fix it, and Solana led me to believe that we needed all fae on Earth to return to Teleran—that having you and others there was making us weak. But when I arrived on Earth, Heather had already been killed, and you were being taken to prison for questioning. You were so overwhelmed; I felt that I couldn't add to it. I was wrong, but I didn't know how to tell you. And then, when we thought Alison was missing and presumed dead, I saw a part of you wither. You were in pieces, and I thought bringing you here and upending everything you knew would have been cruel." I waited a moment before responding to him. There was so much information to process.

"I understand that you didn't intend to hurt me, Haywood. But there was time, and as I said before, I'm not some weak damsel. I'm not someone who can't handle hard things. I've been through a lot in my life and, recently, more than I ever thought I could withstand. But I can, and I have," I said.

"I know I failed you, Clarke. I just want you to know that I did so with the best intentions," Haywood said.

His voice sounded sad and sincere, but I was still angry. I started to think about all those times I'd felt lost, like a puzzle piece that didn't fit anywhere. Those times when I felt a power buzzing inside me but explained it away. When I saw little flames on my fingers that second time in prison, I thought I was losing my mind.

"I can summon fire on my fingers," I said in a daze as I remembered thinking I'd lost my mind. If he'd just told me the truth instead of treating me like some injured bird or, worse, *a child*, then I wouldn't have felt like I was going crazy. He'd known when he had sex with me. Couldn't he have just told me in a postcoital moment? But I knew he wasn't lying now; I could *feel* it.

"You … you can what?" Lachlan asked.

"Summon fire on my fingertips. When I was taken in for questioning the second time, I was freaking out in the interrogation room and freezing. Then all of a sudden, I saw tiny flames at my fingertips," I explained. "I'd thought I was losing my mind, but if what you are saying is true, then it's possible that was really happening."

"I know there's nothing I can say that will make you trust me, but you are fae, Clarke. If you truly conjured flames, then you are the most unique fae in existence," Haywood said, his voice sounding worried. Luck's expression mirrored his, while Lachlan looked stunned.

"What do you mean?" I asked. From what I'd read, fae possessed seemingly limitless power; they were magic and could do anything.

"In Teleran, we have two types of fae: the Estival and the Obscurus. Each kind wields control over different elements. The Estival have power over water and air, while the Obscurus govern fire and earth," Haywood explained.

"Then what am I?" I asked.

"Something rare," Lachlan answered. Haywood nodded. Luck was staring off in deep thought.

I was fae, a rare type.

It hit me that I had somehow always known. Maybe not that I was fae. I mean, when I was a kid, I daydreamed about maybe being the moon princess, a witch, or something like that. I had always wished for another world just out of reach.

My brain felt like someone had shoved it in a blender.

"Clarke, are you okay?" Haywood asked, placing a hand on my forearm.

"Am I okay?" I laughed a mocking laugh. "I don't think I'm anywhere near okay right now, Haywood. I'm angry at you, at myself, hell, at the fucking world, and everyone it in. I cannot believe that I'm about to say this, but I believe you. I feel so much right now that I can barely keep my thoughts straight. I'm relieved because I knew—I knew something was different about me. I thought I was losing my mind, seeing things that couldn't be real, feeling things I couldn't explain that no one would or could explain to me. I have been gaslit into thinking I was crazy for just being myself. And I know I initiated it, Haywood, but we slept together, and you couldn't find five seconds to tell me the truth. I asked you—I think I even begged at one point because I knew you weren't being honest with me. I thought for a minute that you were the one killing everyone. I thought you were going to kill *me*, and that's what you were lying about."

Haywood looked stricken, as if he was going to be sick. Well, join the club, buddy. Luck looked at me sympathetically. I didn't even bother looking in Lachlan's direction.

"I was planning on escaping you as soon as I could, up until you found the murder weapon, and Luck said I needed to go back to the police station for questioning. I convinced myself that I could trust you, that you cared about me, and that I was crazy for suspecting you," I said.

"I do care about you, Clarke," Haywood protested.

"No, you don't get to say that to me right now, Haywood! I can forgive a lot of things, but not right now. I can't trust you, but again, you've left me with no choice. I'm isolated again. I'm alone in a foreign place, so I have no choice but to rely on you *again*," I shouted. "And you've even robbed me of this moment where my dreams are literally coming true. I've always wished magic existed and dreamed for more, but now I can only think about how you betrayed me."

The house seemed to quake with my outburst, but I didn't care. Maybe my power would crush his whole house. Fuck it. I was hurt. I couldn't even revel in the fact that I was a whole different species because some guy I fucked had just ripped my heart out. It was worse that he hadn't even done it on purpose. He'd clumsily broken my heart. I was fuming. I didn't care that I had aired all our dirty laundry in front of Lachlan and Luck; they could kiss my ass too.

"You still have nothing to say? Hold on—is your name even Haywood Taylor? I knew that sounded like a fake soap opera name," I scoffed.

Luck cough-laughed. Lachlan bellowed with laughter. Haywood looked a bit stunned. He narrowed his eyes at Luck and Lachlan before returning to me.

"Haywood is my name; I didn't lie to you about that. But no, Taylor isn't part of it. The fae don't have last names like humans do."

"Well, fine, that's fine then, Haywood Nothing," I said, deadpan.

Luck laughed again.

"Clarke, you have every right to be angry," Haywood said. "I knew you would be. I suppose that's why I put this off. It was wrong of me. I was selfish and wanted to get to know you before the inevitable happened."

"That's convenient: Gain my trust enough to fuck me. And then what? Abduct me and bring me to your realm and keep me prisoner? What am I doing here?" I retorted.

"It wasn't like that," Haywood said, almost pleading.

"Oh, it wasn't? So tell me then: Why did your queen tell you to bring me here? Who the hell am I to her?" I asked.

"My sovereign gave me reasons I now believe to be false, but you are important, Clarke. I think she wanted you here because of the power you possess," he answered.

"What of it? I don't feel any different, and now that you've healed me, I want to go home," I demanded.

"We need your help, Clarke," Haywood answered. "If our world is in danger, then so is yours. The damage would be catastrophic if the barrier between our realms continues to deteriorate."

CHAPTER 13

Clarke

"Help with what?" I questioned.

"I think you can help Teleran from being destroyed. It started about thirty years ago when you were born. I hadn't made the connection until recently," Haywood answered.

"You think *I* caused this?" I reeled back.

"No, of course not, Clarke," he said, "but I don't believe in coincidences. You were born, and our world started to break down. It started off slowly, but it's escalated since you've come into your power. I think it is possible that your magic is tied to this somehow. We don't know the implications for Earth, but if Teleran falls, it could destroy Earth as well."

"What?" I said in disbelief. The news had said the phenomenon might just be an art installation and that officials saw no reason to panic. But really, millions of people could die?

"I realize that all this is overwhelming, but we don't have the luxury of time," Haywood said. "The destruction is escalating. You don't have to help us, Clarke, but I had hoped you would want to. You are free to return to Earth if that is what you choose, yet I don't know how long that would be. I did take the liberty of having Luck erase all the evidence against you, so your case will be thrown out."

"Luck did what?" I asked, shocked.

"She erased and removed the evidence. So if you returned, those cutthroats wouldn't be able to touch you. You tried to hide it, but I know something happened before I got you out of that prison. I saw you wince in pain. I made sure that if you chose to go back, you could do so safely. With the accelerated deterioration, I think you may be safest here, but I won't make this choice for you. You are still in charge of your destiny," Haywood said.

He'd certainly noticed more than I thought he had. I appreciated all he'd done to help me, but apparently, it was all for nothing. If our worlds fell, there'd be nothing left. I couldn't fathom how I could be the source of our realm's salvation or downfall. I was a thirty-year-old student and a part-time nanny, not some savior or harbinger.

"I don't know what to say," I sighed. "Thank you for trying, but even if I wanted to go home now, I can't just stand by and watch it all burn. I don't know how, but I'm willing to try."

"I just want you to have all the facts, Clarke. You have a choice. With time, you will learn to control your powers, and it could be possible for you to live a normal life on Earth, however short-lived," Haywood said, sounding way too hopeful.

"Temporary peace for me while I could've done something to save millions of people would be deplorable. I'd never be able to live with myself. Like I said, I'm willing to try, but I'm going to need help," I said, twisting the sheets in my fists.

"I will help you," Haywood said earnestly.

I nodded my head. I found myself wanting to know more about where we were and who Haywood really was.

"So if you aren't a detective, who are you really?" I asked.

"I am second in command of the Estival," Haywood started.

Luck snickered from her chair. "Second in command?" she questioned. Her gray eyes lifted to his.

69

"I am her second and emissary to Earth," Haywood said, seemingly offended by Luck's comment.

"Sure, if by emissary you mean babysitter. I thought we were being honest here, Haywood. You are only second in command because—" Luck started.

"I'm getting to that, Luck. If you're done interrupting, can I finish?" Haywood asked.

"If you must," Luck said while rolling her eyes.

"As I was saying, the Estival, of which I am second in command, are the light fae of Teleran, not just in looks, as most of us are fair-haired, but also in power—air and water. We can manipulate both, and coupled with spellcasting, we can conjure most things within reason. Our senses are heightened compared to humans. We are fast. And we can manipulate the weak-minded," Haywood explained.

"I can do all those things?" I asked.

"You can, Clarke, and I believe you can do even more. May I proceed with explaining further?" he asked.

I nodded again.

"I've also known of you since you were a child," He blurted. Shock and confusion radiated through me as Haywood continued.

What. The. Fuck.

"My sovereign, Solana, tasked me about twenty-nine years ago with keeping you safe and alive. It's not uncommon for us to keep an eye on those fae who dwell on Earth. To my knowledge, you were the only one living there who did not know what you were. I came to you when you needed me and helped you when I could."

"How is this possible, Haywood? I know I would have remembered you," I said, shaking my head in disbelief. Yet another thing he had conveniently left out during our time together.

70

"Until you reached the age of thirty, coming into your power, you were not able to see me. It was a way to protect you from knowing who you were or alarming you with my presence. The first time you were able to see me was in prison. We spoke. Do you remember?" Haywood asked.

"That was you?" I said, my eyes wide and blinking.

"Yes, and I was so surprised that you could finally see me that I wasn't sure what to do. I knew it was possible since your powers were awakening, but after being a part of your life for so long, existing as a ghost, and then suddenly being able to talk to you, I was thrown. Clarke, you were … well, incredible, and for the first time in my life, I wanted. I wanted something for me, something I chose. I know it was wrong. I had no claim, no right to you. It was like I couldn't reason with myself. Something about who you are drew me in, and I needed to get to know you."

Haywood's brown eyes were deep wells of sincerity. It only served as kindling for my growing waves of emotions. Anger and hurt burst through the cage I was trying to keep them in. With each word from Haywood, my resolve waned, and my emotions won. I had put my trust in someone and had yet to learn my lesson. I couldn't decide who I was angrier with, Haywood or myself.

"If you saw me my whole life, Haywood—I'm sorry, but this is so much worse! Did you see my pain? My struggles? Did you see me wither away into a shell of a person when my parents died? Did you feel my loneliness and despair?" My questions hit their mark, and the hurt I felt reflected in Haywood's eyes.

"There wasn't anything I could do—" He protested.

"I don't believe that, Haywood. You truly didn't interfere with my life at all? You just said you had powers." I knew in my heart that he had. His eyes held regret.

71

"I was following my sovereign's command. But there were times, brief occasions, where I may have used my powers to help you. You wouldn't have known." He explained.

"Tell me, Haywood," I demanded. "Tell me every time you interfered," I said, crossing my arms over my chest, crinkling the white button-down that smelled like him.

"I saved you from drowning, sent bees after a bully who teased you, held you when your mom died, even if you couldn't feel me. I saved your friends' lives who fell off that balcony …" Haywood trailed off when he noticed the tears streaming down my face.

His words felt like verbal assaults on the fragility I was already experiencing, feeding the confusion and disbelief I was battling. I fell into a pit that I feared no one could pull me out of. I didn't know who I was anymore, and Haywood's attempt to explain what the hell was happening only served to make me feel like a hollow shell.

CHAPTER 14

Clarke

My throat was thick as the tears continued to build and fall.

Haywood had been there and saved my life, all the while not being able to talk to me or comfort me. I felt like I was breaking, but I knew I couldn't go to that dark place I often retreated to when my emotions became too overwhelming, when life became too much.

I was so angry at Haywood; I couldn't turn that emotion off just because he was sorry. My heart urged me to forgive him; even though he'd lied so many times, he'd also been there for me. Someone had been looking out for me when I thought I had been left alone in this world, and that someone was Haywood.

Anger flickered, and comfort momentarily soared. Memories and feelings started clicking into place. It's why he'd always felt familiar. All those times when I had felt like someone was watching me, it was him. Maybe that should have creeped me out, but it didn't, because it was Haywood.

If I knew nothing else, I knew he was kind and caring. But, *fuck*, he was so frustrating. I was undeniably hurt, and my heart ached. I yearned for my mother or Alison, someone who knew and loved me, someone I could reach out to. The sadness of their loss was more than I could bear.

This place we were in seemed to amplify my feelings, as if my emotions were wavelengths erupting from me. The room dimmed, and the bracelets glowed on my wrists, making them ache. I rubbed them, hoping it'd soothe them a bit, then took a deep breath.

Haywood had stopped talking and was looking at me worriedly. Had he asked me something?

"Is that all you wanted to say?" I asked, regaining my composure.

"Well, there is probably more I should share, but—"

"I know something you should tell her," Luck interrupted, amusement lighting her face.

"I was getting to that, Luck," he responded with a bite of irritation in his tone.

"There was someone here from the Estival court looking for you. Her name is Leora. She is the daughter of my sovereign," he said.

"What did she want?" I asked.

"She wanted to know why I delayed bringing you to her mother, but I explained that you were injured and were not ready for travel," Haywood said.

"I'm positive that isn't what I was referring to, Haywood," Luck said pointedly.

I was missing something.

"Are you still trying to keep things from me, Haywood?" I asked angrily.

"No, I just …" he started.

"You just what?" I asked.

"Leora was just here looking for you," he said with a heavy sigh. "And … she is my … betrothed," he finally blurted out.

"What?" I whispered.

"I'm betr—" he started.

"Oh no, I heard you. What in the actual fuck, Haywood!" Why was the fact that he was engaged more shocking than an alternate universe or me being fae? "Since fucking when?"

"The contract was signed many years ago. I understand that you're upset, but it's merely a political arrangement. I've never been romantically involved with Leora in any way," Haywood said as if fucking someone while engaged to someone else was nothing.

"Oh, and she has a pretty name. Great. Awesome," I said, mostly to myself. "Just because it's an arranged marriage doesn't magically make it better. Does she know you don't have feelings for her? I don't know how you do things here, but what we did is not okay. Even if it was, I'm still not okay with it. What was I to you? Your last fling before the ring?"

A chuckle erupted from the bottom of the bed, but it was swiftly muffled by a cough. That captured my attention toward the stranger at my feet.

"And you, who the *fuck* are you?" I was getting angrier and more annoyed, but really, who was Lachlan, and why was he here?

"Me?" Lachlan questioned, pointing at his broad and likely hard chest.

"Yeah, *you*, why are you even here? Do you work for Haywood like Luck does?" I questioned.

He looked at me, threw his head back, and started laughing, deep and rough. My lady bits throbbed. *Down, down, girl! Definitely not the time,* I chastised myself. What the hell was wrong with me?

"Fuck no. I don't work for Haywood. Why would you think that?" Lachlan roared through his laughter as he wiped tears from his eyes. It was the most expression he'd shown; it seemed he had a sense of humor of some sort, although I wasn't sure what was so funny.

"Just to clarify, I don't work for Haywood either. Technically, I'm his second in command, his bonded ally," Luck interrupted. I nodded at her in understanding, even though I didn't know what that meant. I turned back to question Lachlan further.

"When you came to the warehouse, I thought Haywood had sent you to rescue me or something. If you weren't there for him, why were you there?" Sure, Lachlan had saved me, but I was starting to worry that I didn't know anything about him, and he was sitting very close to me. I had a track record of being too trusting, and I vowed to do better from now on.

The current of something ancient ran through my veins, and a sense of peace filled me. *You can trust him,* the intuitive feeling seemed to say.

"I was there under the command of my sovereign and leader of the dark fae, Osiria. She bade me to retrieve you from Earth," Lachlan explained as if it was the most fucking obvious thing in the world.

"Okay, wait, both of your rulers wanted you to bring me to them?" They nodded in unison, sounding like a skipping record with their repetitive responses. "Why?" I asked, bewildered. I couldn't just be a fae in a magical realm. Nope, there had to be more mysteries and queens who wanted me for reasons nobody understood. Oh, and our worlds were on the brink of collapse, and I was supposed to save everyone. It felt like an emotional tug-of-war.

"Their intentions are unknown," Haywood answered.

"Oh, well, okay. That's really weird that they both wanted you to bring me to them, right?" I questioned.

"Yes, it's more than a little *weird*, Clarke," Luck chimed in, mocking my use of the word.

"Were you keeping tabs on me as well?" I asked Lachlan, trying to understand what was happening here.

"No, the warehouse was the first time," he answered, a strange gleam in his eyes. Was he lying? It was hard to tell with him. Aside from his laughter earlier, his face was a mask of indifference and seriousness. While Haywood had lied many times, his emotions were always at the forefront and easily spotted. The two men were so different that it was difficult not to compare the two.

"This is too much, you guys: I'm just sitting here in Haywood's shirt; I have powers; you think I might be the key to saving both our worlds; some royal people want me for god knows what; and I just need …" I said, squeezing my eyes shut.

"Anything," Lachlan and Haywood answered in unison. Luck rolled her eyes.

Lachlan had a determined and commanding tone; Haywood's voice was barely a whisper, full of emotion and words that would remain unspoken for now.

"Anything you need, Clarke, you will have it," Haywood said, determinedly.

Luck just snickered and continued to twirl shadows around her fingers. I had many questions for her, but I needed a break first, and these bracelets had to go.

"Could we get these bracelets off? I think they are making me feel weird, and I think they are burning my wrists," I said, continuing to fidget with them. They had to have a clasp somewhere.

"I don't advise that," Luck said to Lachlan and Haywood, who had both moved in my direction.

"Why not?" I asked Luck.

"Those *bracelets* are made of iron infused with ancient fae magic. They are called Vincula bracelets, and we place them on all fae adolescents. This helps them stay calm and learn to manage their magic properly," Luck explained.

"Um, in case you haven't noticed, Luck, I'm not an adolescent. I'm thirty," I said, waving my hand toward myself in explanation.

"That's actually quite young for us," she went on. "Fae come into their power at thirty. Until then, for the most part, our youth are sequestered to keep them safe as they are vulnerable without power and to train them on how to handle their power when it comes. You, unfortunately, must receive a crash course on all that they learn during training."

"Well, they itch, and won't I need my power? Especially if I'm going to help you?" I asked.

"Untethered power is volatile, Clarke. You'd do more damage than good," Luck responded. "But don't worry; we will help you learn how to use it."

"But we don't have time, right? You said so yourselves. Your world is … what? Dying?" I asked.

"Not dying," Luck said with a flinch, "but withering, yes. You are correct that you cannot help us unless you have access to your powers. But you must be trained, or you'll do more harm than good. We will have to make time," Luck answered.

"Well, okay, fine. I'll train, I guess, but first I need a shower. Does this place even *have* running water? I feel disgusting, and I just need … a minute to myself," I said.

I looked up at the two men on the bed with me. They were such a contrast to one another. Haywood, with his light features and deep brown eyes. Lachlan, with his black waves and piercing green eyes. One was light, and one was dark. I found them both devastatingly handsome; apparently, I didn't have a type, or maybe my type was fae.

When neither of them replied, I continued. "I've been beaten and shot, and then I slept for an eternity, and I feel gross. I want to clean up, and after that, maybe we can discuss how I can help Teleran."

"Of course, Clarke, let me help you to the washroom," Haywood said, taking both my hands and moving to help me up. "You are likely still too weak to walk on your own. If you would permit me, I will carry you to the bath."

"Um, I don't think that's necessary," I protested, slowly swinging my legs to the opposite side of the bed. I didn't want his help or to be in his arms.

When my feet hit the slate floor, my knees buckled. I was going down, and I knew it was going to hurt. As I braced myself for the pain, strong arms wound around my waist and hoisted me up. I found myself blinking up at Lachlan's handsome face; my arms somehow worked their way around his neck. The black curls at the nape of his neck brushed my hand, and chill bumps broke out along my arms. I also felt a slight spark similar to when I first met Haywood. It must be because they were fae, and my body was reacting to their magic.

My mouth parted, and Lachlan's eyes darted to my lips. My heart jackhammered in my chest so loud that he had to have heard it. Fae had enhanced senses, right? I hadn't noticed a difference in my own yet, but that could have something to do with the bracelets on my wrists. When Haywood's throat cleared, the moment evaporated, and I glanced at him over Lachlan's broad shoulders. I felt my cheeks warm with embarrassment and a slight twinge of guilt.

"I'll go start the bath for you, Clarke," Haywood said, casting his gaze down and moving past us to the room that I assumed was the bathroom.

I owed Haywood nothing, but actively salivating over someone I had just met in front of him was just cruel and wasn't like me. I swore I wasn't doing it on purpose. The sexual magnetism rolling off Lachlan would've made me weak in the knees if he wasn't holding me.

I had been habitually single before, so maybe that was why they affected me so much. Charlotte men certainly didn't measure up to the beauty of the fae men, that was for damn sure.

Lachlan walked me toward Haywood, who was placing clean towels on the counter of the sink for me. His bathroom was all beige stone and black marble.

"Everything you need should be on the ledge by the tub. I've set out fresh towels for you. Luck retrieved your bag from the alley. I trust it has everything else you need. Please let us know if you require anything else," Haywood said, barely looking at me and walking out of the bathroom.

My heart sank. Was he jealous that I had accepted Lachlan's help and not his? I hadn't done it on purpose. I was falling, and Lachlan saved me from an embarrassingly painful fall. What did he expect me to do?

"Can you, um, do you need help with …?" Lachlan gestured to the shirt that I was still wearing, stumbling over his words.

"Are you seriously asking if I need help undressing, Lachlan?" I asked, my cheeks heating.

We were still close since he was holding me, so I could see Lachlan's bronze face reddening. "Not—no—just—you couldn't stand before, and I just, um, never mind."

A giggle found its way out of my mouth, and Lachlan's eyes softened and then darkened. Oh shit, was he turned on? No, he couldn't be.

"What?" I asked when he continued to stare. "Why are you looking at me like that?"

He closed his eyes and opened them again, clearing the desire I had seen there. "That was the first time I heard you laugh. It was beautiful."

Oh shit. "Um."

"Sorry," he apologized, flustered. "I should leave you."

"Just sit me down. I think I can take it from there." I gestured to the bench beside the claw foot tub.

He did as I instructed and moved toward the door, but he turned back to me just as I was lifting the oversized shirt above my head.

Lachlan breathed in sharply, and I abruptly let the shirt fall back to cover my body again. The moment felt charged as our eyes locked, but Lachlan quickly averted his eyes.

"I didn't mean … just let us know if you need anything else," he said, hurrying out the door.

Fuck, my life was only getting more complicated.

CHAPTER 15

Lachlan

I leaned against the inviting cold of the stone balcony railing, which began to cool the raging fire in my blood. The rolling snow-covered hills of the Estival side of Teleran were slightly pink from traces of the red fog that occupied the Obscurus side.

Even here were touches of my kind that comforted me. I missed home, its familiarity, and the warm, humid air. I even missed the way the moisture clung to my skin. I feared it would be long before I saw the inside of my beloved apartment at Aurantia again.

No matter what happened now, I knew Osiria would find a way to punish me for failure. I wasn't long for this world, and the thought was bittersweet. I had found my mate, only to lose her shortly thereafter. Osiria was not understanding or kind. She would see my delay as a betrayal.

I ran my hands through my hair in frustration as I breathed in deeply. The air was crisp here and smelled of my favorite bakery in Teleran, Pistrani's. They manipulated water to the perfect pH, which did remarkable things to the dough. Too bad it was on the Estival side.

When I was younger, I would sneak past the border to order my weight in pastry. And don't get me started on their coffee. While I loved my people, they preferred tea to coffee, and even when they attempted to make a decent cup, it tasted like bitter mud. While the volcanic soil could grow things properly, the thickness of the red mist choked any plant-life we tried to cultivate.

However, we could make a nice strong ale from our waters. Currently, I didn't need a dull to the senses; I need a kick in the gut. A nice, strong coffee would be ideal. I was losing my mind.

Had Haywood noticed how my body had reacted to Clarke when I held her in my arms? Had Luck? Had either of them felt the charged air when she looked into my eyes?

I had all but announced my claim on Clarke and what she was to me to my mortal enemy, to the very fae who could and likely would use it against me. And now the fucking General of the Estival had laid her eyes on Clarke. I sunk my hands in my hair again and pulled at the roots.

Snap out of it, you idiot.

The problem was I knew I wouldn't. I had seen mated faes before, blubbering fools drooling at the sight of their mated partner, doing everything possible to grant them their every wish and desire in the hopes that they would solidify the bond.

Fate was a cruel beast, hitting one of the mated pairs with her arrow first and making them a pathetic pool of misery until their fated mate chose them and accepted the bond. As luck would have it, I had been hit first.

Fuck.

At least Clarke wouldn't feel any of this. Sure, she'd be slightly drawn to me, attracted to me, but her emotions wouldn't be all over the place like mine were. Thankfully, the bond didn't work like that. I wouldn't want her to choose me just because she'd be miserable unless she did. To sever the bond, she would need to reject it. I had to make sure she made that choice when the time came.

CHAPTER 16

Haywood

After Clarke left to bathe, I reluctantly went to join Lachlan. I needed to reign in my jealousy. Clarke didn't deserve that display. I also needed to know why he was acting so strangely around Clarke. We needed to try to trust one another, and I needed to know Clarke was safe.

I saddled up next to Lachlan, leaning my weight against the balcony's railing.

"Not that I care, but mind sharing what's going on with you? I won't pretend to know you or insult your intelligence by acting like we are anything except enemies, but for Clarke's sake, we need to be on the same page here. It pains me to say this, but we need your help. Clarke needs us, and Teleran needs her. She needs to be protected. I do not need to trust you, but I do need to trust that you understand that," I said.

"I would never do anything to hurt her," Lachlan said, and I felt the truth of his words.

"That I do believe, Lachlan. But I don't know *why* since you've only just met her. I'm correct in saying that, right? You haven't been secretly visiting her on Earth?" I questioned. I would've detected him had he been close to Clarke at the same time I had, but I was only pulled to her when her emotions were severely heightened or when she was in danger. Osiria could have had him keeping tabs on her when I wasn't around.

"No, of course not; I loathe that vile place. The most time I've ever spent there was when Osiria sent me to retrieve Clarke," Lachlan said.

"Yes, about that. Care to tell me why she would command such a thing?" I asked.

"I've told you the truth, Haywood. I don't know. My sovereign doesn't often share her reasons for most of the things she commands, and she spent only seconds commanding me to retrieve Clarke before she practically shoved me to Earth. I've been trying to work out her intentions, but I'm coming up short. If you must know, I do not trust her in this, and I've decided neither she nor your sovereign will have Clarke. Their intentions aren't clear, and judging by the power she possesses, I fear they will seek to use her as a weapon," Lachlan said.

"I agree," I said.

"You agree?" Lachlan's shock was palpable, and relief flashed in his eyes.

"Yes, until we know more about why they want her and, more importantly, what that signifies, we can't turn her over to them. What matters most to me now is finding out how to save our people and helping Clarke figure out her powers."

"I have fewer answers than I did before Clarke woke," Lachlan admitted.

"In that, we are the same," I said, feeling a small kinship with the Obscurus.

"What must we do to trust one another? We cannot hope for success if we are constantly fighting amongst ourselves," Lachlan said, his eyes connecting with mine in earnest.

"Trust is a difficult thing, but I will endeavor to try," I replied.

"So you are ready to betray your sovereign?" Lachlan asked.

"For Teleran and Clarke, I am," I said without question.

"You sound so sure, Haywood. Your honor is known to us. You've followed your sovereign without question. You wish to save Teleran, as we all do. But your desire to help Clarke runs deep. Why risk everything for her?" Lachlan asked.

"I will do it for her because I love her, and I suppose I have loved her in different ways throughout her life," I admitted.

"I have many more questions now, Haywood. You are her … what? Fae godfather? Watching over her for thirty years? And then you fuck—I mean, sleep together. You can see how that is very strange, can you not?" Lachlan asked.

"It wasn't strange, and it's not like I was her caregiver. I just watched over her and kept her alive. Believe me: I didn't want to have feelings for her. She was my mission, my duty. Deny it if you will, Lachlan, but Clarke has a pull to her like a siren. She's magnetic. I've seen the way you've been looking at her. She's gotten to you too. And I'm not some predator who used any knowledge or power over her. She pursued me. Should I have resisted? Of course. But I didn't, and that was my mistake. One I will not be repeating," I explained.

"She hasn't gotten to me," Lachlan denied defensively, "and we aren't talking about me right now. How did she breach your defenses if she was just a duty to you?"

"As I said, she had just learned that her best friend was dead. We later learned that she was only missing. Her heart was broken, and she was attracted to me. I tried not to feel her emotions, but it was like she was screaming them at me … vividly. And when she initiated contact and needed comfort, something to tether her, I could not refuse her. I wanted her too, and her magic, her power, felt like a drug. It sang to my own like they were meant to be joined. I can't

86

explain it. It's just her. I admire her for who she is, not what she is. You'll see. she's not like anyone in Teleran and nothing like the vile humans she had to live amongst for thirty years." I revealed more than I thought I would to Lachlan. Despite his denial, I had a feeling that he may understand.

"So are you lovers or not?" Lachlan questioned. I tried to reign in my frustration.

"Why do you care?" I said, growing suspicious.

"I don't, Haywood, but you asked if I had questions, and you still haven't directly answered me. I would like to think that you have your head in the game. That you will not be remiss in your duty again or distracted."

"No, we are not lovers, Lachlan. We had an unspoken understanding that it was a one-time thing, a heat-of-the-moment decision, a mistake we won't be making again. I will never do anything to harm her. I'm focused, and I will not become distracted."

"How can you be so sure? You said you loved her. How is that not distracting?" Lachlan asked.

"I will always love her as her friend. Anything more is no longer a possibility," I replied solemnly.

He was quiet for a moment and then held his hand out to me.

"Then I vow to help you, Haywood. I vow to help Clarke and save Teleran, whatever that entails," he said.

"Why? Why would you do this, Lachlan?" I asked, stunned. Vows between fae were eternally binding and were not entered into lightly.

"That's simple. Survival. I love Teleran, and since Clarke may be the key to saving it, it seems logical that I should help her learn how to use her powers."

"You make a good point, Obscurus. I vow to do the same." I sighed heavily, raised my hand, and clasped it to his.

"I so vow to protect Clarke Carpenter and do whatever is in my power to ensure the survival of Teleran and the people thereof," I pledged.

"I so vow," Lachlan agreed and nodded his head.

Energy buzzed painfully up my arm, landing at the very center of me.

CHAPTER 17

Luck

While Haywood and Lachlan gabbed on the balcony, I contemplated how much trouble I would get in for murdering my first in command.

What had Haywood been thinking? And why was he entertaining this Obscurus filth? We were all in deep shit now. Sure, I liked Clarke just fine, but her power was something to be feared. Fates, just keeping her here could get us all killed.

Perhaps it was my namesake that had just saved us all from Leora discovering exactly what we were hiding from her, but I wasn't counting on it a second time. Come to think of it, Leora retreated far too quickly for my liking. I had never seen her back down from anything. Her weird lie-detecting power aside, I couldn't accept that she'd just taken Haywood at his word and left.

Before she stormed Haywood's manor, I had been getting ready to intercept her at the palace. I was polishing my throwing daggers when she'd burst through Haywood's front door.

It was a disaster.

There was a time when she would have listened to reason and given me more than just the time of day. Unfortunately for me and Haywood, those days were long gone.

A wave of agony hit me that had nothing to do with the predicament we were in. Leora and I had once been close. We all had been. Her, me, and Haywood. We were a team of rambunctious youths causing mischief and mayhem in the Luna Palace as our charges chased us around.

It wasn't until after we had all settled into our power that Solana called Haywood into her throne room. Of course, I had tagged along. I had heard everything from behind the pillar I had hidden behind. Haywood and Leora were to marry. Haywood was exalted to his current position. I had unceremoniously sunk to the floor, not caring if my thud had echoed throughout the throne room, alerting everyone to my presence.

Before that day, it was the three of us, the best of friends, and I had thought it would last forever like that. That's the funny thing about the last time you do something or experience something: You never realize it's the last time. I hadn't known that it was the last time we'd be adolescents.

After that, we'd forever be burdened with the weight of duty and responsibility. Just a few days prior, Leora and I had shared our last kiss. We used to sneak off and steal time together when Haywood was busy tinkering with his plants. I had thought I loved her and foolishly thought she felt the same way.

I had never been more wrong. After that day, she barely regarded me with a passing glance, and when she did, there was nothing but cold detachment behind those glittering purple eyes. The gleam that I used to see there had been wiped away.

Her training to become the general started the same day I was shipped off to the Guild of Shadows and Haywood began his duties to Solana. We were fractured.

After I returned, Haywood requested that I be appointed as his second. Solana acquiesced. My skills were formidable, and that was perhaps why she had me carted off in the first place.

I didn't resent what I had learned there. The Guild had given me a purpose, and I was damn good at what I did. None could match my speed and stealth.

Being back at Haywood's side, working with him, had been an unexpected joy. I did hate him a little for a while. He had been given the one thing I'd wanted, and he didn't even seem happy about it. He didn't love Leora, not romantically anyway, which I'd struggled to understand. What wasn't there to love? She was stunning and strong, sexy and mysterious.

I thought Leora and I could maintain a friendship at least. But no, for some reason, Leora had decided she hated me. Her jeers and jabs had hardened my heart to her. She was as cold and aloof as her mother. Sure, I served my sovereign as it was my duty, but did I love her? Worship her like Haywood seemed to? No, not at all.

All sovereigns seemed to possess an undercurrent of cruelty, as if the formidable power they wielded corrupted them somehow. Solana hid her true nature a bit better than Osiria did, but it was there all the same. If you asked me, I would have preferred the latter. I would rather serve someone who was outwardly evil than someone who wore a mask of kindness.

Well, the apple hadn't fallen far from the tree with Leora, which was why I didn't trust her hasty exit from Haywood's home. I half expected her to return with her battalion ready to raze his manor to the ground for defying her mother—for defying her.

Hopefully, I was wrong. Maybe she had a weak spot for him now? Perhaps she was in love with him? Nah, no way. She didn't love anything or anyone and wasn't capable.

I chuckled to myself, thinking how she'd react if she found out how head over heels Haywood was with Clarke. I doubted he'd be able to hide it from her.

She wouldn't kill him, would she? I didn't think she was the jealous type, and if rumors were to be believed, she'd had her fair share of lovers over the years. But could she forgive his love?

Defiance rose up when a thought entered my head. I would just have to kill her if she tried to lay a finger on him.

Haywood drove me crazy sometimes—well, most of the time—but he was still my truest friend. He'd boggled our mission with Clarke, but I had to take into consideration that after all these years I had served him, it was the first time his resolve had ever faltered.

He would need to explain why he allowed the Obscurus to linger. I couldn't wrap my mind around why Haywood hadn't turned Lachlan out on his ass yet. So what if he'd saved Clarke's life? That task was done. His usefulness had run out. Did his motives pertaining to Clarke matter so much? I could not give a flying fuck what Osiria wanted with Clarke.

Haywood had filled me in briefly on what had happened while we were apart, but I needed time to debrief him on what I had found. So many things had happened in our short time apart, from Cody abducting Clarke to Clarke getting shot to the Obscurus dispatching Cody.

I knew Cody was scum. However, something wasn't adding up with the timeline of Heather's murder and Alison's disappearance. His motives didn't make sense.

After cleaning up any lingering evidence of Clarke, Haywood, or the Obscurus in the warehouse, I had pocketed a cell phone that had been discarded on the floor.

The screen was cracked, but it still worked. I deciphered Cody's passcode easily—6969—and searched for anything that would tie him to either girl's case. I found nothing at first but a porn app, lots and lots of naked screenshots of various women, and a few pictures of both Heather and Alison. Then I found the video.

It was a short clip of Clarke being groped by Cody as he told her his twisted plan. He had taken her to the warehouse to film her confession to ensure his innocence. Why would he do that if he were guilty? He could've just skipped town.

I saw the two men moving to enter the bedroom again and made a mental note to inform Haywood of the video and ask him what he thought the moment we were alone.

The mysteries surrounding Teleran's demise, Clarke, her missing friend, and our two sovereigns were all connected. I could feel the truth of it in my bones. We needed more information, and I knew just how to make an Obscurus sing.

CHAPTER 18

Clarke

My muscles relaxed as I eased into the warm water, which smelled of jasmine and lavender, but my mind started racing again. Now that I was alone, maybe I could sort out what had just happened.

So Haywood was the cat who had come to reveal who I really was. I chuckled to myself, grateful that I was alone. Maybe I was crazy, but the fact remained that Teleran existed; it was my Narnia. A world awaited me through a doorway in the woods. Everything I thought and dreamed of was true.

Ugh, Haywood, why was everything so complicated? When he'd broken me out of prison, my feelings for him, my attraction for him, had reignited. He'd saved me from whatever that officer had planned during lights out and whisked me away. He'd conceded to letting me get my mother's necklace, even though that ended horribly.

Suddenly, I realized that when he'd said he was taking me somewhere safe, he must have meant Teleran. He had to have been planning on telling me everything before Cody interrupted our plans.

Bang. Crack.

I winced as I remembered the pain of the bullet, burning and sharp. Cody was dead now and couldn't hurt anyone anymore. But my anxiety won like it always did, and my thoughts returned to the night when everything had changed.

Cody had been drunk and unhinged, threatening me with a gun and implying more with this touch, but did that mean he deserved to die? He deserved to be in prison for sure, if not for abducting me, then for sure for killing Heather.

Sweet, innocent Heather. I wish she were here somehow so I could ask her why the hell she hadn't mentioned that she'd dated Cody. It wasn't the most important thing at the moment, but it did bother me. She must have known of Alison and didn't want to make it weird for me at home.

Oh, Alison. I hadn't thought of her at all since waking up. She was out there somewhere. How could I escape Teleran and help find her? How could I assist the fae here *and* search for Alison? Not that I could help her now if I went back to Earth. Everything was such a fucking mess.

I could never go home. The thought hit me, and my heart sank. Nothing would ever be the same again. Not that being trapped in a fae realm was the worst place to be marooned, but never being able to return to my life hurt. I would never be a teacher now and would never have the opportunity to help kids like me. But maybe, just maybe, I had a different purpose. Maybe I could help the fae save Teleran and Earth. I could save countless lives. It all seemed so unreal to me, but a bud of hope opened in my chest. This could be exactly what I'd been waiting and wishing for: a magical life where I could help those who needed me.

I looked down at my hands with a sigh. With these bracelets on, I didn't even have the realness of possessing magic. All of it felt so out of reach, and even though I believed it, it didn't *feel* real.

At that moment, I would have given anything to talk to my mom. I palmed her necklace and imagined her face as I told her what I was. Knowing her, she wouldn't even act surprised. She always talked about how special I was. I could almost see her smiling, shrugging nonchalantly, and saying something like, "You see, my girl, I've always told you there was something magical about you."

Tears trickled down my face. I had forgotten until just now how often she used to say that to me.

Time hadn't healed all wounds; I'd just learned how to live with them. I felt them every day, and they became a part of me, just as my mom was part of me. I cherished the pain; it was my last tie to her, and I would rather have it than not. Missing her spurred my desire to find Alison. Exhausted and spent, I rested my head on the back of the claw-foot tub and fell asleep.

"Oh, my god, girl!" Alison screeched, deafening my ears and causing me to wake up.

"Alison?" I questioned.

"Clarke, you have to find me! You have to save me!" She pleaded.

"Are you okay? Where are you?" I asked, groggy from sleep.

"I'm okay, but whoa, you look like a ghost. Oh my god, are you dead? No, no, you can't be dead, Clarke. You have to save me," she wailed.

"I'm not dead. I'm sleeping, I think, or dreaming. Just tell me where you are. Did Cody take you?" I asked.

"What? No, Cody didn't take me. What are you talking about? I'm in Teleran, Clarke. You have to come get me," she begged.

"What?! I'm in Teleran!" I said as the fog from sleep lifted. The thought that Alison was nearby sobered me.

"You're coming to save me!" she exclaimed.

"Yes, I will! Of course, I will. How do I find you?" I asked as Alison broke out into sobs.

"I don't know," she said, hiccupping through her sobs. "Everything is dark, hot, and red, and ..." Her image began to fade.

"Don't worry. I'm coming to get you. Do you hear me? I'm here, and I will find you. Just hang in there and be strong until I do?" I promised.

"Yes ... but ... no ... don't leave me alone ... Clarke," she begged.

"Clarke? Wake up."

"Luck?" I said, my voice still hoarse from sleep.

"You were shouting in your sleep. Are you okay?" she asked.

"Yes, wait, Alison is here!" I yelped, trying to get out of the tub, suds and all, not caring if Luck saw me naked. Alison was in Teleran, and I had to go get her.

"Wait," Luck said. "Hold on."

Warm water flowed over my body, washing away the suds, and then a large white towel wrapped around my now-dry body, my hair surprisingly also dry.

"What the fuck just happened?" I asked.

"What about *we are fae and have magic,* aren't you grasping?" She asked as she smirked.

I blinked, bewildered. "Most of it," I deadpanned, grabbing Luck and shaking her back and forth. "Alison is here! We need to go tell Haywood and Lachlan. We have to go get her!"

"Okay, just wait a minute. What do you mean? How do you know she's here?" Luck questioned.

"I saw her while I was dreaming, Luck. I can't explain it, but I know it was real."

"All right, Clarke, let's get you dressed, and then we can talk to the others to resolve this. Just take a deep breath and relax," she encouraged.

I realized my breathing had become labored. I used the calming breaths my mom had taught me so long ago. Breathe in slowly. Breathe out slowly. Breathe in slowly. Breath out slowly. Big, deep breath, and let it out.

"Okay," I said, shaking my arms out to relieve the tension.

Luck left me alone. She'd looked at me like I was crazy, and for the millionth time since I had woken up, I was also starting to question my sanity. My dream had felt so real, but I had been thinking about Alison right before falling asleep. I didn't know what to believe anymore. For all I knew, this whole damn thing was a dream, and none of this was real. That possibility seemed more likely.

I peered at myself in the mirror, expecting to look as haggard and exhausted as I felt. Instead, the person looking back at me appeared rested and glowing. Like, literally glowing. My dark lashes looked fuller and longer, framing my vibrantly green eyes. My cheeks were pink from the heat of the bath, and my lips were plump and reddened. My face seemed slimmer, which made sense; I couldn't remember the last time I ate anything. It had to have been with Officer Cain, who had stopped at the fast-food place, and I had no idea how many days ago that was. My stomach gurgled and alerted me that it was empty. I was suddenly very hungry.

A quiet knock sounded, and a second later, Luck opened the door and handed me my duffle bag.

"We're ready to talk about what you saw when you are," Luck said, exiting the bathroom.

Thanking her, I shut the door and opened my bag to

grab some clothes. I had packed my duffle before Cody abducted me. My heart leaped with the realization the things I'd packed had made their way to me in Teleran. How Luck had found it, I didn't know and didn't care at this point. Having the comfort of my clothes, my precious books, and my favorite picture of my mom and me warmed my heart.

I dressed in a hurry, wanting to get to the bottom of my dream. I was happy to be able to stand on my own. My legs and body felt recharged from my bath and nap.

I looked back up at the mirror, inspecting my hair, which looked like I'd received a blowout at a salon.

Then I screeched. The door swung open, nearly knocking me over in the process, and three fae dog-piled into the bathroom.

"What?!" they all exclaimed together.

"What? Are you serious? Look at my fucking ears." They had grown and were way pointier than they used to be. My ears had always had a pointy shape, but nothing like this.

"Well, Clarke, I would've thought that was obvious. You're fae. Your ears are like ours now," Haywood said.

"I mean, yes, obviously, Haywood, but I didn't think my body would physically change overnight." Why didn't I look like this before? I started poking my ears and then, on closer inspection, shrieked again as I took a lock of my hair in my hands. My once chestnut-brown waves had streaks of vibrant red through it. My second thought after freaking out was that Alison was going to love it. She'd always tried to convince me to let her dye my hair something other than my "boring virgin hair," but I had been too scared to try anything.

"I'm sorry, Clarke," Haywood continued. "Some things during the awakening process are so second nature to us that I forget you don't know any of them. Sometimes, physiological changes can occur, not all the time, but given the level of power that you possess, it makes sense that your physical appearance is changing too. Your ears, your hair, and even your face look slightly different now, but more could manifest in the coming months. There really is no way to know until you settle."

"Haywood, you make me sound like some sort of science experiment, like at any moment, I could become unstable and spontaneously combust." Haywood's face paled, and he looked ill but said nothing. "Wait, that's not a possibility, right?" I asked, alarmed.

"One of the reasons I placed the Vincula bracelets on you was to prevent such … incidents. It's not common, but in some instances, adolescents do not survive their awakening. But you will," he assured me. "I have full confidence that you are past the worst of it. The most we should expect is a few cosmetic alterations. We will know for sure once we teach you and train you on how to control your powers. The bracelets will make it easier for you to correctly guide your powers so that you wield them and not vice versa."

I sighed in relief, taking a quick glance back at myself in the mirror. I turned my head to the right and the left. It really did look like I had dumped Sephora all over it. I looked … beautiful.

"Okay, now that we've established you are fae and subsequently look like one, shall we discuss why you think Alison is in Teleran?" Luck suggested impatiently.

CHAPTER 19

Alison

"Alison?" A gentle, melodic voice coaxed me from sleep. Whoever it was, was in for a rude awakening. I was not a morning person.

"What?" I grumbled.

"Wake up, my dear. Your breakfast will be getting cold."

My dear? What the …? My eyes peeled open, and I gasped.

"Who are you?"

The woman in front of me was like model hot, or like celebrity hot. She had dark, almost-black eyes that seemed to glimmer. Her matching hair fell in waves down her back and was adorned with a red diadem.

"Oh, dear, you must still be recovering from your little bump on the head. I'm Osiria, seventh sovereign of the Obscurus. You're in my castle. Hurry, your breakfast is getting cold. I need you feeling strong, as we have much to do."

"Huh? Lady, what are you talking about?" Was I still dreaming? A sovereign was a queen, right? I looked around, expecting to find my colorless black cell and watery floor bed, but instead, I saw a room bathed in red. The floors were red stone, white veined and shiny. Even the sky pouring in through the open floor-to-ceiling windows appeared to be red … red mist.

I breathed in the familiar scent from my dream. It couldn't be, could it? Had someone finally figured out that

I wasn't supposed to be in a dungeon? Was I about to get everything I deserved? It had to be true. I was no longer in a smelly cell but in a plush bed covered with red linens. I looked down to see I was wearing a sexy black nightgown. Not my color, but it wasn't that bad.

"Oh, you poor dear, you must be confused. Do you prefer me this way?" she asked, waving her hand and transforming before my eyes into the wraith from my dreams and the dungeon. Gone was her immaculate face. In its place was a gaunt, hollow, gray complexion and red-glowing eyes. Her manicured hands morphed into grotesque talons that made me touch my face, remembering how they had gouged my skin.

I recoiled. What the fuck was she? From previous conversations with the wraith, I knew they had magic powers and were something called the fae, but I had paid more attention to all she had offered me.

"Perhaps not," she said, and with another wave of her hand, she was beautiful again. "I took the liberty of having you bathed and dressed while you slept. Don't worry. My handmaidens took great care of you and made sure to treat you gently. You were in such a deep sleep that I thought I would let you rest until you regained your strength."

"Neat trick," I said, not allowing my sudden fear to leak through my voice. "I would stick with this look if I were you." Osiria, or the wraith, whatever, narrowed her eyes into slits. *Shit.*

"So you let strangers fondle me while I slept? *Great,*" I said sarcastically, tilting my chin up. I was not about to be intimidated by whoever she was.

"Not to worry, dear, my maidens are good at keeping quiet about delicate things," Osiria said.

"Okay, let me guess. You either didn't realize who I was when I crossed into Teleran, or you're really sorry, made a mistake, and are here to make it up to me," I stated, folding my arms over my perky chest.

"Oh, my dear, we've known who you were as soon as you crossed into our territory."

"Okay, well then, explain to me why, after I did everything that you asked, I ended up in that disgusting dungeon being fed garbage?" I said as I sat up and placed my hands on my hips. I was momentarily distracted by the sheer decadence of the fabric I was wearing. "No one ever even looked at the cut on my head. I demand to see the person in charge now. I was promised a lot, and I'll expect compensation for how I've been treated," I said, airing each of my grievances.

"I am in *charge*, my dear, but do not mistake me," Osiria gritted through her teeth, all warmth evaporating from her tone. "I have been kind to you, but my patience wears thin. I'll leave you to your breakfast. Maldridge will be by to collect you when you're finished. But I expect you to be dressed and ready. We have much to plan," Osiria said, her tone clipped, laced with lethal grace.

"What the hell are you talking about, *Osiria?* What the hell is a Maldridge? Is Cody okay? Is he alive? And, like, plan for wh—?" I yelled.

Osiria's hand struck my face so fast that my last word was cut off, and spit flew from my mouth. Ouch, and gross.

"Apologies, my dear, but I did warn you. I'll leave you now," she said cooly.

And with that, she walked out of the room, her black waves billowing behind her like an inky black cape.

So they didn't like questions here. I got it. I could play along for a while. The steaming breakfast tray sitting on the nightstand beside the bed smelled amazing. I lifted the lid off the black serving platter and drooled for the first time in my life. It was my favorite breakfast: avocado toast with egg whites paired with a steaming vanilla latte. Fuck not eating carbs, I was starving. Maybe this place had a magical diet or something?

I was sifting through the meal when someone breezed right into my new room without knocking.

"Excuse me, have you ever heard of knock—" My words cut off as my jaw slackened, and maybe I drooled for the second time in my life.

The hottest fucking guy I had ever fucking seen had just walked into my room. He was tall, dark, and yummy, with dark auburn hair coiffed back, revealing pointed ears and a deep, burnt-umber complexion. He wore an unbuttoned black shirt revealing a seriously chiseled, hairless chest. As my eyes drifted to whiskey-colored eyes, they paused on his sinfully sexy grin. He made me wish I was holding a fan because it was suddenly hot as hell in here.

"Hello, lovely, how was your breakfast?" the sickeningly hot man asked. Did he just call me lovely? Hmm … and he had good taste. I might be in love with Cody, but there was a slight chance I would never see him again. He could be dead if the wraith/Osiria were to be believed, and while that was a heartbreaking possibility, I would have to be dead not to think of letting this black silk pool at my feet and offering myself up to the god standing in front of me.

There was no mistaking that familiar heat reflecting in his eyes. He liked what he saw, and I wasn't wearing a bra underneath the gown, so my hardened nipples were on full display. Maybe he was my reward for enduring a disgusting prison for however long. A little orgasm did the body good, and he looked like he knew his way around a clit.

"It was fine, but you're finer," I said brazenly while rising from the bed, causing us to be almost chest-to-chest. He smiled, not fazed by my words. "I'm Alison. What's your name, honey?" I said with my best Southern debutant drawl as I ran my hands up his hardened chest. My accent could make a man melt in seconds.

"My name is Maldridge, but to you, my little lava rock, I'm off limits," he said, amusement lighting his eyes as he extracted my hands from his torso.

"Too bad," I said, dropping my shoulder and cocking my head to the side in a pout. The strap on my nightgown slipped, exposing the swell of my right breast.

"Whoops," I said, feigning innocence. Maldridge's eyes heated to liquid amber as he reached out to fix my fallen strap, grazing my arm the whole way up. His big, strong hand rested on my shoulder a moment longer than he needed to, and the warmth radiating from him was molten. I could feel wetness dripping in between my legs. That's when I realized I wasn't wearing underwear.

"Yes, my dear, my affections are otherwise engaged. I've been instructed to direct you to get dressed. Osiria requests you join her in her lounge."

"Oh, me too, about the otherwise engaged thing. That doesn't mean we can't have a little fun, especially if you've been ordered to direct me to get dressed. Which means you're helping me undress first, right?" I said, my words heavy with intent.

"You, my darling, are going to be trouble. Now, quickly, Osiria waits for no one." He gestured toward an open door that I could only assume was the closet.

"Yeah, yeah, fine. So what am I supposed to wear? Also, black isn't my color. Do you heathens not have anything else to wear? Don't you have *any* pink in this place?"

"I'm afraid not, but Osiria did have her handmaidens stock the closet in this room with clothes that should fit you. So if you'd like to get dressed in there, I'll wait out here and escort you to her safely." He took a step away from me as he concluded.

"Safely?" I questioned. We were in a palace, not the dungeons. I should be more than safe. I was the revered guest of the woman in charge.

"A sweet little morsel like you could get into a lot of trouble if you rounded the wrong hallway here," he cautioned, but his words had a playful tone to them. *Sweet?* This guy clearly didn't know who he was talking to. Maybe he wanted me to be the demure damsel in distress. I was happy to play along if that's what got him going. I always did like a bit of roleplay.

"All right, *darling,"* I said mockingly. "I'll go see if there is anything salvageable to wear." I turned on my heels and headed to the closet, but not before dropping the nightgown to the floor and swaying my hips a little more than I needed to. I had an ass that even I wished I could take a bite of, and Maldridge may have said he was off limits, but the sharp intake of his breath as I walked away naked told another story entirely.

Maybe a little fling in Teleran was just what I needed to slough off the grimness from being imprisoned. Cody would never have to know, and I loved nothing more than a challenge.

CHAPTER 20

Clarke

"You guys think I'm crazy, don't you?" I blurted as I took a seat on the edge of the bed.

"We don't think you're crazy, Clarke," Haywood protested.

"It's okay. I'm starting to think the same thing," I admitted.

"You truly think the dream was real?" Haywood questioned as he came to sit beside me on the bed.

"I …" I paused as a memory came back to me. "Hold on. Haywood, holy shit! When I was back in jail, before you came to get me, I had a dream. It was about Alison, and she was begging me to find her. She was in a gross-looking dungeon kind of place. It was dark, but it looked like she was surrounded by shiny, black stones, and just as I was waking up, she said she was in *Telera*. She got cut off when I woke up. And just now, she said she was in Teleran. I don't understand it, but I don't think I would have two dreams like that if they didn't mean anything."

"However unlikely, there is a possibility what you saw was real," Lachlan interjected. He was sitting in the winged-back chair, his legs spread wide and his hand on his chin as if he were deep in thought.

"You believe me?"

"I believe you, Clarke. I know a place that fits your description," Lachlan continued. "On the Obscurus side of Teleran, there is an underground dungeon carved into the black stone foundation of Aurantia, my sovereign's palace," he went on.

"We have to go," I moved to get up from my seat on the bed.

"Wait, we can't just go, Clarke. This significantly complicates things if Alison has somehow been taken captive by the Obscurus sovereign. And, more importantly, there is more we need to talk about," Haywood said.

"More *importantly?* Seriously? Haywood, my best friend, who I thought was dead, could be alive and here. I have to save her," I said.

"I'm pretty sure both our worlds ending is more important," Luck stated, twirling her dagger in her hand. I shrunk back. She was right. I was being irrational.

"Clarke, think. Why would Alison be here?" Haywood asked.

"How am I supposed to know? Did you know she was here the entire time, Haywood? Is that it—just another one of your lies?" I asked, thinking back to my earlier theory, that he was the one murdering and kidnapping everyone. Even if I knew that wasn't the case, it didn't absolve him from other crimes.

"If she is here, I am unaware of it," Haywood replied earnestly. "And if she is here, I find it peculiar that Osiria's second in command knows nothing about who is in his dungeons," Haywood said, narrowing his eyes at Lachlan.

"Of course, I didn't know," Lachlan sounded offended before turning to me. "Clarke, is this your friend from Earth? Haywood filled me in on some details about what you've been going through," he explained. I nodded, and he continued. "Are you sure she said Teleran in your dream?"

"Lachlan, you can't be considering this," Haywood interrupted, dismissing my response.

"Out of everyone here, Lachlan is the only one who doesn't even know Alison. I want to hear what he has to say," I said.

"I can assure you that I have no knowledge of your friend's capture, so Haywood is correct. If she is in Aurantia's dungeons, our problems have just gotten significantly worse," Lachlan stated.

"But how could Clarke see this?" Haywood asked. "Are these visions?"

"I don't know how I can see this, Haywood. Maybe I'm a seer or something. Don't you guys have those here?" I asked. Anything could be possible here. Fact couldn't be that far from fiction.

"We have the Alternae, our elders, who sometimes see visions. They are where our prophecies have always originated," Haywood replied.

"Well, all I know is I've dreamed of Alison twice. I don't care how unbelievable that is to you, Haywood. I've been betrayed by every friend I've ever had except one. I will not abandon Alison to imprisonment or worse."

"Worse," Lachlan said definitively. I looked at him, alarmed. "If you had seen the things I had, you'd know that sometimes death is a mercy when compared to what my sovereign is capable of." Ice ran through my veins.

"If she's truly so terrible, how can you serve someone like that, Lachlan?" I asked.

"If you were on her side, you wouldn't think her actions terrible," he answered. "Before … you, I thought she was the great protector of our people and all of Teleran. She is wise, always reading and collecting scrolls of our histories to better serve our people. At least, that is what I thought. Now, I only know a few things for sure. Teleran will fall if we do nothing. You are far more important than we could've imagined. And we cannot underestimate my sovereign. If she has your friend, it's part of her plan."

"What plan?" I asked Lachlan.

"I don't know," he said. "I feel the truth of your words, Clarke. You believe your dreams are real. I must confess I have read of a gift where fae possess the ability to enter the dreams of others," Lachlan said.

"You can't be serious," Luck responded with a snort. "Those are just stories we tell children, Lachlan. Oneironauts are not real."

"I have reason to believe they are both real and that Osiria is one of them," Lachlan said.

The shock from Luck and Haywood was tangible.

"As I said," Lachlan continued, "my sovereign is wise and hoards much knowledge. I've seen texts on the subject in her chambers, where she keeps her most treasured texts, in her private library. It is a great risk for me even to suggest that Osiria has this gift, but if Clarke also possesses this gift, it may provide a clue as to why Osiria wants her," he replied.

Recoiling like he'd been dealt a blow to the face, Haywood dropped my hand and looked at me like he'd never seen me before, then to Lachlan. "That's not … possible."

"It is not only possible but likely. This shouldn't surprise you, Haywood, as Clarke has many *unique* qualities," Lachlan replied.

"Excuse me," I said, feeling that we had veered off topic. I was still discovering my abilities, both what I possessed and lacked; all they needed was to believe me so that we could rescue Alison. I didn't give a damn if I was something I couldn't even pronounce.

"The *oneironauts* are a myth," Haywood whispered.

"My abilities, while important, pale compared to Alison being held prisoner," I said frustratedly. "I honestly don't care what abilities I have right now. We have to save her, Haywood. She's the only family I have left." My voice cracked, and Haywood's brown eyes held understanding. He knew what she was to me more than anyone here. He'd seen what happened when I had thought she was dead.

"Why in the *hell* would Alison be here?" Luck questioned.

"I feel like everything has gotten even more complicated. Teleran is waning. Both our sovereigns wanted us to bring Clarke here. Neither of us knows why. And now Osiria has Clarke's best friend in her dungeons?" Haywood questioned. "Everything would be so much easier if we had found the scroll with the prophecy," he murmured.

"Could Alison have magic too, Haywood?" Luck inquired.

"I did not observe anything to make me think that could be," Haywood answered. "Clarke, how old is Alison?"

"She is twenty-nine," I said.

"So it's possible that her powers haven't manifested yet because she has yet to turn thirty," Luck said.

"You guys, this is … I don't even know what to say. I would say that sounds crazy, but you're right—it's possible. Anything is possible," I said.

"You're right, Clarke. We will figure this out. But I must be honest: I'm not exactly sure where to start," Haywood said.

"I think I do," Lachlan said as he pulled a rolled-up piece of paper from his pant pocket. He threw it on the bed in between Haywood and me.

"Is that—" Haywood started.

111

"The scroll with the prophecy you've been searching for? Yes, yes, it is," Lachlan said.

CHAPTER 21

Clarke

"How do you have this?" Haywood asked, picking up the scroll.

"Who do you think helps Osiria fill her library of knowledge?" Lachlan replied. "You didn't think she amassed it all by herself, did you?" The two held each other's gaze for a moment.

"Um. What prophecy?" I asked.

"It is said to be the key to saving Teleran," Luck answered.

"We've been looking for this for years, Lachlan," Haywood said. "You said you helped Osiria amass texts, but not where this was found."

"I found it hidden behind a secret door in the Alternae's archives just before I was sent to retrieve Clarke. I was supposed to deliver it to Osiria, but something held me back. At the time, I thought it was because I didn't want to deliver a scroll that promised answers but contained little instruction. Now, I believe it may have been fate that stopped me," Lachlan answered.

"Well, what does it say?" I asked.

Haywood read the scroll aloud: "Down the line, centuries untold, death and destruction will unfold. To prevent this awful fate, unlikely halves must part from hate. From clasping hands of mortal foes, power sang of fate to be sowed. For peace and prosperity, for love, joy, and destiny, a descendant of both their powers will forfeit heart and increase hours."

"What does that mean?" I asked.

"Other than it seems to direct our two sides to work together, I don't see the doom ending instructions it was supposed to provide. Prophecies are often written in nonsensical riddles designed to be so vague that they become unhelpful," Lachlan replied. "I had considered taking it to the Alternae for further instruction, but now I think there may be a better place to find answers. I can't believe I didn't think of it before."

"Where would that be?" Haywood asked, suspicion lacing his words.

"Osiria's library," Lachlan replied. "As I said, she has amassed scrolls and texts containing knowledge we'd once thought lost. It's why her abilities and power rival even your own sovereign."

"We cannot trust her, Lachlan," Haywood sneered. "You know this."

"I'm not suggesting we trust her, Haywood, but if we want answers. If we want to save Teleran, we need to journey to Aurantia."

"We will be caught before we step foot into the palace."

"We are caught at this very moment." Seeing Haywood's puzzled expression, Lachlan continued, "Osiria would've sensed the moment I crossed back into our realm, but she's yet to send anyone, not even a message. She knows I'm here and has done nothing. Doesn't that strike you as strange?"

"I hadn't thought …" Haywood trailed off as he considered their predicament.

"Solana sent Leora to fetch you and Clarke immediately. The only reason my sovereign stays her hand is because she has a plan, and we are likely following it, however unwittingly. She requested that I bring Clarke to her, but I've yet to be punished for not doing so. Something is going on, and I will find the root of it. But I cannot do it without the knowledge to fight back, to keep us all from dying. We must travel to Aurantia, specifically to Osiria's chambers."

"I think I can help with that," Luck spoke up.

"How?" Lachlan asked.

"I know better than anyone how to hide in the shadows and not be seen. Tell me what we are looking for, and I will get it undetected," she answered.

"You can try Master of Shadows," Lachlan quipped, "but know that Osiria doesn't play the game unless she knows she will win. She will be ten steps ahead of us. We cannot let our guard down."

"I never let my guard down, Obscurus," Luck parried.

"Well, what am I supposed to do while you all go knowledge searching? Stay here and knit while my friend is in danger?" I asked.

"Your friend might be in the dungeons of Aurantia," Lachlan responded.

"And?" I prompted.

"Is it not obvious, Clarke? The knowledge we seek and the friend you wish to save are in the same place. So you must travel with us. Accomplishing both goals at the same time," Lachlan explained.

"The journey will be treacherous, but I agree, Clarke. You must come with us," Haywood said softly.

"Lachlan, I'm finding it very hard to believe that my best friend is in your sovereign's dungeons, while you know nothing about it," I said, growing suspicious.

"I suppose you'll just have to try to trust me, Clarke," Lachlan replied, not offering further explanation.

"Whatever. If what you say is true, then we have to leave now. Alison is in danger. And now that we know where she is, we have to go get her," I said.

"It seems our paths are intertwined," Luck said. "We must all travel to the Red Palace to save Teleran and your friend. I suggest we gather in the study. I'm sure Clarke wouldn't mind a change of scenery. The study is where Haywood keeps the good whiskey, and I'll need it if I'm to conspire against my sovereign with an Obscurus," Luck added, exiting Haywood's bedroom.

CHAPTER 22

Lachlan

"Aren't you coming?" Haywood asked, starting to follow Clake and Luck to the study.

"Yes, I just need a minute to collect my thoughts. I'll catch up," I said, not wanting to explain that I wanted to hang back. I was used to being on my own. With the exception of Osiria, I kept to myself and enjoyed my solitude. Being around Haywood, Luck, and even Clarke without a break overwhelmed me.

I leaned back in the chair and dropped my face to my hands.

"Fuck." I was exhausted and unhinged. What game was Osiria playing now, and why had she left me out of her schemes? I felt like a fool. It was apparent Clarke was at the forefront of her plans: She always had leverage and had locked up Clarke's human best friend in our dungeons. It was her insurance that Clarke would come to her if I failed. Why all the secrecy?

Shit.

I was growing more convinced that Osiria knew of the mate bond between Clarke and me and had decided I was not trustworthy because of it. But why send me after Clarke? If she was concerned that I'd meet her and sense the bond, why let us meet at all? Why not just kill me and send Maldridge or one of her maidens to retrieve Clarke?

The web she'd woven was twisted and cunning; I just had to use what I knew about her to untangle it.

Should I tell Clarke of the bond? If it would be used against us, knowing of it might help her.

The bond had already begun to affect her. It was subtle, but I doubt she even realized it.

If I thought managing the bond was challenging while she was comatose, it was ten times worse when her bright green eyes were open and she was awake and speaking. I found myself forgetting to respond or join in the conversation because I loved hearing the sound of her voice, and I loved watching her do … anything.

Damn it.

I loved her mere presence.

If Osiria could see me now, utterly smitten, she'd never let me live it down. As it stood now, she'd never let me live, period.

I had promised to help Clarke save her friend and to attempt gathering the information I was sure Osiria had hidden in her chambers to save Teleran, but that essentially meant marching to my own death.

Osiria was allowing this plan to form and take place, and we'd only pass the threshold of her palace if she permitted it. We were up against an impossible task, yet we had to press on. Teleran was at stake.

Yes, death would soon be visiting me, but not until I did everything in my power to help my people and my mate.

I wished I had some way to gather intel on *why* her friend was in the dungeons of the Red Palace. Osiria did nothing without a motive.

My propensity for solace worked against me in this respect. I was feared, yes, and my commands were followed dutifully, but I didn't have anyone I could call on for help. My sovereign kept a tight circle; very few were allowed close to her, but none of us were friends.

Maldridge, her current lover, would rather cut my throat and take my place than help me with anything. Her maidens were mute, their tongues removed. They were really silent assassins that my sovereign passed off as servants. They are her true warriors, a close-guarded Obscurus secret. While Solana had her guard, Osiria had trained the females of our court to be fast and lethal. She dressed them in ridiculously ancient-looking garments with veils to conceal their identities and make them appear like mere servants. And while they attended to her needs, they also trained and fought. They knew how to kill before their victims knew what was happening to them.

The realm had no idea of the threat they posed. I had once stood among them, a shining example of the strength of the Obscurus. We were formidable, ruthless, and cunning.

They were all obstacles now that would make our mission nearly impossible. A shudder ran through me as I became disgusted with myself at how far I had strayed from the man I had been just days prior. I would be remembered only as a traitor, a turncoat at the end.

I could hear the others down the hall discussing and planning and decided that if I wanted this mission to succeed, they needed my input. It's not like any of them had been to Aurantia before.

If by some miracle, we found a way to decode the prophecy and acquire the knowledge to save Teleran, I could bargain for Clarke and her friend's life. Osiria could kill Haywood and the shadow one for all I cared, and I knew she'd never let me live, but I had to tip the scales in Clarke's favor.

I ran my fingers through my hair. I couldn't succumb to defeat. The odds were stacked against me, but I had to try.

CHAPTER 23

Clarke

I uneasily followed Luck to Haywood's study. An overwhelming sense of dread and anxiety filled me. I needed to get a grip but felt pulled in countless directions.

Well, I just had to buck the fuck up. Breaking wasn't an option. Alison was here, and she deserved more than my fear, lack of understanding, and disbelief of the situation. If she were truly alive and in Teleran, I had to be strong for her. I needed to save her from whatever fate had brought her here. And Teleran and Earth would be destroyed if we did nothing; I had to ensure we both had a home to return to.

My discovery of who I was had to take a backseat. The realm I came from was dying, and there were more important things than my shrouded identity.

My mind was set, and I was determined. We would save Alison and take her home. She was the last person who loved me, and she needed me. I vowed that I would not rest until she was safe again.

When Lachlan finally joined us, chaos erupted. The innate animosity between the Estival and Obscurus fae seemed to run deep.

Everyone was talking over each other, and nothing was getting accomplished. Even though I knew the frustration and loud voices weren't directed at me, I was still easily triggered. I wanted to retreat to a quiet, safe place, a tactic I had crafted as a child to escape my father's booming anger. I didn't have time to go there right now. Alison's life was at stake, and I wasn't that scared little girl anymore. I had real power deep down.

"Hey!" I yelled, causing everyone to stop talking abruptly. I stood up and nervously smoothed out my shirt. "Thank you. I can't pretend to know how you all feel, but I think I understand what it's like to see your world and everything you know crumble. I also can't pretend to know anything about fae politics or the extent of the danger we will face. But I do know I was brought here for a reason. We need each other. Alison is here. She's in danger and afraid. That much was clear when she reached out to me in my dream. And even if Alison were safe and back on Earth, we won't have a home if our worlds merge. We all need to cut the shit and focus. What's happening is bigger than us.

"We won't accomplish anything if we fight among ourselves. Let's just agree that we are all facing impossible odds and more than uncomfortable circumstances. And frankly, if I can try to work past everything I've ever known being a lie and coming to terms with magic existing and me being a fae, then what I'm asking you all to do doesn't seem that hard. You're from different sides of the track? Big fucking deal. Get over it."

Luck blinked at me, apparently stunned by my bluntness.

"I'm sorry, Clarke. You're right," Haywood said. "If we aim to save Alison, Teleran, and Earth successfully, we will attempt to put aside our differences. Won't we?" He gave Lachlan a pointed look.

"Of course, I will do the same. I gave my word." Lachlan let out a heavy sigh. "Clarke, forgive me. What I was trying to get across was that between all of us, I should be leading us on this venture, especially once we cross over to my realm."

"Thank you both for your apologies. I truly don't care who leads us; it's just that we need to get moving," I said.

"So it's agreed then. I will be leading," Lachlan said smugly.

"Fine, so what path are we taking, *leader?"* Haywood directed at Lachlan.

"The most direct route takes us straight through Altfevis," he answered.

"What is Altfevis?" I asked.

"Altfevis is a festival, a celebration for all of Teleran's fae to come together—something I had been planning for the better part of a year," Lachlan responded.

"I would liken it to your music festivals but with a bit more … exhibitionism," Haywood explained.

"Okay, well, let's go the most direct way. Unless there is a reason we shouldn't," I said, trying to sound unbothered by Haywood saying *exhibitionism*. I really should see a doctor after all this, someone to explain why everything turned me on now. I wasn't a prude, but ever since I had turned thirty, I had been having sex dreams like crazy, and my libido was off the charts. I was thirty and thirsty. I swear, with these two sexy fae in this room, I was afraid I would start doing something embarrassing, like rubbing up against the furniture to get me some relief. A thought hit me. Haywood said that my awakening had started when I turned thirty. Was my awakening making me abnormally horny?

A choked sound escaped Lachlan, and Haywood emitted a pained noise.

"Um…" Haywood started.

"Did I say that out loud?" I questioned, mortified. A sharp nod from Lachlan confirmed that I had. *Damn it.*

Lachlan looked at Haywood, and Haywood looked back at Lachlan. The two of them seemed to be carrying on a silent conversation.

"We should tell her, Haywood," Lachlan urged.

"I think we should honor the lady's wishes, Lachlan. She is clearly embarrassed and doesn't appear as if she wants to discuss this," Haywood responded.

"Okay, you *have* to tell me now," I said.

"Fae adolescents can become quite … sexually charged during their awakening. It's the extra energy building up in your body. Your emotions may be heightened as well. What you are experiencing is completely natural, and there's nothing to be ashamed of," Haywood answered.

It was my turn to choke, and then I really didn't know how to respond. It explained so much. My sex dreams, the vividness of them, practically jumping Haywood after hearing of Alison's death, and my intense attraction to Lachlan. Well, now that I knew this was just a side effect of my body's change, maybe I could work to control it somehow.

"As interesting as this conversation is, let's move on to planning, shall we?" Luck said, effectively saving me from further humiliation.

I settled into one of the green and purple velvet wingback chairs in the study. In the center of the chairs stood a small round wooden table adorned with a tea service that featured four steaming cups of tea. Lachlan and Haywood joined me.

"Since our journey takes us through Altfevis, we have an ideal opportunity to camp and rest. We can hide in plain sight there and regroup. After that, I would take us north past the Guild of Shadows and approach my side of Teleran from that route. A hidden path through the bogs will help conceal our approach. The path leads directly to the prison. Luck and Clarke can sneak in and grab your friend, while Haywood and I retrieve what we need from Osiria's chambers. If we time it right, we will arrive at Aurantia toward the end of Altfevis, when Osiria is planning to make her appearance. So while her chambers will be guarded, she will not be present."

"You make this sound so easy," I remarked.

"Too easy, in fact. He left out the part about how the bogs emit poisonous sulfuric gas that is deadly to my kind and potentially to you since we are not sure what vulnerabilities you have," Haywood said, sounding suspicious of Lachlan's plan.

"Well, by all means, *friend,* if you have a better path, I'm all ears," Lachlan responded.

"I never said I had a better path. I'm simply stating the obstacles so that Clarke is clear on what to expect. You also failed to mention that since the Obscurus are planning and hosting this year's Altfevis, the crowd will be obscene at best." Haywood said, turning his nose up in disapproval.

"I'll be fine, Haywood," I argued. "I'm not some blushing virgin here. And I love a good party. I'm sure I can blend in just fine if you guys can."

"You'll have to make it convincing, *mae,"* Lachlan said, sounding effortlessly seductive.

"Don't call her that!" Haywood spat.

"Call me what? What is *mae?"* I asked. I glanced at Luck, who had been sitting silently in her chair, legs tucked underneath her while stirring her tea, seeming contemplative in her own world. She did not meet my gaze.

"A common term of endearment. A slip of the tongue, and nothing more, I assure you," Lachlan responded indifferently, doing nothing to calm the glaring Haywood.

"Okay. What did you mean by making it convincing? We are just passing through and camping," I said. I was still curious about what mae meant, but more importantly, I needed to keep Lachlan and Haywood from each other's throats.

"Unfortunately, that won't be enough. We will have to partake of some of what's on offer at the festival, or the hiding-in-plain-sight plan won't work," Lachlan replied.

I swallowed. "What's on offer?" Was this some kind of orgy party?

"Don't let him scare you, Clarke," Haywood said reassuringly. "We will get our own tent and appear to be sampling the thoroughfare. Nothing untoward will happen. I'll ensure it."

I let my shoulders sink, feeling a little relieved. I was more than okay with throwing back some drinks and even enjoyed a little recreational drug every now and then, but nothing too hard. I liked weed and had dabbled with psychedelics but had been too scared to try anything else. If this festival had things like weed or shrooms, I would be fine with joining in.

"Nothing will happen … unless you want it to," Lachlan said, suddenly very close to my ear. That last part was so quiet I knew that he'd meant it for only me. I could feel his warm breath caress my skin, and I knew if I turned my head, his lips would be dangerously close to mine. *Do it,* my new instincts screamed. *Nope*. I would just ignore him if he'd said anything else. And judging by Haywood's calm demeanor as he sipped his tea, he hadn't heard Lachlan.

I picked up my cup and took a sip. Warm, honeyed herbal tea slipped past my lips and down my throat, warming my body and soul. I let out a pleased sound that was nearly a moan, and Haywood almost dropped his teacup. I was too afraid even to look to my left to see Lachlan's reaction, but I could feel the heat of his gaze.

"So when do we leave?" I questioned, redirecting the conversation.

"Nightfall will be best," Luck said, finally contributing to the conversation. It'd been nighttime when I'd woken up; I guess I'd been in the tub for longer than I'd realized.

"The shadow speaks the truth," Lachlan said. "I suggest we all rest until then. We won't have soft beds to sleep on between here and Aurantia."

"I have rooms for each of you," Haywood said. "Pick whichever you'd like. We leave at first light."

And with that, we all set off in search of a place to rest before embarking on our journey to save Alison and Teleran.

PART TWO

The Journey

CHAPTER 24

Clarke

After we decided to wait until nightfall to leave, I stood and walked back toward Haywood's room, which he had offered me. Brass sconces lit the hallway with firelight, illuminating the dark green walls.

I'd wanted to argue that we should leave as soon as possible. Alison had already been in that awful dungeon for who knew how long. But Luck said we would need the cover of night for our safety, to conceal us while we left Haywood's home. I suppose she knew better than I did. Better to have a successful rescue mission than a hurried one that somehow got us captured and unable to help Alison at all.

And I guess I could use a good long nap before our week-long journey. I assumed we'd be sleeping on the ground in tents from here on, so I might as well try to enjoy Haywood's heavenly bed.

I was thankful they left me alone; maybe I could calm myself enough to sleep. I was also grateful for the bracelets on my wrists, even though they made my skin itch and burn a little. They helped me feel detached from being a fae. I didn't *feel* different, and somehow, that made what I needed to do easier. I really couldn't focus on myself anyway. My goal was singular—get Alison safe and out of captivity and save the world, or worlds. Simple enough.

I threw myself onto Haywood's bed and gazed up at his enormous circular skylight. Daylight streamed through, yet the sky still swirled with pinks, purples, and blues. It reminded me of photos I had seen of the northern lights. As a painting formed in my mind, my eyelids grew heavy, and I surrendered to the deep sleep my body craved.

. . .

I sat straight up in Haywood's bed, clutching my chest. A light sheen of sweat covered me, and my heart raced. Suddenly, Lachlan appeared in the doorway, looking out of breath. Had he run all the way here from where he'd been sleeping?

"Clarke, are you okay? What's wrong?" he asked with concern.

"I'm okay; I attempted to connect with Alison again. I can't remember everything, but I could feel what she was feeling," I explained.

"You did? What did you feel?" he said, coming to take a seat next to me on the bed, his tone soft.

I took a deep breath. "I don't know. I felt a mix of emotions, but nothing made sense. It scared me, Lachlan. We have to help her."

"We will. I promise you, Clarke," he said, resting his large hand on my forearm in comfort. A jolt ran up my arm, and my eyes flickered up to his. He held my gaze and then cleared his throat, averting his eyes and severing the charged air between us.

"So, dream walking?" I said as a way to break the tension building and the awkward silence that had stretched.

"I don't know everything about it, but I will share all that I do," he offered. "Back when oneironauts were more than myth, the gift was still a rare one to possess. I'll caution you, from what I know, it's not just dreams; some were said to have been able to enter their waking minds and bend them to their will. Remarkably, you have this ability, and it amazes me that you can do it with the bracelets," he said almost reverently. "My sovereign has many texts on the subject, and perhaps while we are in Aurantia, we could find some for you to read. With training, you could manipulate the space around you as if you were physically there. Theoretically, you could use all your senses and feel things even though they are technically happening in your mind or even someone else's mind," he explained.

"You're talking about mind control? I don't think I would want to do that," I said honestly. "I couldn't smell the dungeon this time, Lachlan. Could that mean something bad?"

"Not necessarily. It could be that the connection wasn't as strong as before. Your state of rest and hers might not have been synced. It's hard to tell when so few have ever possessed this ability.

"On this journey to help your friend, we will help you learn more about your powers and find out what other abilities you have. Even with the bracelets, you'll still be able to harness your magic, which is evident now since you've already dream-walked with them on. The power will be muted, and you will not feel its full force, but that will help you get used to it."

"Thank you."

"Thank you?" he questioned.

"Yes, thank you. You hardly know me, yet you're willing to do so much for a stranger. You have a kind heart, Lachlan."

He dismissed my praise with a scoff.

"Don't be modest, Lachlan," I said with a teasing smile. "You've decided to help me without asking for anything in return. I can only assume it's because you are a kind and amazing person. I mean, Haywood and I are … *friends* …

130

and Luck, well, I guess we are friends adjacent. And anyway, Haywood owes me. So, maybe, if you disagree with my assumption of your character, what is motivating you?"

"Let's be clear. I'm not a good *person,* as you put it. I'm simply righting a wrong. You were shot and could have died because of a mistake I made, so in my mind, I owe you a debt as well. In Teleran, we do not leave our debts unpaid; our words have meaning, and our intent drives our magic and power. To renege on our word is to negate our power. That would never be done lightly. Fae covet and revere power. It is how our sovereigns are chosen in the first place; the most powerful rule the least. It is the order of both Estival and Obscurus. You also forget that we need you. You are important to both of our sovereigns and may be the key to saving our world. So you say I require nothing in return? That's not exactly true. Does that *satisfy* you? We are mutually benefiting from this arrangement."

Well, fuck, he had me there. But why did he have to say *satisfy* like that?

I had to get my baby fae urges under control before this fae made me spontaneously combust. His tone of voice, every word, was laced with pure sex. How was I supposed to travel with him for a week? As it was, I had to use all my self-control to stay still and not excuse myself to take the edge off.

Ugh, I needed Alison so badly right now. I craved some girl-talk, like, pronto. Maybe Luck could serve as a surrogate friend for now? I didn't know if I could trust her, though, and what would she think of my wavering affection? Maybe this was normal here? After all, they had a yearly festival filled with all manner of debauchery. I realized Lachlan was waiting for my response, so I ceased musing.

"I guess that answer can *satisfy* me, yes," I said, noticing how the sun was beginning to set. It would soon be time to leave, and I buzzed with anxious energy. I could entertain a little excitement for the opportunity to see the world of the fae. I still had to wrap my head around the fact that I had somehow come from this world. Did my Mom and Dad adopt me? Could one of them have been fae and didn't know? Or worse, they knew and just never told me.

Maybe this journey to rescue Alison would lead to self-discovery as well. I was fae. Teleran was my true home. That fact would eventually set in, right?

"So are we ready to go? Where are the others?" I asked Lachlan.

"Haywood and Luck are still asleep, but I'm sure they'll be up at true sundown," Lachlan answered.

"What, like vampires?" I joked. When Lachlan didn't immediately answer, I became alarmed. "Wait, vampires aren't real, right?"

Lachlan fiddled with his shirt, straightening it. "There are a great many mysterious things in Teleran."

That was not an answer. What if he was a vampire fae? I'd read books where vampirism was a manifestation of fae powers. I imagined Lachlan biting my neck. Why was it hot in here all of a sudden? I was suddenly aware of his size. He was so much bigger than me, standing almost a foot taller with shoulders so broad that I bet he had to turn sideways to get through doorways.

I shifted nervously. My traitorous vagina was making me think up all sorts of things it needed and wanted me to ask Lachlan for. I was painfully aware that Lachlan and I were alone. How would we pass the time? Flashes of our sweaty bodies colliding took me off guard, and I stifled a gasp. I, unfortunately, couldn't stop the warmth creeping into my cheeks as I blushed furiously. Lachlan either didn't notice or was polite enough not to ask questions or comment.

"Have you had the opportunity to look outside?" he asked, effectively changing the subject.

I had been so consumed by the changes in my body, the overload of information, and the many revelations from Haywood that I hadn't even thought to visit Haywood's balcony. Sure, I had glimpsed the colorful sky through the skylight, but that had been all. Suddenly, I was filled with vibrating excitement. The fae were real, their world was real, and I was in it. It was still so unbelievable.

"I haven't. I've been too distracted," I replied sheepishly.

"Well, allow me," he said, extending his hand toward me. I placed my hand in his, and the fluttering of my heart increased. Luckily, he didn't seem to notice as he helped me off the bed. Never letting go of my hand, he led me out through the French doors and onto the balcony. I gasped, taking in the scene. It was so magnificent and quaint all at the same time. Rows of pale pinkish stone buildings lined a cobblestone row. From where I was standing, I could see signs highlighting the businesses occupying the buildings. The smell of the bakery below wafted up and invaded my nostrils with the most delicious scent. Past the buildings, I could see snow-crested hills and a giant oak tree … that reminded me of …

"I've been here," I said softly, unable to believe it.

"What do you mean? You've been to the Estival side of Teleran before?" he asked.

"I thought it was just a dream. I didn't know it was real. I woke up under that tree over there and smelled the bakery."

"That's incredible, Clarke. When do you think your dreams started turning into dream walking?"

"I don't know, but it makes so much sense, Lachlan. After everything you all have told me, all of the unexplained things started happening after I turned thirty." Some of the strange occurrences that had happened to me prior were all Haywood, like when I thought I had sent bees to attack Virginia or made the leaves twirl; that was him all along.

"Are there more dreams you now recognize as real?" he asked, his expression difficult to place.

"Um," I didn't want to tell him about the sexual dreams I had been experiencing, so I decided to keep that to myself. And I *really* didn't think they were real; I didn't have a boyfriend or anything, and there was no way I would involve a stranger in my dreams like that. "I don't think so, but maybe the more I see of Teleran, the more I might remember something from my dreams," I mused. Lachlan didn't say anything in response but just nodded his head and leaned against the stone ledge of the balcony.

He turned toward me, a boyish grin lighting up his usually severe expression. "Want to go down there?" he asked.

"I thought it wasn't safe. That's why we were waiting until nightfall to leave, right?" I asked warily. I wanted to explore but was concerned about something bad happening. Nothing could deter our journey to save Alison, even if my heart was pounding with anticipation.

"It's nearly full night, and Haywood and Luck are still asleep. We could drop into the bakery and grab some items for our journey. I promise that no harm will come to you while you're with me. Besides, most of the fae are traveling to Altfevis, so few should be left in this town."

"I am hungry. As long as you think it's safe." The streets did look empty, and I'm sure Haywood and Luck would appreciate special treats for our trip.

"I do," he said, leading me back into Haywood's bedroom.

"I'll be surprised if they have anything I can eat," I stated.

"What do you mean?" Lachlan asked.

"Well, I used to have a lot of stomach issues, when I was a kid. If I ate anything containing any animal products or byproducts, I became violently ill. It was pretty embarrassing. So I stick to a mostly vegan diet now. Do you have anything like that here?" I asked hopefully, expecting him to say no.

Lachlan looked at me with an amused smile. "Only primitive humans eat animals. I wasn't aware there was a term for our diet, but I can assure you, no one here eats anything comprised of animals. I'm sure we'd all fall ill, as you said, if we did."

"Wait. Are you making fun of me, or are you being serious?" I asked.

"I assure you that I am very serious. Our magic comes from the beating heart of nature. To kill and consume its creatures would be barbaric. Why would we kill and eat the creatures who bring us joy and serve as our loyal companions? Their living essence fuels nature and, in turn, fuels our magic. There is an energy and order to Teleran. You are fae, Clarke. Your body is not meant for human customs, and rejecting them is the most natural thing."

I loved his straightforward way of explaining fae culture to me, as if he'd anticipated what my questions would be.

"Wow … so you're saying there's a bakery here where I can eat everything?" Lachlan nodded, amused, as I bounced on my toes. "Well, what are we doing in here? Lead the way, big man."

Lachlan looked at me and burst out laughing. His entire body shook, and the cracks of his hard shell revealed a glimpse of the fae that lay underneath. I knew it—big man was a big softie.

CHAPTER 25

Lachlan

I was torturing myself. I knew I was, but I couldn't stop. Severing the bond should've been my top priority.

I chided myself, *You can't still be considering this, can you?*

I had to figure out how to break this bond, not just for myself but for Clarke. Even if we succeeded in our mission, I couldn't see any chance of escaping with my life. If she knew, if the bond were solidified, the pain of losing me would be unimaginable. I couldn't do that to her. She'd already endured so much and lost so much. Was I a fool for trying to steal this moment with her? Yes, but it couldn't be helped. If my days were truly numbered, grabbing a few moments of joy with Clarke by taking her to one of my favorite places would be worth it. I would cling to this memory in the afterlife.

I walked her through the back entrance of Haywood's home as she remarked on the splendor of everything we passed. I had to admit, he had good taste, if not a little excessive. His greenhouse had a river running through it, for fate's sake. I could see Clarke wanted to explore, but the others could wake up any moment, and I selfishly wanted to take her to Pistrani's, my favorite bakery … alone.

I rushed her toward the rear exit, guiding her with my hand on the small of her back. The subtle touches I kept stealing did nothing to lessen my growing affection for her.

I was a glutton for punishment. I would take as much as she allowed before I met my end.

When she opened the door to the outside, I ran into her back as she abruptly stopped and gasped loudly. My arms wrapped around her waist to steady her.

"What is it?" I asked anxiously, suddenly fearing the worst. Had Osiria or Solana sent soldiers to abduct her? Were they here to deal out our punishments for disobeying them? I reached for the sword at my hip only to find it empty. I had left it in Haywood's bedroom.

Damn it.

"It's even more beautiful closeup." she said, her voice breathless.

"Oh." I peered around her shoulder. "Yes, I suppose it is." I hadn't thought about what it would be like for her to experience Teleran for the first time, and she was doing it with me with my hands on her body.

A strange peace filled me as she admired the splendor before her, and who could blame her? The Estival side had a certain appeal, although the cold made me yearn for the warmth of home. If Clarke longed for Earth, she hadn't said. In any case, her world was an overpopulated cesspool. What was there to miss? I suddenly hated that she had been forced to live there for so long.

She turned to me, my arms still wrapped around her waist, and I nearly dropped to my knees. The expression on her face was a blend of bewilderment, joy, and … were those tears? Was she sad? This woman was an enigma. She grasped the lapels of my jacket. Was she … was she about to kiss me? My heart pounded in my chest as it burst with desire. I licked my lips, envisioning her soft and delicate mouth joining mine as I tasted her, teased her with my tongue, and brushed her perfectly smooth skin with my stubble.

138

"Lachlan, it's snowing!" she exclaimed, radiating childlike wonder. So she wasn't sad or turned on, just very … *happy,* and no, she wasn't about to kiss me. *Damn it!*

"Well, technically, it has snowed," I corrected, gesturing to the packed white terrain flecked with the same pale pink of the stone buildings surrounding Haywood's home. Clarke shivered, she wasn't dressed for the weather. I looked around and noticed a pair of boots and a large coat in the mudroom adjacent to where we stood. After retrieving them for Clarke, I helped her slip into the oversized coat. It was Haywood's, and I disliked that she'd now be wrapped in his scent.

"I'd recommend changing your shoes if we are venturing out in the snow," I suggested.

"Can you lean down?" she asked. I looked at her quizzically. "I need to hold on to something while I slip my feet into these boots," she explained. I leaned down, and she placed her hands on my shoulders. She wobbled a bit while trying to balance, and I allowed myself to grin at her human-like qualities. It was endearing. Fae didn't *wobble,* but none of us were raised believing we were humans. What would it be like to see all this anew?

I observed her as we stepped through the threshold. Her long brown waves cascaded down her back, and the red streaks in her hair complemented her well. Her long, dark lashes drew me into her jade eyes as they sparkled with delight. She wore an ornate, red-jeweled necklace. While it didn't match her casual attire, it suited her beautifully.

"This is just amazing, Lachlan," Clarke said. "You don't understand. Where I'm from, it rarely snows anymore. It snowed more when I was a kid, but never more than a few inches." Clarke twirled in a circle in her clunky boots.

I smiled at her. "Let's hurry. I don't want the shop to close before we get there."

She stopped spinning, obviously remembering the excitement of devouring some of Pistrani's pastries.

She walked over and linked her arm with mine. "Well, let's go then." She had such an easy, affectionate manner about her that made me feel things I wasn't prepared to experience. Her taking my arm was probably more of a way to steady herself while navigating the unfamiliar landscape than a need to be close to me, but I entertained the fantasy all the same.

Our boots crunched in the snow, and I savored the hushed sounds on the way. Clarke was right: Snow was magical. It brightened the twilight sky and softened the sound. It was a stillness, and I very much enjoyed experiencing it with her. She made me see it with fresh eyes, as it was all new to her.

"What's with all the pink?" Clarke asked.

"It's from my side of Teleran; the fog there is red. Trace amounts of it flow to the Estival side, turning everything a shade of pink," I explained.

"Oh, that's cool. It just reminded me of Alison. She lives in a building that is almost the same shade of pink and wears pink almost exclusively." Her smile was sad. "But it's beautiful. I would love to bring her here. She would love it."

I had to admit that the town surrounding Haywood's home was idyllic. The soft pink stones, vibrant but weathered, had a certain charm. The normally bustling market was deserted this close to night, which was both safer for Clarke and for me.

We approached Pistrani's and pushed open the heavy wooden door. A bell chimed overhead, and I heard the baker shuffle his feet on the gray, cracked stone floor as he wandered toward us.

"Lachlan, my boy!" Gustav bellowed heartily as he rounded the pastry case. He embraced me in a firm hug, his familiar scent of tobacco, sugar, and cinnamon enveloping me. He pulled back to look up at me. Gustav was round, short-statured, and green-skinned, with large tusk-like teeth protruding from his underbite.

"Let me see you. You look well. Is this pretty lady the reason for it?" He gestured toward Clarke.

"It's nice to meet you. I'm Clarke," she said with a smile, holding her hand out to the old man.

"Come here, my child. Friends hug, and if you're a friend of Lachlan, you're a friend of mine," Gustav chided.

Clarke smiled warmly and embraced Gustav as his large green hands wound around her. "Welcome to Pistrani's, named for my forefather. I'm Gustav."

"Thank you. Pleased to meet you, Gustav," Clarke said, smiling brightly.

"Now, my boy, I just took some fresh pastries out of the oven. It's as if I knew you were coming," Gustav said with a wink.

The scent of a chocolate-sweet concoction wafted through the toasty bakery air, and I could feel my mouth begin to salivate.

"Oh!" Clarke exclaimed. "Whatever that is smells amazing!"

"It's a layered pastry filled with hazelnut chocolate, my child," Gustav explained. "Right this way. I'll load you up. Your special table is all set for you, Lachlan. You're both in luck; I was just about to close up, but I got ahead of tomorrow's baking. So now you can enjoy freshly baked pastries and a bit of privacy." Gustav winked at Clarke.

141

I grabbed a dozen assorted pastries for the road. Magic could do many things, but it could not replicate what Gustav could do in a kitchen.

I moved to pay him.

"Your money's no good here, my boy. Put that coin away," Gustav chastised. The old man had never let me pay, even though my position now granted me enough coin for whatever I needed; it had not always been that way, and I once had to rely on the kindness of others. None had been as kind as Gustav. He was one of the lesser fae—lesser only in power, not heart. It was the reason for his appearance. In Teleran, the more powerful you were, the less physically adorned you became.

As soon as we were out of earshot, Clarke leaned in conspiratorially and asked, "Is Gustav an Estival like Haywood and Luck?"

When I nodded, she continued, "He has green skin and fangs. Am I missing something?" she asked. "Do you all have fangs? Do you all really look like that, and are you just glamouring me to appear normal so I don't freak out? Am I going to grow fangs?" she asked, running her finger over her teeth in inspection.

I couldn't hold in my chuckle but covered it with a sharp cough. I smiled a big smile at her to show her my slightly elongated incisors. She inhaled sharply.

"To your eyes, I imagine we have exaggerated features. Our ears," I said, tapping the elongated tip of her right ear, "our teeth," I gestured to Gustav, "and a few other parts are a bit larger than you're used to seeing."

Her eyes flew open and locked with mine, her cheeks flamed red, and then she averted her eyes. I knew exactly where her thoughts had ventured, and while I didn't necessarily mean what she'd taken as a sexual innuendo, I didn't hate that she was likely imagining the size of my penis right now. Her face gave everything away, and I loved how unguarded she was. However, she could also be remembering a certain appendage attached to a certain Estival.

Damn it.

Jealously flared, and I desperately wanted to redirect her attention back to me.

"I know we're in danger, and everything's kind of messed up right now, but this is seriously so freaking cool," she said as she slowly took in the bakery. The few circular wooden tables were empty, and a mop and bucket sat discarded. I would have to remember to thank Gustav again for letting us come in this late.

"Can I take you somewhere?" I blurted out.

"Um, Lachlan, you have taken me somewhere." She waved her hand around the bakery, smiling with amusement.

"Grab our pastries. I would like to show you something," I said as I walked toward the back entrance of Pistrani's.

"I'll be honest with you, Lachlan," Clarke said, stopping me. "You've brought me through a town built with pink stone that was covered in snow, I'm about to eat a pastry the size of my head that won't make me sick, and magic exists. This might just be the best date I've ever been on."

I coughed out a laugh.

"No, sorry, that's not what I meant. We aren't … you're not … I just meant, you're a guy and you've taken me somewhere, and usually that's a date. I didn't mean we were on a date. Oh, no, I've made this weird. I do that … sometimes … and then I ramble and make it worse."

I reached out and put my hand on her bicep, attempting to get her attention. "Clarke," I interrupted, "it's fine. And I know what you mean. Teleran is dazzling. Please permit me to dazzle you further."

Her eyes lit with amusement and relief.

I led Clarke out to the back of Pistrani's. It was a special place I visited as a kid to eat and hide from the Estival, who wouldn't have wanted me on their side of Teleran. But I could never resist this spot, and when Gustav showed it to me, it became my refuge from the world.

I opened the heavy wooden door at the back of the bakery, stepping onto a small porch that overlooked the shallow river flowing behind the village. It had started snowing again.

I overturned two empty storage crates for Clarke and me to sit on, lowering myself onto one. Clarke settled down next to me. It took a bit more courage for me to turn and look at her to see what she thought of my little oasis. When I did, she was gazing straight at me with a huge smile.

"So this is what Gustav meant by your special table," she observed, taking one of my hands into her small, delicate ones. "Thank you for bringing me here. It's amazing, Lachlan," she said, her voice breaking.

"I don't think I would have if I'd known it would make you cry," I said jokingly, trying to lighten the heaviness of the moment. The smile she gave me was bright, wide, and teary. "Let's dig into our feast. Who knows when Luck and Haywood will wake up and come looking for us? This may be the last bit of peace either of us gets for a while."

She chuckled and nodded, considering that, and reached between us. We each took out a pastry and started to eat.

"Oh, my god," Clarke said in a moan that was muffled by a mouthful of dough. "This is the best thing I've ever put in my mouth."

I started choking on my pastry.

She started cackling and choking. "I'm sorry, I didn't mean … well, I did. No, I'm serious, this is amazing," She mumbled while continuing to chew with her mouth open.

"I didn't say anything," I replied, fighting a grin.

"You know what's funny? My mom would've hated it here," she said.

"Your mom? Why?" Her outburst seemed to come out of nowhere, but I noticed she was touching her necklace. She had done that a few times since we'd left Haywood's house, and I wondered if the necklace was a gift from her mother.

"I'm sorry, that was random. I think about her a lot. She passed away when I was eighteen," Clarke explained.

"You don't need to apologize. Please go on with what you were saying," I said, eager to learn more about her.

"She hated the cold. She was always whisking me away to the beach any chance she got. Our favorite thing to do together was to lie in the sun and listen to music. It's probably why we lived in the South. It's mostly hot, and our winters are really mild. Like I said before, it never snows there anymore."

"Then she would love my side of Teleran."

"Oh yeah? Why's that?" she asked.

"It's always warm on the Obscurus side," I said, longing for the climate of home as I shivered. While the snow here was beautiful, I could only handle it in short bursts.

"Then, yeah, she would love it. I can't wait to see it. Is that bad to say? I know we aren't safe, but I'm excited to see this world."

"You can feel excitement and fear simultaneously. There's nothing wrong with feeling joy in the midst of danger."

She smiled at me again. *After this,* I told myself, *after this moment, I'll back off.* This moment with her would have to be enough.

"I suppose you're right. So much has changed for me in such a short time. A few weeks ago, my biggest hurdle was passing my exams and getting to work on time."

"Exams?" I asked.

"I was finishing my college degree. I was going to teach history," she answered, then sighed. "But then Heather was killed, and my life was upended. At that time, I thought I had experienced the worst days I ever would, but then Alison went missing and was presumed dead. My world just crumbled."

"But now you know she isn't dead and might be here." She nodded. "Fate is weaving quite a story for you, Clarke."

"That's one way to think about it. I'm living in my very own fairy story," she said with a laugh. "I keep thinking this is all a dream, that I'm going to wake up from a coma or something."

"But this isn't a dream, Clarke. You know that, don't you?" I asked.

"I know that … I think it's starting to sink in," she answered. "It's just hard to focus on me right now when I know Alison could be in danger."

"You must focus, Clarke. You must train. We need you just as much as she does," I said.

"I will. I promised I would. I'm actually looking forward to the training. It'll help direct my mind to something other than imagining the worst possible scenarios of what could be happening to Alison."

"That's a positive way to look at it, and if you need a distraction, Altfevis will be helpful too."

"Thank you, Lachlan," she said.

"For what?" I asked.

"For this," she gestured to our surroundings. "For this moment of peace amidst all this chaos."

"You're welcome. I'm afraid you'll need to reflect on this in the days ahead. We face an unknown adversary— whatever is causing our worlds to merge must be stopped."

"What … the …" an out-of-breath Haywood said as he crashed through the bakery's back door, Gustav on his heels.

"I'm sorry, my boy, this riffraff barged through before I could stop him," Gustav apologized.

Clarke and I sprang from our seats. Clarke's boot struck the bag of extra pastries we'd left on the ground, sending it sailing into the shallow river.

"Fuck!" Clarke shouted.

I shoved Haywood, who knocked into Luck, whose hair was sticking up everywhere. It looked like they had woken up and tumbled out of bed to get here. "What is your fucking problem?" I shouted at Haywood.

"You're my problem!" he said, pushing me back. I stumbled into Clarke, causing her to trip on her oversized boots and fall backward into the stream. It wasn't a far fall, just off the old porch of the bakery.

Luckily, the stream couldn't have been more than six inches deep, but it was rocky and freezing.

Haywood looked horrified. "Clarke! I'm so sorry. Let me help you," he said, stomping off the ledge and charging into the cold waters to help Clarke, who was already pushing off a large stone to stand.

"I'm fine, Haywood, just wet and cold," she said, annoyed.

"You idiot!" Haywood directed his ire toward me.

"You pushed me! I didn't knock into her all by myself!" I shouted back.

"Okay, you're both idiots," Luck said. "Come on, Clarke. We need to get you dry and warm. Let's leave these two to measure their dicks in peace."

Haywood and I glared at one another as a chuckling Clarke left with Luck. There was no contest, however, and if needed, I would be happy to prove it.

CHAPTER 26

Clarke

The sun had fully set when Luck and I exited the bakery. The walk back to Haywood's home was short, but this time, I took in the enormous structure in front of me. The snow and the quaint pink stone village had distracted me before, and I hadn't even glanced behind me to see what his home looked like. Well, home isn't exactly what I would call it. Maybe a mansion? It stood at only two stories, but it seemed larger somehow. It was an iridescent purple color outlined in black. The gothic-looking mansion glowed warm from the light within, making it feel inviting despite its imposing size.

This place, Teleran, was unreal. Everything was either larger than life or charmingly understated.

The pink stones of the village surrounding Haywood's home were rough-hewn, making them appear ancient, and they could be for all I knew. The cobblestone path, lit with burning torchlight, was miraculously clear of snow and so worn that the cobbles were inset into the earth, leaving a smooth walkway. Had carts and feet worn it down over time? The air was clear and clean, like it often was in the mountains on Earth. Everything seemed more vibrant, and I could breathe easily as the air appeared to be clear of pollutants. My lungs felt like they'd expanded to their fullest potential, as if I'd taken my first real breath in a long time.

As a shiver ran through me, I remembered that I was drenched and still freezing. Luck opened the back door to Haywood's home, and I felt the comforting rush of warm air. As we walked through the long hallway, we passed a room I hadn't seen on our way out. It was entirely green, reminding me of the color of Lachlan's eyes. I laughed a little, thinking Haywood had a Lachlan-colored room in his home. It had green, black, and white diamond tiles on the floor and a giant cerulean stained-glass domed ceiling, casting the entire room in green. The most unbelievable part was the small pool in the center of the room. His house felt like Mary Poppins's bag: endless, with surprises around every turn. It was a good thing that Lachlan had led me out of here and that Luck was leading me now. I would get lost if I had to navigate it by myself.

I guess it wasn't exactly a surprise that his house would be magical since he was fae, something I was still trying to come to terms with. Somehow, it felt as natural as breathing to believe that magic and magical beings existed, but it was another thing entirely to see and experience that in reality.

The fact that I was one of them still hit me weirdly. I had always felt like an outcast, as if I didn't fit in anywhere. Now, I seemed to have found a reason for that, but I was still the outsider. Not that Luck, Haywood, or even Lachlan had purposely made me feel that way, but they grew up in Teleran, had always known they were fae, had powers, and lived where that knowledge and power could thrive. I had been crippled by not knowing.

I was a thirty-year-old newborn, and I felt inadequate. They kept telling me that I was super powerful, but I didn't feel it. I knew it was because I was wearing the bracelets. I understood they were for my protection and possibly theirs, but I would have loved nothing more than to be free of them so that I could feel the change in my body. At least the weird attraction to Lachlan had calmed down. I mean, I would have to be dead not to think he was gorgeous, but I didn't feel the need to climb him like a tree at the bakery. It felt like we were new friends, getting to know each other. It felt … natural. I think he really could become a good friend to me. Even though we'd just met, I trusted him. He seemed to be genuinely kind, even though, at first glance, he looked a little harsh and scary. He had a resting bitch face for sure.

As we ascended Haywood's staircase, I cringed, knowing I was dripping water all over his beautiful home. Just as the thought left my mind, I was instantly dry, the puddle gathering under me gone.

"Holy shit!" Luck exclaimed, hopping back from my side.

"What happened?" I said, bewildered.

"You used air magic, Clarke!"

"I didn't *do* anything." How had I done that without trying?

"What were you thinking right before it happened?" she asked.

"I was thinking that I was ruining Haywood's beautiful home with all the water I was tracking in," I admitted.

"That's all it takes. Haven't the boys explained anything to you yet?" Luck questioned.

"No, they keep saying they are going to train me on our trip to get Alison but haven't told me anything about how my magic works."

"In their defense, I don't think any of us truly understand how *your* magic works, but I do know how ours functions. It's based on intent, and it's that simple. *If you can will it, you can wield it.*" She laughed. "Corny, I know, but that's what we were all taught when we were young."

"It seems almost too simple."

"It's not meant to be hard; it's meant to be innate. We were born this way, and so were you—you just didn't know it," she said with a sad smile.

CHAPTER 27

Haywood

When I woke, still exhausted, I feared the worst: that Lachlan had betrayed us, as I'd predicted he would, and had taken Clarke to fulfill his duty to Osiria. There wasn't a rational bone in my body when it came to Clarke. She was my weakness, and I continuously made mistakes because of it.

The rage I felt when I saw them sitting together at *my* bakery, having the outing I had dreamed of taking her on, was like nothing I had ever experienced. Normally, I wasn't prone to anger or violence. But the desire to kill Lachlan at that moment was strong.

Clarke's expression crushed me when my actions caused her bag of pastries to fall into the river. I calmed down after seeing that she was okay, until Lachlan pointed out my folly in front of her. Then embarrassment and jealousy made me act like an imbecile.

Luck intervened, removing Clarke from the situation and allowing Lachlan and me to handle our mutual disdain like gentlemen.

"We don't have time for this," Lachlan choked out through gritted teeth. How was that animal able to restrain itself better than I was? Who was I becoming?

I cleared my throat and straightened myself. "You're right," I said, feeling pained.

"I'm sorry—I didn't quite hear you. Could you say that again, and maybe louder this time?"

"I said you're right!" I shouted. "We don't have time for this. We certainly didn't have time for you to gallivant through the town with Clarke, where anyone could have seen her," I said exasperatedly.

"Come on, Haywood. This is hardly a bustling metropolis. Anyway, I made sure we weren't seen, and Gustav can be trusted. He is an old friend."

"You have friends on the Estival side?" I said, astonished.

"I few," he said, shrugging his shoulders as if that sufficed as an answer.

"Fine, well, we should rejoin Luck and Clarke and depart as quickly as possible."

"By all means," he said while briskly brushing past me and into the bakery. He waved goodbye to the baker as he exited the front door.

I rushed to catch up with him, not loving his easy dismissal.

"Oh, and if you feel the need to bring this up again or accuse me of derailing our mission, I did this for her," Lachlan said, throwing a tense glance behind him.

"Why? Do you really expect her to jump into bed with you after plying her with sweets?" I said, hating how irrational I sounded, but it was impossible to suppress my jealousy.

He sighed, turned toward me, and rolled his eyes. "If you're quite done, I'll continue." He paused and continued when I stayed silent. "We have no idea what this journey holds for us or her. Do you realize we are essentially embarking on a suicide mission? Osiria commits murder for breakfast, tortures for lunch, and you honestly don't want to know what her final course entails. All I was trying to do was show Clarke a bit of peace before the chaos consumes her. I wanted to show her a glimpse of beauty when horror likely awaits. For all we know, her friend is being tortured and will probably be dead by the time we get to her. My sovereign doesn't set up a bed and breakfast for her captives. She can be sadistic when delivering punishment. I hope I am wrong. I hope that all is well. All I want is to help her and save my home."

He was right again. It hadn't yet occurred to me *why* Osiria held Alison captive, or that we'd be *killed* for seeking out the knowledge to save Teleran.

In my court, justice was more refined. We didn't even have a dungeon to speak of, just rooms with bars to serve as our cells. But I couldn't remember Solana ever keeping anyone there for long. Certainly, no one was ever tortured. I had known the Obscurus were uncivilized, but torture … I shuddered at the thought.

If this was a common practice, what would happen to us if we failed or were caught? What if we were successful? What then? I had not ventured into thinking about what would happen *after* we rescued Alison and saved our realm. I was determined to grant Clarke every desire and whim of her heart, not thinking of the consequences. Regardless, I would still help her. After all, I had vowed to do so. Even if I died trying, Clarke would escape this.

"I am … sorry. That was a kind gesture, and I didn't pause to think. If I'm honest, I had thought you'd betrayed us, taking Clarke to Osiria."

Lachlan's shock was evident, and something like hurt showed through his eyes before he looked away.

"I would never betray her or our vow, even without the magical repercussions. Death will come for me whether I fulfill them or not, so I care very little for my well-being. But for hers … I care and will ensure her and her friend's safety before I draw my last breath."

His tone was ominous, yet I didn't question him further. I thought it best to continue our walk to my home and leave as soon as Clarke was ready to leave. His self-deprecating talk about death made my chest squeeze uncomfortably. Was I coming down with something as my magic continued to weaken, or was I starting to care about him?

As we approached the back door, it swung open to reveal a completely refreshed and dry Clarke and Luck with our packs and provisions for our journey.

"How did you get dry so quickly?" I asked Clarke.

"This one figured out air magic … and fucking fast, if I do say so myself," Luck responded for her, pride coating her words.

Clarke blushed and averted her eyes. Fates, she was adorable.

"So … point the way, oh, leader," Luck said, turning to Lachlan, who nodded and gestured for us to follow him.

The four of us walked toward what I hoped was not certain death.

CHAPTER 28

Clarke

Under the cover of night, we approached a river behind the small, pink-stone town. Through the darkness, I noticed a moored boat that appeared a bit small, but I assumed it would fit us, if not a little snugly. It seemed like no one was having trouble seeing in the dark, another fae trait, I assumed. I was looking forward to that ability manifesting, among other things. I was walking sandwiched between Haywood and Lachlan.

"Why are we traveling by boat again?" Haywood questioned Lachlan.

"This river will take us to the site where Altfevis is being held. And this way, we won't leave tracks—harder to trace us."

That shut Haywood up. It seemed like he was just being difficult for the sake of it. I couldn't blame him; he and Lachlan weren't exactly friends. I only hoped their animosity wouldn't hinder our collective mission.

Our footsteps on the dock were the only sounds in the eerily quiet night.

Lachlan stepped into the small boat first. Haywood reached over to help me into the boat, but I stubbornly ignored his hand and nearly face-planted as I stepped into the vessel. Lachlan caught me, which was becoming a habit. Trying to be an independent woman who defiantly refused any help from Haywood out of spite was challenging when I was as clumsy as a newborn deer.

I thought fae were supposed to be graceful. I felt as though I were trapped in someone else's body, or like I was wearing a suit that was too big for me, and I kept tripping over the extra fabric. Maybe when I trained and eventually got to take the bracelets off, I'd feel more at home in my skin.

We all settled in the boat, and I looked toward the water as it lapped against the side. The water appeared dark red, almost like blood. The absence of light must have been playing tricks on my eyes. I wasn't sure if Teleran had a moon or if it shared Earth's moon, but there was a faint glow from something that made the night not completely pitch black.

Just as we cast off from the shore, the boat abruptly stopped.

"You're supposed to untie the boat before casting off, Haywood," Lachlan chided.

"I did," Haywood replied.

"Going somewhere?" questioned a voice through the void. It wasn't a voice I recognized, and I was instantly terrified. Everyone had told me that their sovereigns were after me, but no one knew why. If they had caught us before our journey even began, I would never get to Alison in time.

Haywood's back went ramrod straight. Lachlan pulled a crooked-looking blade out of nowhere, while Luck positioned herself between me and the direction of the voice.

"Leora, this isn't what it looks like," Haywood spoke first. Leora … Leora, I recognized that name. *Oh, shit!* Was this the girl Haywood was engaged to? What was she doing here? I tried to keep my hands from shaking, but Haywood's voice had been full of fear. If this woman scared him, what could she do to me?

158

"What it looks like, my *intended,* is that you're stealing away in the dead of night with an Obscurus and what appears to be the very recovered female my mother requested you bring directly to her," Leora said, ire punctuating each syllable.

"So it is what it looks like, but allow me to explain," Haywood responded.

"No, I don't think I will, Haywood. All of you, out of the boat. Now," she commanded. "What I *will* do is deliver her and you to my mother," Leora said as we all slowly filed out of the boat onto the dock.

"Leora, please, you don't understand," Haywood pleaded.

"I understand that you managed to lie to me. That you deceived my mother and are attempting treason," Leora spat.

"Leora, don't you think that is a little extreme," Luck interjected.

"Oh, is that you, *Luck?* I didn't see you there," Leora said with a snark.

"Sure you didn't," Luck snarked back. "I know you're upset, but we have a good reason for deceiving you and going against Solana's wishes."

From nowhere, a light appeared, and I could see Leora for the first time. Holy shit, she was gorgeous. Her skin glowed against the light, which was shaped like a ball and hovering a few inches above her curved hand.

"Unlike these two, I owe you no allegiance, *General.* If you want her, you'll have to go through me," Lachlan asserted.

My lady parts quaked at the sight of the huge fae ready to fight for my honor. I wasn't a damsel in distress type of girl, but Lachlan made me kind of want to be one.

"You are a fool if you think you can best me, mongrel," Leora hissed.

I sucked in a sharp breath as a sword made of water appeared in Leora's hands, dangerously close to Lachlan's throat. He didn't move, though.

We were so fucked. I was about to be captured, and god knew what they'd do to my new friends for trying to help me.

"That may be true, but you still can't have her," Lachlan protested, not bothered at all by the blade at his jugular.

"Do something," I urged Haywood through my teeth. He looked paralyzed. Was he that afraid of his fiancé? I mean, she was terrifying. Her beauty did nothing to hide her fierceness, and Lachlan had called her "General." Did that mean she was head of an army or something?

Luck palmed an ornate dagger and placed her other hand on a gun holstered at her side, both of which were previously concealed. More magic, I supposed.

The tension in the air was so potent you could've choked on it. That should've made me restrain myself, but it seemed like I was about to throw my self-preservation to the wayside.

"I'm not going anywhere with you," I said in what I hoped was my most assured and commanding voice. There was definitely no whimpering or fear there—nope, none whatsoever. I absolutely was not afraid of the fae with the fancy magic light glinting off her silver battle gear and her perfectly highlighted cheekbones that were so sharp they mirrored the weapon she was holding in her hands.

I had a really terrible, not-thought-out-at-all plan. I was always protective of my friends to a fault. And these fae, while our relationships were complicated, were quickly becoming people I cared about. I had to do something, even if it was stupid.

I could control water, right? I had no idea what I was doing, but Luck said I could basically use my power to do what I wanted. She'd said to trust my intent, and right now, I wanted her to take that sword away from Lachlan's neck. I figured fae were hard to kill, but I wasn't prepared to test that theory, not on him.

"Oh, she speaks. How charming that you think you've a choice in the matter. In case you are as dumb as you look, allow me to spell it out—you don't," Leora spat, her purple eyes glistened with rage.

I raised my hands and willed the sword back and down, hoping it wouldn't graze Lachlan in the process. I repeated the command over and over in my head while attempting to steady my breath. And much to my surprise and the astonishment of everyone else, the sword not only moved from Lachlan's throat but disappeared altogether.

Leora reared back like I had struck her. Fury erupted across her beautiful face as she raised her own hands in my direction. Haywood stepped in front of her and took her wrists in his hands.

I felt my own rage well up; I would not go quietly.

"Your eyes," Leora said, recoiling from me. "Her eyes hold flame, yet she conjures water. What trickery is this, Haywood?"

"Leora, please listen to me. If you truly do not like what I have to say, then you have my permission to cut down everyone on this dock," Haywood pleaded.

"Um, excuse me, I do not give my permission to be cut down." Luck perked up, holding up her dagger in protest.

"Quiet, Luck," Haywood chided as Luck sank back behind him. She didn't discard her weapons, though. Luck was ready for a fight.

Taking a deep breath but not calming the fury on her face, Leora said, "You have one minute, and I'm only conceding to this because I want to know how someone who is wearing Vincula bracelets has access to that magnitude of magic. And how she seems to hold Estival and Obscurus powers. Furthermore, no one should have the power to holster my blade. So begin explaining how the impossible just occurred, Haywood, and take heed: These words very well could be your last, betrothed or not."

CHAPTER 29

Clarke

Damn, this girl was intense. I hoped Haywood could convince her not to kill us more eloquently than he had convinced me not to be mad at him. It seemed I wasn't the only one itching to pummel his face in. If circumstances were different, I would've loved to sit down with Leora and commiserate over the conundrum that was Haywood. Although, on second thought, that would involve me telling her about us hooking up, and she looked like a stab-first, ask-questions-later type of fae.

"Are we just going to stand here while you attempt to talk your way out of this, Haywood? We are sitting ducks here," Lachlan pointed out. He made an excellent point. From what I gathered, we were in a hurry, and I wasn't even sure if their night lasted the same number of hours as my nights on Earth. It could be just an hour for all I knew of Teleran.

No one seemed to acknowledge Lachlan as Haywood started speaking. "There is something *off* with your mother's order concerning Clarke. You must feel it if I do. You are too wise, and your gift to ascertain a lie is unparalleled."

Either Haywood truly meant those things about Leora, which made me tinge with a small amount of jealousy, or he was laying it on thick. Regardless, it seemed to be working because Leora stayed silent.

"As you know, your mother has had me watch over Clarke since she was a child. She commanded me to keep her safe but never said anything about bringing her here.

Around the same time Clarke's powers started to surface, your mother requested I retrieve her and bring her to Teleran. Because I had stood as her caretaker of sorts, I foolishly thought it was to keep her safe as she transitioned into her powers and to help with what was causing Teleran's deterioration. As you can see, Clarke can use a great deal of power while wearing the bracelets, which shouldn't be possible. It also means her power level could rival that of our sovereigns, making her a threat to both crowns. She is no normal fae, and I think your mother knows this. I don't know to what end, but she desires to use Clarke or, perhaps, rid her of her competition. I've become … protective of her, as you can imagine, after knowing her for her whole life, and I couldn't, in all conscience, deliver her to your mother without knowing her intentions. Please understand, I didn't mean to mislead you when you came to my manor. I was telling you the truth; Clarke had been gravely injured and has just recently been able to travel."

"Travel? I'm curious, Haywood. Where are you going if not to my mother?" Leora asked, her anger seeming to evaporate.

"To Aurantia," Lachlan responded.

"Are you willingly traveling to imprisonment? Are you all mad? If you wished for death, I would be happy to oblige you," Leora grinned wickedly. If I were in one of my fae novels, my bowels would've gone watery at the malice in Leora's purple eyes.

"Mad we may be, but that is where we must go," Lachlan said. "Osiria also tasked me with retrieving Clarke for her. I thought little of it, to be honest. I'm not in the business of rejecting my sovereign's wishes. Let's just say she's not as lenient as Solana. I had no prior knowledge of Clarke before I was hastened to the human world to save her from an unknown threat and bring her to Osiria. However, after meeting Clarke, seeing her uniqueness, getting to know her, and realizing our sovereigns both have hidden agendas when it comes to her, I could not, as Haywood said, in good conscience, follow through with my orders. As to why we are traveling into the belly of the beast, so to say, it isn't only for Clarke. Osiria possesses knowledge that could help us save Teleran. We travel to attain this from her chambers. We have also learned that she holds a human friend of Clarke's in her dungeons. We mean to rescue her."

"Why would you risk your position for someone you've only just met? Haywood, I understand. He's always had a bleeding, human-like heart, but the Obscurus are vicious by nature," Leora questioned.

"I love my home just as you do. I will fight, scheme, and betray anyone who seeks to destroy it. I will uncover the truth about this human's capture and obtain the knowledge to save Teleran, if it exists, and face the consequences when they arise," Lachlan answered.

"I didn't realize a beast could express such *conviction* and treachery in a single sentence. What talents you have," Leora chimed, almost sounding amused. "You would sell out your sovereign, stealing her knowledge for the good of the realm, an honorable endeavor for Obscurus filth. I thought you only cared for yourselves." Leora scoffed.

"Do not mistake me, General; I am a selfish bastard, but Teleran is my home. I will not see it fall or its people wither and die. And as for knowledge, perhaps this will entice you not to betray us." He held out the scroll with the prophecy to Leora.

"Is this?" she said, staring down at the paper.

"It is," Lachlan answered.

"You are full of surprises, Obscurus," Leora said, still inspecting the scroll.

"So will you aide us, General?" Lachlan asked.

"Well played, dog." Leora paused, considering. "It seems we should be on our way." She said, moving past us toward the boat.

"Pardon? What are you—?" Haywood questioned, bewildered.

"Have I not made myself clear, Haywood? It's obvious that I must accompany you on your treacherous journey if for no other reason than to protect what belongs to my mother."

"Leora, you can't mean you are coming with us. There is hardly room for starters, and what of your duties?"

"You know as well as I that my *duties* are my mother's poor excuse to keep me busy. There have been no attacks on our adolescents in centuries, Haywood."

"I just meant … Leora, I've made a vow to help Clarke—" Haywood explained.

"As have I," interrupted Lachlan.

Haywood continued, "And we intend to see this through. We *will* rescue Clarke's friend and obtain the knowledge to save Teleran."

"Yes, so you've said," Leora sighed as if we were exhausting her. "Teleran is my home as well, and I have as much right as any to protect it and its people. To speed up the process, of course, I offer my aid. Not that you've asked, but I'm sure that's what you were implying."

"Leora, I assure you that is not—" Haywood persisted.

"Haywood, either you accept my help and allow me to accompany you, or I will take Clarke now by force."

A growl sounded from Lachlan.

"Can someone calm the beast, please? He's not worth the energy it would take me to conjure my blade again," Leora said, boredom lacing her tone.

I placed my hand on Lachlan's shoulder, and he flinched. I guess big man did not like being touched. He was super tense. I couldn't imagine what it felt like to be on the wrong side of the fae realm, receiving commands when he wasn't used to taking orders, but he did eventually calm under my touch.

"Ah, the female is good for something after all. She can be in charge of the beast on this trip. Now, where were you all headed? I assume you were taking the northern route, passing the Guild, and continuing on through the bogs?" Leora asked.

"We were, in fact. How did you know that, General?" Lachlan answered.

"There isn't any other way to attempt an approach to Osiria's dungeons that would result in a successful stealth mission. Which would be the only way to escape with your life," Leora continued.

Lachlan looked at Haywood pointedly but said nothing.

"I don't like this," Luck said to no one in particular, crossing her arms across her chest.

"No one cares, *Luck*. Everyone back into the boat," Leora commanded. "Haywood, be a dear and push us off the dock," Leora said while leaping like a gazelle into the boat. How an armored-clad fae could jump into a boat without rocking it or making a sound, I didn't know.

"We sail for Altfevis first," Lachlan informed Leora. "We plan to hide in plain sight."

"Wise," Leora responded. "It will also throw off anyone who may be tracking you."

167

"Yes, well, let's just hope we pass through unnoticed," Luck said.

"Oh, Luck, you don't need a festival to help you with that," Leora said cruelly. Yeah, there was definitely a story there. The murderous look in Luck's gray eyes signaled violence was imminent.

If Leora noticed, she said nothing.

I suppressed a laugh as I looked around the boat at the five of us sailing toward a huge party in a tiny boat. Haywood was squashed between Luck and Leora, stiff and uncomfortable, in the most laid-back outfit I had ever seen him in. Usually, he wore some kind of suit, but now he was dressed in khaki pants paired with a blue T-shirt and the large dark-green coat I had worn to the bakery.

Leora was gleaming in full battle gear, while Luck's shoulder-length blonde hair stuck out of a blue wool beanie. Her clothes looked similar to Haywood's, making me think she'd raided his closet in our haste to leave.

Lachlan, who was next to me in the back, reminded me of the first time I had seen Haywood wearing an all-black outfit, slacks, a shirt, and a black denim jacket.

Other than Leora's armor, the clothes the fae wore weren't so different from what humans wore on Earth.

"I have a question," I directed at Lachlan. "We are supposed to be 'hiding-in-plane sight,' right?" he nodded his head in response, his black curls bobbing at the motion. It made me want to reach up and tug one to see it spring back into place, but I didn't think Lachlan would appreciate my impulse. "Well, other than Leora, who is wearing shiny armor, how are we supposed to fit in at a party?"

"Magic, remember?" Lachlan said, playfully nudging my arm. I swear this guy was hot and cold. "If we need something, Teleran will provide it."

168

Great, because that made perfect sense.

As we floated along the river in the darkness, my thoughts drifted to Alison once more. How could she have been taken captive here, and why? I hadn't had time to sit and think about why she was here, only that she was, and I needed to help her. A chill ran up my spine as worry filled me. Why would the fae want her? Why would they imprison her? How did she get here? Was she abducted in New York on her work trip and brought here? Did it have something to do with me and the reason the rulers here wanted me?

I couldn't figure it out. I didn't have enough information, and I didn't think any of my new companions did either. I guess we would find out sooner or later when we found Alison. There would be time for answers later once we were all safe.

CHAPTER 30

Clarke

"Clarke?"

When I opened my eyes, I found myself in a gray, misty place. It reminded me of the prison I had been in, just without the bars. A bed sat in the middle of the room, and a smoky cedar and cinnamon scent filled the air.

"Clarke?" the voice questioned again, and I turned toward it.

"Lachlan? Where are we? Are we at Altfevis already?" I asked.

"Um … no, I think we fell asleep," he answered, gesturing to our surroundings.

"Oh, no, Lachlan, I'm sorry. I didn't mean to bring you into my dream. I can't control it. The only other person I've done this to is Alison. I must have dragged you in since you were next to me." I apologized, feeling overwhelmingly embarrassed.

"It's okay. Where are we?" he asked.

"It looks like the jail I was in. It was all gray too. I'm not sure why my subconscious would bring me back here." My subconscious was a fucked-up bitch for bringing Lachlan into my dream and taking us to a place I'd hated and feared.

The mist started to clear a bit as I walked closer to Lachlan and noticed he was shirtless and not wearing any—"Oh my god, Lachlan! Why are you—are you—um … I think you're naked." I said, my gaze fixed on the ground. Desire urged me to peek, but she could just shut the hell up.

Lachlan simply laughed and looked up at me with a mischievous smile. "This is your dream, Clarke. Isn't that something I should ask you?"

"Oh my god, I didn't … I'm sorry, here." I reached for the pile of blankets on the bed and thrust them toward him.

The mist kept his lower half obscured, but it wasn't entirely opaque. *Things* were outlined, and I could feel my cheeks heat. Lachlan's chuckling stopped suddenly after he looked up to take the blanket from my hand to cover himself with.

"Fates!" he exclaimed, covering his eyes as he tilted his head straight up.

"What? What is it?" I asked, alarmed, looking from side to side, expecting to see a giant monster or something equally scary.

"You're … um, I think you're naked too," he said, his voice gravelly.

I looked down and screeched. "Oh, shit! Oh, shit!" I said, leaning down to grab the remaining blanket on the bed.

"Okay, I'm covered," I said reassuringly after fashioning myself a strapless toga in record time.

Lachlan leveled his head back down, and as soon as we looked at each other and our blanket-makeshift outfits, we both burst into laughter.

"This is beyond awkward, Lachlan. I'm so sorry. This has never happened before, and I swear I didn't mean to bring you here."

"Clearly, your mind had other ideas," he said, pointing out the bed in the middle of the room. I burst into hysterics.

"Don't," I said through choked laughter. "It's bad enough that I brought you here against your will, naked. Your teasing isn't helping."

"I know. I'm sorry," Lachlan said through his laughter. "Wow, I can't remember the last time I laughed like that."

"You know, me neither, and now my stomach hurts."

"So you truly don't know how to get us out of here?" Lachlan said, sobering.

"No, normally someone wakes me up, or I wake up," I answered.

"So you're saying we're stuck here?" he asked, somewhat resigned.

"It looks like it, at least for the time being," I yawned. "I know I'm sleeping, but I'm still so tired."

"Ah … yes, the effects of the bracelets, I'm afraid. Honestly, I feel the same way. I haven't had this much excitement in years. Before this, I was a glorified secretary. Osiria's tasks for me had dwindled of late. I was mostly searching for the prophecy for her."

"Oh, I didn't even think about that. Are you going to get fired or something for helping me and stealing from her office?"

"Or something," he mumbled. "Don't worry about that. I am prepared for whatever consequence awaits me. Teleran is more important than my position; you are more important," he said. His expression shifted to shock, and my heart melted. I didn't think he meant to say that last part. "I mean, it's important to find your friend and discover why Osiria has imprisoned her," he corrected, "a fact she kept from me."

"And that is unusual for her to hold things back from you?" I asked, choosing to ignore how he made me feel when he said I was important.

"Before all of this, I would have said yes. But now I'm questioning everything I've ever known. Before this, I would have said we were close. Perhaps not friends, but confidants. I am her second in command, not her general like Leora is to her mother. The Obscurus don't have an organized army. All of us are trained in combat. Osiria is second to no one in power and is one the wisest in all of Teleran. As for those who guard our sovereign, let's say that none would dare cross those who serve her.

"You admire her."

"I did—that is I *do*. It pains me to say that I no longer trust her and have clearly lost her confidence." Sadness lit his green eyes.

"You love her." A strange pang of emotion vibrated in my chest at the realization.

"I suppose that I do in some way. I love who I thought she was. After meeting you, seeing the depth of her deception, the enormity of what she's concealed from me, I no longer believe I knew the real her at all."

"I'm sorry," I said. "You are risking so much, and it looks like you are losing more than anyone to help me and your people."

"Don't be sorry. I choose this."

"Yes, but you chose this to help me."

"I did, and to help Teleran survive. It was my choice. Don't feel bad because of it; I regret nothing."

"Okay, I'll try," I said with a weak smile.

"Well, since we are both exhausted," he said, effectively changing the subject, "it seems that there is only one thing to do." He nodded toward the bed, then erupted in hysterics again. "Your face! I truly meant that we sleep. The things your mind conjures up." He said, still laughing.

I started laughing with him. The lightness drove out the heaviness of our conversation. The comfort I felt with him was unlike anything I had ever felt before. Normally, even with Alison or my mom, a part of me was still guarded. Not that either of them had done anything to make me feel like I needed to keep my guard up around them. It was just how I was—I think because of the mental gymnastics required to survive childhood with my dad.

In some moments, he would be so kind and jovial, and I'd think that version of him was there to stay. But time and time again, something would trigger him, and he'd turn back into a relentlessly cruel monster. He'd shatter my heart, which he'd just started to repair with his fleeting kindness.

I had never truly let the walls around my heart down for anyone. Why Lachlan, whom I had known for only a few days, was making them feel like they were effortlessly falling away, I couldn't fathom. Some part of me didn't even want to understand. It just felt so good to let my heart stretch to its full size, with no walls holding it back. A warning in the back of my head said I was headed for heartache and that I should rethink the path I was traveling on, but I was no stranger to heartache. It was the foundation I was built on, and it granted me strength and made me who I was.

My attraction to Lachlan was secondary to the kindred spirit I sensed we shared. Even when I embarrassed myself around him—something that would typically make me rethink and rehash every word to death, spiraling into an anxious mess—I felt at ease.

It wasn't me; it was him. I had a feeling that no one had seen this side of him, that it was something special only I was privileged to see. And even if I hadn't pulled into the dream on purpose, I secretly wished we could stay here, safe from the outside world and all the problems that came with it.

"Come on, Clarke, I promise I won't bite," Lachlan said, already seated on the bed under the blanket that covered his body. I wrapped myself more securely in my own blanket and shuffled towards him, almost tripping but righting myself before sliding my body onto the bed.

I laid down next to Lachlan, whose body radiated delicious heat. A little shiver wracked through me as the cold mist flowed over me.

"Are you cold?" he asked, sounding concerned.

"I'm fine," I said, lying.

"Come here," he said, extending his arm out. I looked at the space between his shoulder and bare chest; his tattoos were mesmerizing, like pieces of fine art. I scooted over to him, careful not to dislodge my blanket. I laid my head on his chest, and he let out a small sigh and rested his arm on the small of my waist, pulling me closer to him.

"Is this okay?" he asked, his voice sleepy.

"Hmm …" I mumbled, already falling asleep. He chuckled, and his warm breath tickled my face. I breathed in his cinnamon and cedar scent as I drifted off to sleep in Lachlan's arms.

CHAPTER 31

Alison

"Hello, dear. Come take a seat," called Osiria's sweet, saccharine voice through the doorway.

I had dressed in a black gown with thin straps and a deep V-cut neckline with a hint of lace covering the decolletage. I picked it because even if it wasn't my signature pink color, I looked hot as fuck in it.

I had almost got myself off in the closet just looking at how it hugged my sculpted, tight body and showed off my perky, round tits. Much to my frustration, Maldridge barely spared a glance in my direction as he led me down the gleaming red marble hallways. I suppressed the urge to pout. I knew he was just fighting his urges because he was attempting to remain faithful to whomever he was with, but he was mistaken if he thought I would entertain his rejection much longer.

The hallway near my room had been empty, but we turned into another corridor where three women lined either side of two large, gilded doors. They were all clad in black dresses similar to the one I wore, except the lace covered them all the way to their necks, almost as if it was trying to choke them. Their pale and bony hands peeked out of lace bell sleeves. Were these Osiria's servants? How rich were these people? Sure, they were all magical and whatever, but a whole palace built out of marble was a bit ostentatious even for my tastes, and even Daddy and I didn't have servants. But I had to admit the thought of this amount of wealth becoming my new normal sent a shiver of excitement down my spine. And to think all I'd had to do was betray my closest friend and murder that mousy little brat, Heather.

Without question, I would have murdered a thousand Heathers to have this, which is why I was sure this meeting with Osiria was going to be a negotiation of sorts. She would demand more from me, and I needed to put on my game face like my dad had taught me.

As I stepped through the doorway, I was greeted with a lilac and mint scent—Osiria's scent. Stretched out on a lavish, black velvet chaise lounge, she silently indicated that I should take a seat on an identical chaise opposite her. Between them, a hunk of shiny black stone serving as a coffee table was piled high with fruits, gold goblets, and pitchers of wine. My mouth watered at the sight.

"Sit, my pet, you must be hungry," Osiria directed. "Maldridge, be a dear and pour the wine."

Maldridge quietly obeyed, filling both our glasses to the brim.

The whole scene reminded me of a heightened version of the board meetings I had attended when my dad entertained a new acquisition. He'd ply them with wine and gourmet catering, making them feel at ease, right before he convinced them of a deal that mostly benefited him while making them feel like the whole thing had been their idea. He was brilliant in that way, and I hoped that I was like him.

"I'm still full from the lovely breakfast earlier, but I can always have more wine," I replied. I tried not to sound too rude reminding her that I had just eaten. Like, did she not remember, or did these people eat all the time? I had to admit the red grapes spilling over the shiny black tray were calling my name. Maybe I was still a little hungry.

Osiria either didn't hear me or didn't care as she continued talking. "As you are aware, I'm *interested* in your friend from Earth."

"Clarke? Why? I thought you just wanted me to fuck up her life. Aren't we here to talk about me?" Even this woman was obsessed with Clarke. My ears grew hot as my temper flared.

"We are here to talk about you, my dear, but in truth, it is Clarke that I need. At this very moment, your role is to be very pampered and well-fed bait for her."

"I'm not fucking bait!" I squealed. What an insult. I was Alison Villareal! I wasn't some weird bargaining chip to lure Clarke anywhere.

This time, the backhand was delivered by Maldridge, who had taken a seat next to me on the chaise.

"You will address my sovereign with respect," he spat.

Damn, I needed to remind myself that these people liked to hit. I swear my vision blackened for a hot second when he hit my cheek, which was now hot and stinging.

I was fuming and a little turned on. In another setting, I didn't think I would mind getting thrown around or spanked by those big, strong hands. It wouldn't be the first time I enjoyed being manhandled.

Cody had always toed the line of being too rough during sex. Most of the time, it excited me. But once in a while, he'd get a crazed look on his face and squeeze my throat a little too hard. But then I would cum while seeing stars dance in my vision, and all would be well again.

"Um, yeah, sorry, I guess," I managed to reply.

"Of course, you are more important than bait. That is, however, the role you will play until Clarke arrives. She is an integral part of my plans, so we need her. She unknowingly holds the key to what comes next."

178

"What comes next?" I asked.

Osiria's full, red lips curved into a small grin, revealing bright white teeth with exaggerated canines as she sipped from her wine goblet.

"Before the Great Catastrophe, Earth was our home. Afterward, it poisoned our lungs, robbed us of our magic, and desecrated all life, leading to the demise of much of the fae. Our elders at the time decided we needed to create a realm far smaller than Earth to hold us temporarily. Using their combined power, they formed Teleran. While it has sustained us for centuries and is appealing in its own way, it was never meant to hold us indefinitely. Even now, it withers. The fates have given us this sign that the time has come to reclaim our birthright. Humans are weak and foolish, mere custodians of a place that was never theirs to begin with. I realize this is a lot to take in. You are only a human, after all. But my dear, you are special, and you will become *more.*"

My ears perked up. Finally, she was going to talk about something interesting … me.

Osiria continued, "As soon as you got close to Clarke, I felt you. Your darkness called to me, and I knew you were a kindred spirit. Like calls to like. You are so full of hate, twisted, and unremorseful. You are strong, Alison. I knew right away that you would do what needed to be done, that you craved the abyss as I once did. That is why I brought you here. Not only because you are a weakness for Clarke, and having you here will grant me control over her, but also because you will become a formidable ally. However, you must be willing to bind yourself to me and serve me as you have already done. I need something more assured from you. Then and only then will you receive everything you deserve and more."

"I already completed one task for you," I countered, "so I'd say that you owe me something for that now. As for your next task, I would like to see the contract in writing." She'd thrown me in a dungeon after I'd helped her before. I'd be getting more assurance this time.

"We seal our contracts with magic, my dear. And as far as receiving what you deserve, I assure you that you won't have to wait long to get what's coming to you," Osiria said.

"You keep saying that, and you promise power, and you supposedly have magic, but I've yet to see the proof of that."

"Maldridge, the lady would like proof of our power. Would you be willing to supply a demonstration for her?"

"Gladly, my sovereign," Maldridge replied as he raised his hands toward the fireplace.

With a flick of his wrist, a roaring fire appeared, and I gasped. The fire flew toward his hands, and he held it without getting burned. When he stretched out his hands, the fire returned to the fireplace.

I was speechless—me, speechless—for five seconds.

"So this is the power I will get along with a fancy marble castle like yours? As long as we can get pink marble, of course," I said, trying to restrain myself from bouncing up and down.

"Of course. Whatever you desire, you shall have," Osiria answered. "But first, as I've said, you must bind yourself to me."

"What would I have to do to *bind* myself to you?" I hoped it wasn't anything sexual. I had never hooked up with a woman before. But honestly, the lady was hot; maybe it'd be fun. And if she included Maldridge in the mix, I might really be okay with a little ménage action.

"You need only to take my hand and repeat after me," Osiria said, extending her hand toward me.

"Before I get all committed to this baiting Clarke thing, I need to ask you something."

"Ask your question, dear, but make it quick," Osiria said through a vicious grin.

I took a deep breath. "When I was still in the dungeon, you told me that Cody was dead or would be soon." I paused, suddenly afraid to hear her answer. "Is he … dead?"

"Yes," she said with as much warmth and care as if I had asked if it was raining outside. My heart sank. Everything I had done, everything I had sacrificed, and everyone I had betrayed to bring us both here, to Teleran, to become powerful and perfect for Cody, to give him—us— the life we always wanted … for nothing. Sure, I had entertained the idea of fucking Maldridge and would've done it given the opportunity, but that didn't mean Cody wasn't the love of my life. A fissure ran through me, cracking my perfect heart. Cody was … dead.

"How?" I asked, my voice shaky and small. Usually, I wouldn't let anyone, especially not this woman, know how much I cared about something. I was showing weakness, but I couldn't get my emotions to cooperate. My heart was breaking.

"I have reason to believe those who travel with Clarke are responsible. Once they get here, you will have justice."

A murderous itch twitched my hand as I remembered the satisfaction I had felt when I'd stabbed Heather.

"If they did this," I sneered, "I will destroy them."

"Of course you will, dear. I have no doubt. So what do you say? Do we have a bargain?" she asked, holding her hand out once more.

"We have a bargain," I said, taking her hand without hesitation. Maldridge, who had taken up residence on my other side, pressed his leg closer to mine.

"Wonderful, my dear. You've made the right choice," Osiria said. "Repeat after me: *I vow to serve you, Osiria, and obey you in all things.*" Her words felt like a warm caress; I sensed them from my head to my toes.

"I vow to serve you, Osiria, and obey you in all things," I repeated, wondering if I had ever obeyed anyone in my entire life. I always found a way around it and ended up doing whatever I wanted whenever I wanted. This would be no different. I felt a shock straight to my heart at that thought, and red mist formed a helix around both our arms, sealing them together. Pain radiated up my arm, and I held my breath so I wouldn't cry out, but it hurt like hell until Osiria let go.

"Now we may proceed," she said, retaking her seat on the chaise. "We know Clarke is in Teleran, but I can't sense where. I do have a plan to ensure she ends up here, but I don't like surprises. I need to be prepared for her arrival."

"So what does that have to do with me? I'm just the bait, right?"

"Not just bait, my dear. I'm preparing something special for Clarke's arrival, and I will require your assistance."

"When will I get the power you promised me?" I blurted. With Cody dead, it was the least she could do.

"Be patient, pet. All will be revealed to you soon. In the meantime, rest. You will need it."

Osiria needed *me*—of course, she did. I was awesome, and soon, I would have power like hers. Cody's death was devastating, but I had to be strong. I would do this to honor him. Maybe I could reverse time or raise him from the dead with my newly acquired magic.

"Maldridge, will you be a dear and take Alison back to her room? I have much to prepare for, and my head is starting to ache. Draw the blinds before you leave, would you?"

"Yes, my sovereign," Maldridge replied, rising from the chaise and closing the blinds on the floor-to-ceiling windows. The curtains, made of heavy oxblood velvet, seemed to block out all light, as the only illumination when he shut them came from the crackling fire in the hearth. As he escorted me out of the room, I glanced back at Osiria and could have sworn her black eyes glowed red, mirroring the flames. I shuddered and quickly turned, exiting the room.

CHAPTER 32

Clarke

I stirred awake, jostled by the small boat's rocking. Dawn had just begun to crest above the horizon, casting warm light that made the lavender field along the river glow. The water was crystal clear, with pink shimmering swirls throughout.

The air felt warmer, prompting me to shrug off the jacket Lachlan had draped over my shoulders while we slept. Something about the beautiful lavender fields stretching over the hills on either side of the river evoked a strange sense of déjà vu. I sat up straighter, inadvertently waking Lachlan. Haywood, Luck, and Leora were deep in a heated discussion and paid no attention to us.

"What is it?" Lachlan asked, noticing my wide eyes.

"I've been here before, in a dream," I replied.

"This is the second place you've remembered from a dream. Did anything significant happen that you can recall?" he asked.

"No, I saw some of the fae, and they saw me. They appeared more … adorned than all of you."

"What do you mean adorned?" he narrowed his eyes in question.

"Well, they had gold dust on their faces, some had flower petals as masks, and some had hair that looked like the Milky Way galaxy."

He chuckled. "You'll see all that and more when we get to Altfevis."

"And you all look normal because you're stronger. The fae I saw were more like Gustav."

"I'm not sure what your definition of normal is, but I'm confident that over time, you'll come to notice our differences from the plain and dull humans you're accustomed to. For example, I doubt you're used to bright-red-striped hair," he said, taking one of the strands between his fingers, causing me to shiver.

"Actually, it's pretty common. Alison was—*is* a hairstylist. On Earth, I guess you could consider what they do as magic. But it's not really, just chemical reactions and science."

"Huh." He seemed to consider. "Well, I haven't spent much time on Earth to see anything remarkable, but I'll choose to believe you," he said with a smirk and a wink like he really didn't believe me at all.

"Oh, look who's awake," Luck said, turning to us.

"I'm sorry, guys; I didn't mean to fall asleep," I said while wiping my eyes.

"It's okay, Clarke. I'm glad you got some rest," Haywood said. "We are only a couple of days away from Altfevis. We will stop soon to rest and start your training. Are you sure you're ready for this? Ready for Altfevis?" he asked.

"It's just a party, Haywood. I may not be in the partying mood, but I can fake it for Alison. I'll just tap into the last time she and I partied together. And I'm actually pretty excited about the training."

The memory of the last time Alison and I went out was bittersweet. It had been my thirtieth birthday, and she had gotten me some weed gummies as an additional present alongside my gorgeous red heels. We had drunk our weight in champagne. My feet and sides ached from dancing and laughing so much, a sign of the best nights.

She'd been pissed to learn that the shoes she'd gifted me had been the one physical piece of evidence tying me to Heather's murder. And in true Alison fashion, she was even more pissed that they were now ruined, having been soaked in blood and thrown in an evidence bag.

"Have you fools not informed her?" Leora said.

"Informed me what? They already warned me about the giant orgy. Don't worry—I'll steer clear of that."

"Not just that, silly girl. They infuse the festival with fae essence, a drug made of pure magic. You'll be intoxicated as soon as we enter the territory. You'll feel happier and freer than you ever have. We are all used to it, having to make sure to keep our wits about us as we hold such high positions in our courts. Don't get me wrong: *Everyone* lets go of their inhibitions at Altfevis. It's how the peace between us has lasted this long. We all dine, drink, and fuck our way into not killing one another," Leora said.

I blinked. "Okay, well, I trust you all to be my party buddies then."

"What's a party buddy?" Lachlan asked, the others looking intrigued as well.

"You know, a party buddy, someone who makes sure you don't take the party too far or do something you'd regret while your inhibitions are lowered," I explained.

"Sounds boring," Leora commented.

"I don't need someone watching my back," Luck said.

"I can do that," said Haywood and Lachlan in unison.

"Why don't you two idiots be each other's party buddy?" Luck joked.

"Yeah, I think it might be best if I stick with the girls anyway," I said reluctantly. Leora looked like she'd rather do anything than be close to me; honestly, the sentiment was mutual. I didn't need my inhibitions lowered around someone who was engaged to my one-time lover.

Both Lachlan and Haywood looked downtrodden at my suggestion, but I ignored them.

"I believe it's best for us to stay together. If we become separated, we could jeopardize the mission if someone searching for us discovers our location," Haywood interjected.

"And I think this is a good place to camp for the day," Leora said, jumping from the boat, throwing down her pack, and removing two pieces from her cumbersome armor.

"We should press on," Lachlan disagreed.

"She's right, Lachlan," Haywood said, climbing out of the boat. "We risk discovery if we travel in the daylight. These banks are unoccupied, and we can set up camp and rest until nightfall."

"Fine, it'll provide the opportunity to start Clarke's training," Lachlan replied. As he moved to join them, he paused, turned back, and extended his hand toward me.

"Really?" I exclaimed, suddenly excited. The training montage from Rocky played through my head as I took Lachlan's hand and leaped to the shore. I landed with a heavy thud and winced, wishing I had landed more gracefully.

"Yes, really," Lachlan answered. "We'll start small, see where your limitations are while wearing the bracelets. And then we can see which weapon suits you most."

"I get a weapon?" I was overly excited, but I couldn't help it. I was about to become one of those badass fae from my books. I could just envision myself as a sword-wielding assassin, a multiple-magic wielder, or a sharp-shooting, curvy goddess.

"Who said you'd be training her?" Haywood said, breaking through my fantasy.

"I never said I alone would be training her, but you must admit, Haywood, that she has a unique opportunity here. She will be the only fae in Teleran to receive training by an Obscurus, an Estival, a master from the Guild of Shadows, and the general. We are masters at our crafts and have strength in different areas. I, of course, have fire and earth magic paired with my studies of our ancient histories and knowledge from working with Osiria for centuries, and you have your knowledge of herbs and plants coupled with your air and w—"

"The Obscurus has a point," Leora interrupted. "But I have yet to determine if she deserves my talents. If there is an order to her training, I will go last. In the meantime, I'll observe and take her measure."

Well, fuck.

"I suppose you think that you are first in line?" Haywood questioned.

"That honor was yours if I remember correctly," Lachlan said under his breath.

Did he mean …? My cheeks heated as an enraged sound burst out of Haywood. "You idiot!" he said, lifting his hands toward Lachlan and wrapping them around his throat.

"Stop it!" I yelled, moving to separate the two.

"Apologies," Haywood stammered as he stepped away from Lachlan. "I don't know what came over me."

"It's fine. I spoke out of turn. It won't happen again," Lachlan said, rubbing his throat. "Clarke, you can rest and prepare yourself while we set up camp." His voice sounded cold and detached.

I reached for Lachlan's forearm, as the others walked away to set up camp. I wouldn't let his comment about Haywood and me go unchecked. I thought we were friends, but then he brought up something private, almost loud enough for Leora to hear.

"Hold on a second," I said, stopping him and turning him toward me. My new friend, who had taken me to eat pastries and made me feel less embarrassed about bringing him into one of my dreams, was nowhere to be seen.

"Did you need something?" he asked.

"Yeah, I need something. What was that back there? Are you jealous or something? Why would you say that?"

He hung his head in shame. "I am sorry for my outburst. It was a poorly landed joke, nothing more."

"Well, I would appreciate it if you kept jokes at my expense to a minimum. We are supposed to be working together. I thought we were past the pissing contest."

"We are. I haven't forgotten our mission," he replied, turning and walking toward the others. I followed. His expression turned stony as we approached the waiting Haywood. "I am a being forged from magic. I'm nothing like your human men, and the sooner you realize that, the better. You are among creatures you do not know in a realm that would sooner destroy you. I will help you because I've vowed to do so in hopes that you will assist us in saving Teleran in return. Do not mistake me; we aren't friends. I won't bend to your every whim like Haywood does. I am Obscurus. I am not tame. You'd be wise not to make assumptions that will only lead to further disappointment."

Well, that came out of nowhere.

"Fine. Not friends. Got it," I said and moved past him without another word.

There was nothing left of the fae who had held me in my dream and had been so warm and gentle. I guess playtime was over, and it was time to get serious. They were all risking so much for me; there was no room for hurt feelings. While I knew I hadn't mistaken our flirting or charged glances, I wasn't foolish enough to entertain anything with a fae again. I had been too trusting my whole life, and I had constantly been burned by my own actions.

After our trip to the bakery and our conversation, I thought we were becoming friends, but I wouldn't be making that assumption again. He was acting like a jilted lover. And that made my attraction to him wilt. Who the hell did he think he was? No matter what I thought I had felt for Lachlan, I would not make the same mistake I'd made with Haywood. I would just have to overlook his jealous grunts and growls. I would train, grow stronger, discover my powers, and utilize everything at my disposal to rescue my true best friend, my family.

I imagined myself building back the wall around my heart brick by brick and sealing any cracks with fresh mortar.

CHAPTER 33

Lachlan

Fuck! Why had I said that? If Leora had heard me accuse Haywood of fucking Clarke, she could change her mind about helping us and likely challenge us to claim Clarke for her mother.

I had woken up in the dream with a nearly naked Clarke, and the possessive beast inside me took over. I was jealous of a claim fate had placed on us. It was absurd, and if I didn't reel myself in, Clarke would hate me. The hurt and confusion I'd seen in her eyes were unmistakable. She clearly thought of me as just a friend, if she thought of me as anything at all.

I wasn't a friend; I was a clumsy oaf, breaking what had been building between us. Maybe it was for the best that she saw me this way before I did something stupid and professed my undying love for her.

My selfish nature was winning over, and while it would be easier to accept her hate rather than the friendship we could have, I no longer wanted that. If Clarke was offering friendship, I should take it. The coldness in her tone, however, suggested that I'd ruined that too. I suppose it was for the best.

I volunteered to train her first, not out of the claim the bond was screaming at me to fulfill, but because I wanted it over with. I had to be close to her during training, and her expelling magic would make the bond go wild.

When she'd intervened with Leora on the dock and caused the sword at my throat to vanish, potentially saving my neck, I almost exploded. The need to pull her to me and taste her mouth was deafening. No one had ever come to my defense before, not that I had ever needed it, and she did so with such fearlessness.

Now I had thoroughly pissed her off, and fuck if that didn't turn me on too. Her kindness and gentleness were beautiful, but her anger was … my cock throbbed and hardened.

I deserved Haywood's wrath. The ache in my throat where his hands had been was almost comforting; maybe a little punishment and pain would do me good. Perhaps after training Clarke, I should seek him out and convince him to spar with me. It was too easy to provoke him. When it came to Clarke, he was wound tight as a bowstring, and I was no better. How were we going to survive this journey together?

Leora approached me after I finished setting up our camp. I braced myself for a fight, but the gleam in her eye was more mischievous than malicious.

"What have I done to warrant the general's attention?" I joked. Luck and Clarke were claiming their tents and getting settled, and Haywood began gathering food from the nearby vegetation for dinner. Leora and I were left virtually alone. I wasn't afraid of her, but I knew keeping the peace would require my effort.

"You're not hiding it well, you know," she said quietly but directly.

"This should be fun. What could I possibly not be hiding well, General?"

"Foolish dog," she cooed. "Your attempt to conceal the truth is glaringly obvious. If Haywood weren't blinded by his infatuation with her, he would have noticed it the moment you were in the same room. And as for Luck, well, she has her own distractions."

My heart jackhammered in my chest, but I kept my face aloof. "I'm not sure what you're referring to—" I began.

"If you bed her, there will be no hiding it," the general interrupted. "Even now, you betray yourself with your scent. You reek of the bond."

"There's no way you can smell that." The words spilled out, and my heart sank as Leora grinned wickedly. I had just confirmed her suspicion.

"Don't worry, beast. This can remain our little secret. I mention it only to caution you. The path you are on will inevitably lead to pain and destruction. Too much is at stake."

"Do not mistake me, General. I know all too well what is at stake," I growled.

"Down, boy. No need to raise your hackles. I'm actually curious to see how this plays out. I truly haven't been this entertained in centuries." She walked away chuckling to herself.

Fuck. That exchange solidified it: I needed to put as much distance between Clarke and me as possible. The thought ripped a painful hole in my chest, but I had no choice.

Removing this bond once and for all was more paramount now than ever. There had to be a way.

Leora would never keep my secret. Would she?

Everything I'd feared when my eyes first met Clarke's, when I realized what she meant to me, was coming true. One of my greatest enemies now knew my deepest vulnerability. I had to make this right somehow, for both Clarke and me.

CHAPTER 34

Alison

I hadn't realized I was crying until I felt Maldridge's hand on my shoulder. The grief I felt over Cody's death wasn't surprising; I had loved him deeply—had sacrificed and done unspeakable things for him and our future. It couldn't all be for nothing. I would gain this power in his honor.

I jerked away from Maldridge and turned my head so that a curtain of my perfect blonde hair hid my face.

I was beautiful when I cried, of course, but I didn't want to appear weak. I wasn't weak. I was just feeling a lot at the moment. I normally kept my feelings locked up because fuck that shit. I was awesome, my life was awesome, and I didn't do *sad*. And if I ever did, I definitely didn't do it with an audience.

I kept walking toward my room, and sorrow was replaced by anger. I took pleasure in thinking of all the ways I would destroy whoever was responsible for Cody's death. I would drive a knife into their hearts just as I had Heather's. Just imagining it made my heart race in anticipation.

At first, I'd hated to admit to myself how good that hot, thick blood spraying over my hands and face had felt, but now I could freely admit it. It felt fucking awesome. When I was snuffing the life from Heather's body, I kept picturing Cody staring at an old picture of her and him.

I had been willing to do anything Osiria had asked of me to achieve my dreams, but when she said I needed to kill Heather, I had to admit I was happy. Helping Osiria had eliminated two objectives of Cody's misplaced affection, and I was indebted to her. Now, I would be more in her debt, but if it meant I got to give Cody the vengeance he deserved, I would do anything.

I would need to ask Osiria where she kept the weapons. Someone like her had to have a whole fucking armory. I was lost in my thoughts when I realized Maldridge had stopped walking.

"We have arrived at your room, lovely," Maldridge said, placing his big, warm hand back onto my shoulder. "Do you require anything before I leave you?"

I paused as I thought of how to answer him.

"You could fuck me," I said pointedly.

Maldridge chuckled. "You really are trouble." Somehow, we were standing closer. I could smell him, and wow, he smelled as yummy as he looked, like a crackling fire and spearmint gum. I moved in to capture his mouth.

Maldridge clicked his tongue. "Greedy little thing. You move to take what I have yet to consent to," he said. But I noticed he didn't say no.

"Your hard dick digging into my stomach says otherwise," I said as I ran my hand over the very solid and very large bulge in his pants.

Maldridge hissed and grabbed my hand away, positioning it above my head.

Before I realized what was happening, my back landed hard against the now-closed door of my room as Maldridge pushed his body flush with mine, his mouth hovering over my ear. "I thought I told you I was otherwise engaged." His breath tickled my ear in warning. How the hell had he gotten us into my room so quickly? It had to be part of his magic powers.

"Again, your dick is telling me another story," I teased, rocking my hips against his rock-hard cock.

"You fucking brat. Shut your mouth, or I'll leave that dripping wet pussy unfilled," he warned.

"What is this? Dry humping my thigh isn't going to get me off." I was baiting him, riling him up. It was the perfect way to make sure this fuck was going to be hard and rough; it was the only way I got off. I loved an angry fuck. Hate-fucking was always more fulfilling than making love.

Another inhuman sound escaped from Maldridge as he effortlessly bent and tossed me over his shoulder, striding toward the enormous bed draped in red silk sheets. I presumed one of the modestly dressed servants had made it while we were in Osiria's lounge. I couldn't wait to destroy it.

As I was thrown onto the bed, goosebumps prickled along my skin. Then Maldridge was on me. His weight felt incredible.

"Are you sure you want to do this, lovely?" he asked, looking me dead in the eyes.

"Shut up and fuck me, *lovely*," I mocked. Taking his bottom lip in my mouth, I bit down hard enough to draw blood.

His smile was lethal as blood dripped from his split bottom lip. He reached between us and ripped apart the black gown I wore. I had chosen not to wear anything underneath, and the look on Maldridge's face told me he more than approved. Of course, he did.

He took in my toned, tan skin and perfect, perky breasts. Hell, I was just as turned on as he looked, just imagining my naked body.

His mouth trailed down my form as he explored, bit, and teased until I was a writhing mess. He feasted on my pussy until I pulled his head to my mouth. I tasted my arousal and a metallic tang from his lip that was still bleeding.

"Stop playing around and get your dick inside me now," I commanded.

I tore his shirt from him while he made quick work of his pants and underwear.

When his dick sprang up hard and ready, I gasped. He was big and beautiful, like a work of art. I took him in my hands, feeling the silky velvet skin encasing a thick steel rod. My pussy quaked with excitement. I guided him to my entrance, and without warning, he jerked his hips forward and fully sheathed himself inside me. I screamed, but his hand swallowed up the sound.

"As much as I crave your screams, lovely, you'll alert the whole palace, and I don't want to lose my balls. I'm very attached to them."

I simply nodded. I felt rather attached to his balls at the moment as well. I closed my eyes, immersing myself in the feel of him and the deep stretch inside my body.

"Eyes on me," Maldridge demanded.

My eyes flew open and took in the gorgeous man grinding on top of me.

His rhythm picked up, and all I could do was hold on. It was by far the best ride I'd had in a while, maybe the best ever. He clearly knew what he was doing.

His hand captured my moans as I called his name, like a plea. A mouth-watering eruption was building, and I craved the release it promised.

My muscles coiled tightly as his thrusts increased, and I felt myself detonate. Electricity pulsed up my spine. Maldridge soon followed, spilling his hot cum all over my tits and torso.

We both panted as he lifted himself from my body and walked to the enormous bathroom. I turned to see his glorious ass as he walked away. He returned with a towel and threw it at me.

"I thought you said you were going to fill me," I complained. I wasn't sure what kind of magical sperm they had in Teleran, but I was pretty sure my IUD would still work. I wanted to feel the aftermath of him drip down my thighs for the rest of the day.

"Perhaps next time," he said. "Clean yourself up, lovely, and do us both a favor: Shower. We don't want Osiria smelling me on you and decapitating us both, do we?" He smirked as he dressed and quickly exited my room.

My mouth hung open. Did he just say Osiria? Fuck, was that the person he was involved with? She'd kill me for sure.

Shit! I quickly wiped up Maldridge's cum and scurried to the bathroom. I turned the shower on and let the water run until the steam filled the bathroom, making sure the water was scalding hot. I washed my body five times and emerged with red-tinged skin.

I didn't see a hair dryer in the bathroom, and when I came to think of it, there was no evidence of electricity at all. There were lights but no plugs. I guess everything in this place ran off magic or something. Luckily, my hair dried perfectly straight with or without blow drying; it just wouldn't have the normal salon-quality voluminous blowout it usually had.

I wiped the condensation from the mirror and looked at my face. My cheeks were still rosy from my orgasm, and my hair fell past my shoulders almost to the small of my back. My blue eyes were bright and luminous, my lashes were still long and black from my last lash tint, and my skin was glowing.

I was right: I was even prettier in Teleran. And I had just experienced one of the best fucks of my life, I was living in a palace with servants, and I was the newly appointed most important person to the queen. I smiled at myself in triumph.

CHAPTER 35

Clarke

"Does this even look right?" I asked Luck. She was teaching me how to stand still and use the shadows to become invisible. Lachlan had wanted to train with me first, but I had asked Luck to start instead. I wasn't ready for any one-on-one time with him anytime soon.

"Yes, now tuck your limbs in and hold them close to your body. Don't sway; stay out of the light," she instructed.

It was a bright day, so finding shade had been difficult. I stood under a large tree, attempting to stay in its shadow.

During her time with the Guild of Shadows, Luck had mastered drawing the shadows to her, using her powers to bend the light. If I possessed the power of shadows, it had yet to manifest.

"Can I take these bracelets off yet? I think I'd do better if I could use my power at full strength." The Vincula bracelets still got super hot when I trained, and I could feel how much they held me back.

"If you can do this much with them on, I think it's safest for you and us to keep them on for now," Luck answered.

I hadn't really thought of that. Using my power with the bracelets was all I knew.

"You'll need to practice staying still, Clarke, but otherwise, you have the gist of it. As a fae, these abilities come naturally to you; however, your brain and body need to catch up. Your movements are still clumsy, like a human."

"Just what a girl likes to hear, Luck. She moves clunky," I deadpanned.

"You'll never learn if I coddle you. I'm not Haywood," she said with a knowing grin.

"Yeah, I'm glad you aren't," I said, grinning back. "Thank you. I genuinely want to learn. I need to learn. I appreciate your patience."

"Let's take a quick break, and then I'll show you how to throw a dagger," she said, taking a seat on the ground and propping herself up with the tree trunk.

"Sounds good to me. Any chance you brought us anything for lunch?" I asked hopefully. "Are there any pastries left from our provisions?" I wished we'd had the foresight to bring Gustav along; I was craving one of his magical concoctions like crazy.

"No, we are out. You had our last one yesterday; it's all you've been eating for days," Luck said.

"It's not *all* I've been eating. Haywood made a delicious stew last night. It's just that I'm starving, and those pastries are so savory that I can't help it," I said.

"Your magic is probably burning up everything you're consuming. Make sure you are eating enough." She handed me a sandwich from her pack.

We sat silently for a minute while we both ate.

"I found Cody's phone while cleaning up the scene in the warehouse," Luck said, breaking the silence. "I was able to decode his password, and I saw the video," she continued. She looked at me.

I'd forgotten all about that video. The shock was evident on my face, and I was speechless.

"You saw that?" I asked, feeling embarrassed. I didn't know how much he'd got on film, but I couldn't imagine it was anything I wanted anyone to see.

"I did. I thought I would show it to Haywood, but since we aren't on Earth and Cody is dead, I feel it's no longer relevant and thought it should be up to you who sees it," Luck explained.

"If it's all the same to you, I'd rather not relive or rehash that night," I replied.

"Do you want to watch it?"

"No, absolutely not." I replied.

"Do you want to talk about anything else that happened that night? Did he—"

"No," I interrupted. "He … implied, and he touched me, but …" I swallowed the lump in my throat. "Lachlan and Haywood got there in time," I said, relief flooding the anxiety that had built as flashes of that night ran through my mind.

"I'm happy to hear that," Luck said as she retrieved Cody's phone from her pack and handed it to me. "It's only fitting that you should be the one to destroy it then."

I turned the phone over and willed my water magic to seep into it. Destroying it caused a weight that I hadn't even realized I'd been carrying to lift.

"Thank you," I said.

"Don't mention it," Luck replied, taking the phone from me. She used her shadows to send it to a place where I'd never have to see it again.

Silence descended once more. I savored the lilac-scented breeze and took another bite of my sandwich.

"So what's going on with you and Haywood?" Luck asked. I choked on the piece of food I was eating. I suppose it was a matter of time. I was about to get the *what are your intentions with my best friend* speech.

"I was wondering if you were going to bring that up. To be honest, I care for him, but he broke my trust. In the past, when someone did that, my heart closed to that person. I couldn't help it. And in any case, our worlds are on the brink of collapse, and my closest friend is in danger. My love life is hardly the most important thing right now."

"It is if it distracts from the mission. Distraction equals death, Clarke. And don't think I haven't noticed what is happening with the Obscurus," she said, lifting a questioning brow.

"Nothing is happening with Lachlan," I protested. "I mean, he's hot, but so are all of you. And, yes, there is a small attraction there, but I promise you, I'm focused," I asserted with conviction.

"I didn't mean you. Those males are so bewitched, it's a wonder we made it out of Haywood's manor in one piece."

"Well, what about you?" I asked defensively.

"What about me?" She asked, narrowing her gray eyes.

"Oh, come on, Luck. You could cut the tension between you and Leora with a knife."

Her eyes widened, but a mask of indifference quickly replaced her surprised expression. "That's not up for discussion," she said coolly.

"Fine, then you can't question my focus when yours is clearly *distracted* too."

"Fine. Let's get back to training," she said, pulling a dagger from some hidden place in her outfit. It was a wonder how she could move around with weapons concealed everywhere without stabbing herself. "Here," she said, extending a dagger that could only be described as beautiful. It had green and blue inlaid jewels and was made of silver metal. "It's a Faeval blade, one of the strongest and well-crafted in Teleran. It was forged with titanium and magic to create a near indestructible blade. Normally, you'd need to undergo rigorous training at the Guild of Shadows to earn one, but since we don't have the time, you can have my spare."

"I can keep it?" I questioned.

"Yes, you need to learn how to defend yourself, and a dagger is the easiest weapon to conceal. However, you must first learn how to use it."

"I know how to use it; stick them with the pointy end," I said with a chuckle, quoting Arya Stark from *Game of Thrones.*

"Yes, obviously," Luck said, without humor. She clearly hadn't been soaking up any television while on Earth. "I will teach you where all the vital targets are on the body, and how to hit a target. You'll know how to wound, kill, and incapacitate."

My pulse kicked up a notch as I felt the dagger warm in my palm.

Two hours later, I had knicks in places I didn't want to think of, and only three direct hits on the targets Luck had set up. At least I was hitting the vital points on the creepy dummy she'd made. It spewed a red substance when I hit the correct area. Luck assured me that it wasn't real blood, but it certainly looked like it.

I was so tired at the end of the day that I took my dinner to my tent and left the others to talk among themselves around the fire.

I sat on the ground and used a small chair as my dining table. I had barely shoved one spoonful of soup into my mouth before I started to fall asleep.

And that's where Haywood found me the next morning, my face halfway in a now-cold soup bowl, drool hanging from my mouth, and my stomach growling because I'd barely replenished the calories I'd burned training the day before.

I couldn't remember if I had ever heard Haywood laugh before. With all the dire circumstances surrounding the bulk of our time together, there was hardly time or cause. My heart squeezed to hear it.

"I'm sorry. I didn't mean to laugh at you. Let me show you what I saw," he said as a vivid snapshot of my disheveled appearance flashed in my mind.

"Whoa, you can just send pictures to my brain like that?" I gasped.

"Along with our base magic, we also possess special gifts like Luck and her shadows and Leora with her lie detection," Haywood explained. Every day, I learned somehow new about their seemingly limitless magic and abilities.

"I thought your magic was growing weaker. Does using your gifts deplete it further?" I asked.

"I suppose it could tire me out if I were constantly using it, but I haven't used my magic since we left my home. Sometimes, letting a little off the top eases the pressure. In any case, that was the equivalent of using your energy to yawn, barely a blip on my reserves," he explained. "I came to tell you it's time to train with me, but if you aren't up for it, we can take a break today."

"We can't afford to take a break, and I'm fine. I just pushed myself a little too much yesterday with Luck."

"If you're sure, I'll leave you to clean up. Meet me outside when you're ready," he said.

A few minutes later, I stepped from the tent into a beautiful morning with bright skies and warmer air than yesterday. Haywood was waiting for me with his back turned.

"I hope this is okay. I didn't know what we would be working on and …" I trailed off as Haywood turned around to face me. The sun had caught his face just right, making the orange ring in his deep brown eyes sparkle. His blond hair was unbound, blowing in the light breeze. Damn. Then he smiled at me, his perfect white teeth gleaming, and a dimple appeared on his left cheek. There was no denying he was beautiful, but at that moment, he looked more than that; he looked ethereal as he leaned closer to me.

As much as I didn't trust him and had closed my heart to the possibility of him, warmth still crept into my face. His smile turned into a smirk, another expression I hadn't seen from him before, and I knew he'd realized why I had stopped mid-sentence. Hope flared in his eyes, causing me to regain my composure. I needed to be smarter now. I was in a foreign realm, discovering that impossible things were true every day, and I needed to learn how to manage my magic so that I could be strong enough to save Alison. I couldn't get distracted.

Haywood noticed, and his expression shifted to the serious one I was more accustomed to.

"Today, we will work on conjuring water and air. Follow me," he said

And I did.

CHAPTER 36

Clarke

"What the fuck, Haywood!" I screeched as a fuck ton of cold water fell on my head, soaking me through. Cold wind hit me next, and I started to shiver.

"Fight back, Clarke. Remove the water and attempt to dry it off with air. You did it before; you can do it again."

"I'm trying, but nothing is working," I complained through chattering teeth.

Warmth traveled up my body and instantly dried my skin. It felt like a physical caress, and a low moan escaped my lips before I could stop it.

Haywood's eyebrows shot up to his blond hairline.

"You did it!" he exclaimed, picking me up and twirling me around.

"I didn't," I protested.

"I did," a familiar, deep voice said as Haywood put me down abruptly.

"If you keep helping her, she'll never learn," Haywood chided.

"She was shivering. She won't learn anything if she becomes ill." Lachlan grumbled. He had been avoiding me since I decided not to train with him first.

"I thought fae didn't get sick," I stated.

"We don't, but you are different. Who knows what can happen to you that can't happen to us?" Lachlan explained. "You are stronger in many ways, but we must consider that perhaps you have weaknesses we do not. Magic has a balance, and we have yet to discover yours. Why disturb the scales by allowing your body to freeze needlessly?" He paused a moment to let his point sink in. "It's time to light some fires, Clarke," he continued.

"We are not done here, Lachlan," Haywood protested. "She has yet to conjure a single drop of water today."

"Maybe all the training is too much, too soon? Are we wearing you out, Clarke?" Lachlan asked, grinning wolfishly as concern darkened Haywood's gaze. Haywood was ever the protector, always worried about me, but Lachlan seemed to enjoy challenging me while allowing me to decide where my boundaries were.

"She's fine, Lachlan. I wouldn't do anything to cause her harm," Haywood answered defensively.

"She shouldn't be able to use her powers this much with the bracelets on. We are pushing her; we don't know her limits yet," Lachlan argued.

I hated when they started talking about me like I wasn't there. Lachlan did it the most, as if avoiding speaking to me directly.

"Yeah, *she's* still standing here," I interjected. "I'm also fucking sick of these bracelets. Just because I've been training doesn't mean I've gotten used to them."

"You should be able to take them off soon. It's just hard to know how long you need to wear them since you are so powerful. They protect you and us because we do not know what will happen when you take them off," Haywood explained.

"When you say it like that, Haywood, you make me feel like a ticking time bomb," I said.

"We just want to keep you safe. With your training, once the bracelets come off, you will have a better chance at controlling the magnitude of power inside you."

Haywood said. "Even though your training is important, if you need a break, you will have it."

"I'm okay, I promise. I just fell asleep while eating dinner last night and forgot to grab something for breakfast before we started training today," I explained.

"You didn't even feed her, Haywood. What good are you?" Lachlan prodded, humor woven into his words.

"I-I," Haywood stammered. "Forgive me, Clarke, I didn't think to ask you this morning. We should break for lunch early."

"Works for me," Lachlan said as we all walked toward the fire pit in the center of camp.

"If you want to eat. Light the fire," Lachlan said.

"Are you serious?" I complained.

"No fire, no food. I could hear your stomach growling from inside my tent. It woke me from a deep sleep, so I know you are properly motivated," Lachlan said, folding his arms over his expansive chest.

"Finc," I said, raising my hands. Luck had said it was all about intention, and I wanted the roasted vegetables with a warm slice of sourdough bread I knew we'd brought.

While I was willing the fire pit to light, the logs that served as seating around it burst into flames. Then the bread and brussels sprouts that had been in our food pack fell from the air above us like rain. Panicking, I envisioned the flames being extinguished, and a torrent of water blasted up at us from below.

I looked up at the two drenched fae in front of me, the ruined bread scattered around us, the mud pooling near the fire pit, and brussels sprouts floating in it.

I cackled, snorted, and laughed so hard that I had to bend over. Haywood and Lachlan looked at each other and began doing the same.

The levity of the moment burst as Leora came into view, practically fuming. She was drenched too. I couldn't help but feel a little afraid of her, and the sharpness of her purple eyes told me she was not amused.

I straightened up. "I'm sorry, Leora. I'm really struggling with conjuring today."

"You struggle with conjuring every day. Now, tidy yourself. It's time to train with me," she said, giving a cutting glare.

"If that's true, what made me suddenly worthy of your training?" I quipped.

"Don't question me, girl. Thank the fates for your good fortune and follow me," she said caustically.

"She hasn't eaten, Leora. She'll tire out," Haywood argued.

"If she cannot conjure properly, our suicide mission is doomed, and so is her friend. We do not have time for failure. Failures don't eat," she replied icily.

"She's right," I said, moving to follow her. "I'm fine. I'll eat later."

A small, unsoaked piece of bread appeared in my hands. I knew it was from Lachlan. Confused as ever, I walked away with Leora to get my ass kicked.

CHAPTER 37

Clarke

We'd been traveling for a few nights, camping and training during the day. Tomorrow night, we'd reach the outskirts of Altfevis.

I had ping-ponged between the four fae, learning moves and attempting to wield the power inside me that I still felt disconnected from. Other than commands and instructions, Lachlan barely said two words to me while training.

"Here," Leora said, tossing me a flagon of water. I knew she hadn't checked to see if I was looking before she threw it, a subtle show of disdain. But I sensed that I was secretly growing on her; she just wasn't ready to admit it.

My muscles were sore, and I felt … good and strong. My stance was more sure-footed and less wobbly.

I was so exhausted at the end of the day that I slept through the nighttime boat rides. My sleep was so deep that I didn't have any more visits from Alison. I also hadn't pulled Lachlan into another dream, which was probably for the best.

Not only was the first time extremely embarrassing, but also, since then, he'd been acting so weird toward me. Any time he had to show me something that required physical contact, he'd recoil as if my skin had burned him. When I asked him if anything was wrong, he made me feel like I was dumb for even asking. I had stopped trying to be his friend and accepted him as just a temporary, albeit reluctant, teacher.

At the moment, the fire inside me seemed more substantial than any other powers I had. He'd taught me how to summon a small flame and made me practice lighting different things over and over until it felt like second nature.

Haywood had been completely fine with being more hands-on. Maybe it was my feelings toward him, but water felt by far the weakest of my powers, nearly out of reach. Other than controlling Leora's sword to save Lachlan and accidentally summoning a torrent of water, I had barely summoned anything of substance other than sweat.

The times I trained with Luck were my favorites. Not only was she the one fae who had no weird feelings toward me, but also the skills she imparted made me feel like a badass. She taught me how to stand so still that I could render myself invisible. No, really—actually invisible. She'd also gifted me a cool corset similar to hers in which to conceal my dagger. My aim was also improving.

Leora's training was grueling and taxing. She hadn't let me touch the sword that hung holstered at her side. I wondered why she even had it, considering she could conjure a far more deadly one with her water power. Nope, my future best friend just had me running and doing jumping jacks. She said it was important to increase my endurance. It was one thing to wield a weapon, but if I couldn't evade an enemy while fighting them, I would die regardless of my skill with a blade.

When I'd asked her if I would be getting some fancy armor of my own, she just scoffed, saying something about not having time to teach me how to use a forge. When I pointed out that she probably could just create a set with magic, she rolled her eyes and stalked off.

Overall, I was starting to feel capable. My new friends assured me that we wouldn't be discovered, that I would never need to fight, and that the combat training was just a precaution.

The next morning, as we set up our final camp before reaching Altfevis, I began to feel a different sensation pulsing through my body. A drizzle began falling, the first time I experienced precipitation other than snow in Teleran. A rumble of thunder echoed from a distance, and the pulsing beneath my skin intensified. I glanced down at the Vincula bracelets, which were emanating a warm glow. I had grown accustomed to the burn from my magic clashing with the resistance of the bracelets, but this was painful, somehow stronger. Lightning struck mere yards from our encampment, and I jumped, startled by its proximity.

A charred smell, like burning wood, filled the air in stark contrast to the scent of the rain, which smelled like eucalyptus and made me crave deep, cleansing breaths. I realized that I hadn't had a panic attack since starting training, and a smile tickled my cheeks. What if I didn't need my breathing exercises anymore? What if I was getting stronger, not just in my body but in my mind as well? I touched my mother's necklace that rested against my chest. I wondered what she would think if she could see me now. I knew for certain she'd be proud. Sometimes I missed her so much it hurt. Somehow, being in this place made me feel closer to her than I had in years. I couldn't explain it, but the feeling made me feel lighter, more whole, and less empty.

Footsteps through the damp grass made me turn from the direction of the lightning strike.

"Clarke, why don't you come inside the tent? The storm is picking up," Luck said.

"I didn't think of that. I was just enjoying the sensation of the rain." I had always loved rainy days just as much as sunny days.

I followed Luck back to the big tent that could fit us all for meals and mission planning.

"It's getting worse," I heard Haywood say.

"What's getting worse?" I questioned while moving the tent flap aside to enter.

Haywood sighed, appearing like he was going to evade my question. "The breakdown. We've never had storms like this before. If it rains here, it's normally light. And as far as lightning striking anything, well, that's never happened. It's most concerning. We don't know what timeline we are up against."

"Yes, just on my way to your home, Haywood, I noticed an old wing of the Luna Palace had disappeared," Leora said.

"Things are appearing on Earth randomly. Just before we came here, castle structures popped up in New York and in the Indian Ocean," I explained.

"What else have you seen, Clarke?" Luck asked.

"I'm trying to remember. One of our seven oceans turned pink and blue, some buildings transformed into pink bubble-like structures, and there were giant auras in the sky that almost looked like mirrors to another world. I guess they were the tears you were talking about," I explained.

"Could you see parts of Teleran through them?" Luck asked.

"No, I saw them on TV, so they looked warped in the center."

"We have to stop this," Leora said.

Lachlan grunted in agreement. We all stared off in silence, worried about what would happen to our worlds if we failed. The storm picked up, mirroring our growing fears.

. . .

"Wake up, girl," Leora's voice pulled me from a deep sleep. I knew I had been dreaming, but the images were foggy.

"What?" I asked, wiping the sleep from my eyes.

"Since we are headed to Altfevis today, we must start your training early," she responded.

"I thought we had to start getting ready for Altfevis early?"

"Luck and I will help you get ready later. Right now, we are training." Leora made an impatient get-moving motion.

I stood up, put on my black tights, my favorite band T-shirt, and my red Converse shoes. Then I joined Leora outside, where the sun was barely cresting. She led me to a clearing not far from our camp.

"Here, hold this," handing me a pillow that appeared to be stuffed to the brim. "This will have to suffice as a training pad. Bend your elbows, pull your arms into your body, and hold the pillow tightly to your chest," she instructed as she positioned me.

"What the hell are we—?" I started to ask before Leora's open palm slammed into my chest where the pillow was. The impact knocked the air out of me and sent my body sailing into the dirt.

"What the fuck was that?" I asked, standing back up and rubbing my ass.

"I'm teaching you how to receive a hit. It's just as important as being able to land a blow. You need to understand what it feels like so that when it happens to you for the first time, you can sail past the shock and go straight into kicking their ass," she answered, a wicked gleam in her eye. Suddenly, I had a sinking feeling that someone had told her about Haywood and me and that she was about to show me just how angry she was about it.

"First, your stance is all wrong. Spread your legs, with your left foot slightly forward, and bend your knees." I tried to follow her directions. "Not bad. Now, push back slightly when you feel the impact. Stay in your stance and breathe."

I took a deep breath. "Okay, I'm ready," I said, nodding.

Leora came at me again, thrusting her palm forcefully into the center of my chest.

The impact was still jarring, but my body was balanced, allowing me to absorb the blow with only a small step back. Then Leora unleashed herself. I had to focus all my energy to remain upright and dodge her strikes. I was genuinely starting to worry that she had brought me out here to kill me. I wondered if I screamed whether the others would hear me or not.

"Would this be easier without these bracelets on?" I asked Leora.

"Yes," she answered matter-of-factly.

"So can I take them off?" I asked. I'd been training for days. Maybe I was ready.

"No," Leora responded as she dealt a rather harsh blow.

"This feels more like punishment than training," I groaned. My tone was light-hearted yet probing. If she were angry, maybe it would be better to hash it out.

"Why would I want to punish you, Clarke? You're supposed to save us all," Leora asked, while flashing me a knowing glance. Fuck, she knew, she fucking knew, and I was going to die. One mistake and that was it. She was going to kill me out here in the middle of nowhere. She took another swing, and this time I ended up on my ass.

"Listen, Leora—" I began. Leora leaped into the air and landed on top of me with a thud. I shielded my head with my arms, bracing for the impact of her blows. Instead, Leora burst into laughter.

"You … should've … seen … your … face," she said between cackles. This was the first time I had heard her laugh, and it was easily the creepiest thing I had ever heard.

I lowered my arms and looked up at her. She remained straddling my torso.

"I don't care that you fucked Haywood, you stupid girl." She stood with predatory grace and extended her hand to help me off the ground. I was still too stunned to speak.

"To be honest, I'm glad he has found comfort in other fae over the years. I'm not remotely interested in Haywood that way, but it was amusing to see the fear on your face," Leora said.

"I truly apologize," I said, regaining my voice. "I didn't know you were engaged until I arrived. I'm not a homewrecker."

"I respect your attempt to apologize, but there's no need. I've fucked half my battalion, some all at once, and don't intend on stopping when my mother forces our union. I don't expect Haywood to be faithful. It's not necessarily the custom of the fae to be monogamous. Unless, of course, you are mated. That is a rare thing indeed for fate to mate your soul to another and rarer still for those souls to find one another," she said with a knowing glint in her eyes.

"Fated mates are real?" I asked, geeking out. It was one of my favorite book tropes. Although each of those books said fated mates were rare, weirdly, every character seemed to have a mate. It was a funny contradiction, but it often led to great smut, so no one cared.

"Yes, it's real. Now, can we return to training? I'll hold the pillow, and you take your turn hitting me."

"Leora, I don't want to hit you," I protested.

"You can't hurt me, and this is vital to your training. I'm sure a small part of you wants to get back at me for attacking you and teasing you about Haywood. Did you think I was going to kill you out here?"

"No, I didn't think that," I lied.

"You did! Oh, how delicious. Now, ready yourself, girl. Get back into your stance, keep your hand flat, and step into the hit. Use your whole body."

It didn't feel natural at first, but eventually, I got the hang of it and even made Leora retreat a step once or twice. It made me feel powerful to take a hit and remain standing, and if I used my whole body behind my strike, I could also land a seriously painful blow. She also taught me how to use my elbow. She said it could be my sharpest and most powerful weapon.

"So now that you have mastered those techniques, you must continue practicing them until they become second nature. In reality, you will panic in a real scenario, and I want these steps to be your first response," she said.

I nodded my head. The others had started to wake up, and I could smell breakfast cooking on the fire. My stomach rumbled.

"Before we finish for the day, I want to show you one more thing. Lachlan, could you come here for a moment?" Leora called.

My heart dropped. I hadn't even heard him enter the clearing. This couldn't be good. Lachlan jogged over, his hair was mushed from sleep, and he was wearing fucking gray sweatpants. Of everything to have a thing for, why the fuck was it gray sweatpants? They were the most generic thing, and they weren't even a color. But for some reason, they were the hottest fucking thing on a fit man. He was also in the process of pulling on a black T-shirt over his tattoo-clad torso, another kryptonite for me. I wiped my mouth inconspicuously just to make sure I wasn't drooling.

"Did you summon me, General?" he asked Leora sarcastically.

"Pretend to choke Clarke," she commanded.

"Excuse me?" Lachlan asked at the same time I asked, "The fuck?"

"I'm showing her something important, and I need help positioning her while she does it. So I need you to put your big meat hands on her throat. Is that too difficult for you, beast? Can you handle basic commands like a good dog?" Leora teased. They'd come a long way from wanting to murder each other. Dog and beast sounded more like pet names than insults now.

Annoyance flashed in Lachlan's eyes, but Leora didn't balk. Of course not. Women were more powerful in Teleran.

"Fine," he said, walking toward me with a growl. He wasn't doing himself any favors; his demeanor was sometimes more beast than man. He brought his big, beautiful, strong hands to my throat. His hands did crazy things to my body. He was so close now that I had to avert my eyes. "Clarke, is this okay?" he asked.

I looked up, and fuck, those goddamn eyes lasered straight to my fucking soul.

"Yea-yes, totally fine," I said, awkward as fuck. Why was I such a bumbling wreck around him? And why did I

219

like this so much? That settled that. As soon as I got home, I was looking for a therapist or an exorcist. I needed some serious help.

He stepped in closer to me, and his smoked cedar and cinnamon scent washed over me. His nostrils flared. Oh my god, was he smelling me too?

Fuck. Fuck. Fuck.

We'd yet to cover it in my training, but I knew fae senses were heightened. My favorite books always mentioned that they could smell arousal. *Think about non-sexy things, Clarke!* Like Alison, yes, Alison locked up in a sad, dark cell. Whew, that was working, sort of.

Leora cleared her throat.

"Clarke, the first thing you need to do if you are attacked this way is to scrunch your neck," Leora said.

I tried to do this without laughing, but I failed. Lachlan gave me a small grin, the first one in days, and my heart melted into a puddle on the ground. Almost as if he sensed the shift in my mood, he put a mask of indifference back on so quickly that I might have imagined the grin.

"This is serious, Clarke," Leora scolded.

"I know, I know, I'm sorry, Leora," I said, now sober from my fit of laughter.

"Now, turn your head as far as you can. You do this so he has less of a chance of rendering you unconscious. Good, now raise the arm closest to your face. With all your strength and speed, turn in the opposite direction with that arm and bring it down. Your elbow is now level with his groin, and you can render him inert or impotent depending on how hard you strike him." She watched me go through the motions once. "Now, repeat this five times. I'll be right back; I need coffee," Leora said while walking away, leaving Lachlan and me alone.

220

"It's okay, Lachlan. You don't have to do this. I'll just tell Leora we did it. You can go do whatever you were doing before she interrupted you." It's not that I thought Lachlan didn't like me. Well, actually, yes, I did think that. I wasn't so naive as to think everyone wanted to be my friend.

Just because we were forced into a temporary partnership of sorts didn't mean he enjoyed my company. He truly seemed to despise the time we spent together. I had made peace with that but didn't want to withstand more of his disdain than I needed to.

Lachlan, however, stared at me like I had grown three heads. His hands were still on me, but they were no longer around my throat; he'd moved them to my shoulders, holding me in place.

"She's not forcing me to help train you. I said that I would. Remember?" Lachlan said.

"Yes, but I know you don't like it, so I'm letting you off the hook," I replied.

"I don't like what?" he asked, still not getting the picture. Did I really have to spell it out for him?

I stepped out of his reach and said, "I know you don't … like me. You said we weren't friends, and that's perfectly okay. I know I'm not everyone's cup of tea. I actually didn't have many friends growing up because I'm a little different—"

"Clarke—" Lachlan attempted to interrupt.

"You don't have to explain yourself. I still appreciate everything you're doing for me. You've been a great teacher, and—"

"Clarke!" Lachlan said, raising his voice. I realized I had been nervously rambling.

"What?"

"You think I don't like you?" he asked, bewildered. No, not bewildered. I must have been reading his expression incorrectly.

"Well, yeah, I mean, you were nice to me at first and took me to get pastries, and I know I weirded you out when I brought you into my dream, but I promise, I'm trying really hard to understand how I did that. I didn't do it on purpose, and I really didn't mean to pull you into it naked, and you didn't have to hold me or anything and—"

"Clarke, stop." Lachlan interrupted me again. He had reclaimed the steps I'd taken backward and stood close. I looked around and realized we were very much alone.

"I'm sorry," he said sincerely. "I've been dealing with some personal transitions and didn't mean to hurt you. I do like you … more than I should permit myself to." He traced my jaw with his hand and cradled my face in his palm. The gesture made me feel like I was the most precious thing in the world to him, but that couldn't be right.

"I don't understand …" I started but trailed off as the clank of Leora's armor approached us. I stepped back out of Lachlan's space. His eyes never left mine.

CHAPTER 38

Clarke

"Haywood, I'm supposed to meet Leora and Luck to get ready for Altfevis," I whined.

After training with Leora and that awkward exchange with Lachlan, Haywood had shown up in the clearing.

"I just want you to try a bit of water conjuring before we go," he insisted.

We were on the outskirts of Altfevis, and Leora and Luck had promised to help me get dressed and ready. They'd noticed my growing nerves about it.

I had relied too much on Alison to help me get ready for our nights out, to the point that I had forgotten how to tame my mane of frizzy waves by myself. I didn't want to stand out at this festival for the wrong reasons. Haywood was determined to help me control my water magic, but he made me anxious. Things had been friendly enough, but I still didn't know where we stood. I cared for him, but not romantically.

"I have to be honest, Haywood. I think I know why I can't conjure water around you." I really didn't want to tell him the truth, but learning to use my powers was more important. I couldn't be afraid to express how I felt. I was beginning to understand how this magic worked, and it seemed like it was tied to my mood. Somehow, I'd begun associating my water magic with Haywood, which was why it was the weakest.

"I'm not angry with you anymore," I began.

"Clarke, that relieves me more than I can express," Haywood said, stepping closer.

"I'm glad, but that's not everything. I'm not angry, but I'm uncertain how I feel about you. I can tell you want more, and while I'm still attracted to you, I really just want to be your friend." I tried not to notice his wince. "I understand why you lied to me. I recognize how difficult it must have been to explain all this," I continued, gesturing to our surroundings. "That's not why I don't want to be with you that way. I was in a dark place when we hooked up, and I need to apologize because it feels like I took advantage of you."

"Clarke, no, I—" he interrupted.

"No, wait, Haywood. Let me say this." I paused. "I want to start over as friends."

"I would be honored to call you my friend, Clarke," Haywood said warmly.

I sighed in relief. I moved to hug Haywood when something burst through the woods and into the clearing. A blur of motion came barreling toward me from the right. I lifted my hands just before a bear-like creature with antlers rammed into me.

It froze in midair.

"What the fuck is that?" I asked, breathlessly.

"It's an Onikuma," he replied. "It's similar to the bears on Earth, but it has antlers like a deer."

"Why did it try to attack us?" I asked, my heart still pounding.

"Animals are our friends. You were probably caught off guard just as it was. It likely runs through these forests regularly and may have been fleeing the crowds of Altfevis," he said. "It would have collided with you, but it didn't."

"Oh," I said, feeling a bit embarrassed for overacting.

"I think you are missing a vital point, Clarke," Haywood said.

"What?" I asked.

"You froze the Onikuma."

"I froze the bear." I had successfully used my water magic. "Haywood, I froze the bear!" I said, jumping into his awaiting arms, surprised not to feel the usual urge to pull away.

"I knew you could do it!" he said.

The hug was just a hug; it didn't feel like more. I stepped away from him and smiled.

We backed away from the bear as Haywood lifted his hands. It unfroze, shook its body, and stared at us in confusion.

I could've sworn it smiled and winked at me before it ran out of the clearing into the woods. What. The. Fuck.

I turned toward Haywood, who had a broad smile on his face.

"Friends?" he asked.

"Friends," I said, feeling lighter than I had in weeks.

CHAPTER 39

Clarke

"You're being ridiculous, Clarke. Just stay still," Luck said.

"I'm sorry, Luck, but you are literally ripping my hair out. Can't you just use your magic and give me a blowout like you did in Haywood's bathroom?" I asked.

"We are supposed to do this without magic, but your hair is proving too difficult," she said, waving her hand to transform my hair into smooth, flowing waves.

"I can hear both of you from my tent. Do you want to alert all of Altfevis that we're here?" Leora asked, breezing in with several dresses over her arm.

"No one can hear us over that music, Leora. Calm down," Luck said.

It felt natural like three girlfriends getting ready for a night out together. I'd thought the makeup here would be magically done, but Teleran tradition was to prepare for Altfevis without magic. Something about the ritual made it special.

"So who's going to help me with my makeup?" I asked, eying them in the mirror.

"I can help with that," Leora said.

I blinked my shocked response.

"Oh, I can help you take down an enemy, but you doubt my precision with cosmetics?" Leora asked. "I'll have you know, I have the finest eyeliner flick in all of Teleran," she continued. I didn't doubt it; it made sense that her precision and steadiness as a warrior translated into other skills.

"By all means, flick away, Leora," I said with a chuckle.

As she worked on my makeup, Leora asked, "So you and the Obscurus dog, huh?"

I flinched back from her.

"What are you talking about?" I asked.

"Lachlan. Are you blind, girl? He gazes at you endlessly," Leora continued.

"There have been some moments," I conceded. "But we are literally trying to save worlds here. I'm not interested in pursuing anything with anyone right now."

"Of course you're not," Luck joked.

"What about you, Luck? Are you making time for romance?" I asked. I couldn't believe she was teasing me about Lachlan when she wasn't owning up to her feelings toward Leora.

Her eyes widened as she looked at Leora in the mirror. Leora's hand halted as she met her gaze. Their eyes locked, and something passed between them.

"Anyway," I said, breaking the tension, "the way you all acted in the beginning about him being an Obscurus … well, are Obscurus really bad? Is there a reason you all hate each other so much? It seems that besides your magic and weather, you're pretty similar."

"It feels more like a tradition to hate each other," Luck said. "It's just like anything—no one is completely good or completely bad; we all have elements of both. The Obscurus are known for their short tempers, but they aren't evil."

"So why all the training and the Estival army? Do you guys go to war? Lachlan told me that all Obscurus are trained in combat; is that why?" I asked.

227

"Close your eyes, Clarke," Leora scolded. "I may be talented, but if you keep moving your face, I can't promise the results will be my best work."

"No, we don't fight wars," Luck said. "You know how you didn't come into your power until you turned thirty?" she asked. I nodded. "It is the same here. The powerless must be protected. Even after thirty, some fae's power don't amount to much."

"Like Gustav?" I asked.

"Look up, Clarke," Leora directed as she applied concealer under my eyes.

"Yes. Just like on Earth, the smallest creatures develop physical traits that make them seem more formidable. It's the same here," Luck explained. "Like the adolescents, both are protected by the most powerful and seasoned warriors."

"And the Guild you trained at, Luck?" I asked.

"Look straight out," Leora said while she used the mascara.

"It is for those who exhibit qualities better suited to stealth. When someone demonstrates that they possess such talents, the Guild assists in cultivating them. We focus on their strengths. Additionally, we accommodate most of the adolescents in our dormitories," Luck explained.

"Now, if you two are finished with your history lesson, look at yourself, Clarke," Leora said, turning me toward the mirror.

"This looks so great, Leora! Thank you," I said. As promised, she'd achieved a smoky eye, and the best-winged liner look I'd ever seen. She'd also painted my lips bubble gum pink, a color Alison would approve.

"And to complete the look, you'll be wearing this," Luck said, holding up what looked like strips of multi-colored fabric.

"I can't wear that," I protested.

"You can and you will. Trust me, the Obscurus will be eating out of your hands tonight," Luck teased.

"I told you, Lachlan doesn't want me, and even if he did, this isn't the right time. Aren't you two close to Haywood? You don't think that would be cruel?" I asked.

"I thought you said you and Haywood agreed to be friends?" Luck asked.

"It is more than obvious that you do not want him, Clarke," Leora added.

"We did, but—"

"What do you want, Clarke?" Luck asked. "It seems you've had very few true choices since you came here," she noted. "If the worlds weren't ending and Alison was right here beside you, what would she tell you?" Luck asked, causing my throat to grow thick at the thought.

"She'd tell me to 'hit that,'" I chuckled.

"Hit that?" Leora asked.

"She means 'fuck him,' Leora," Luck explained.

We all burst into laughter.

"I like this girl. She's direct and to the point. I look forward to meeting her," Leora said through her laugh.

I smiled at that. I had felt like I had one close friend, but now it felt like I had four, maybe five, including Lachlan.

I couldn't deny the pull toward him, how he made my heart race, the ease I'd felt when we'd first met, or the dream we'd shared.

Maybe the girls were right. It may be time to seek out something for myself for once.

CHAPTER 40

Alison

I woke up with an exquisite ache between my legs. The memory made a wetness pool between my thighs. I looked around my room, hoping to see Maldridge somewhere. Maybe I could convince him to visit me again. I yawned, pushed off my blanket, and went to use the bathroom. I was still naked and could see bruises forming from where Maldridge had gripped me. There were scratches on my neck. My usually soft, silky blonde hair stuck out on the side of my head. I grinned. Sex with Maldridge had been the most fun and satisfying experience I'd had in a long time, and hell, maybe ever.

I opened one of the drawers under the bathroom sink, found a brush, and began working on the tangles in my hair when I heard the door to my room open. Not bothering to cover myself, I walked out of the bathroom to find Maldridge. He stopped dead in his tracks when he saw me, his eyes heating with a desire that I knew echoed my own. I hadn't bothered to get dressed yet and had clearly made the right decision. It was go time.

As I approached Maldridge, his expression changed to the more serious one he'd sported when we first met. Had that been only days ago? Usually, I didn't catch feelings this fast for anyone. It made me question how much I'd loved Cody.

At the time, he'd been the most impressive man I'd met in Charlotte. He had money, power, the right family, and connections—he was my equal.

But I was no longer in Charlotte. I was in Teleran, living in the castle of the most powerful queen. I was about to get power myself. Maldridge's appeal was limitless, rivaling anything I could've ever imagined.

I'd also never climaxed that many times with anyone. He was power. He was sex. He never backed down. He pushed me to my limits.

Speaking of those limits, I was more than ready to push some of those as I stepped into Maldridge's personal space. He hadn't touched me yet, but I assumed he was prolonging the inevitable. There was no way he didn't want more of what I was offering him.

"I need you to dress, lovely, and quickly," Maldridge said.

"You're fucking kidding me, right?" I said, gesturing to my naked body. Like, here are multiple entry points, easy access, that need filling.

He sighed loudly. "I'm not *kidding* you, Alison. Osiria has commanded me to take you on a tour of the palace. She wishes for you to see all that is ahead for you."

"Well, why didn't you just say that?" I asked, scurrying off toward the closet. Even though his use of my name made me drip with need, I wanted to see more of the splendor I would receive.

Maldridge was waiting by my door when I emerged from the closet. I chose a devastatingly tight black minidress to pay him back for leaving me hanging.

We left my room and turned down the vast red marble hallway.

"I'll show you the throne room first," he said, leading me toward two enormous, intricately designed black doors. When we got closer to them, they opened on their own.

Maldridge looked back at me as if expecting that to impress me.

"What? The doors are beautiful, but we have automatic doors on Earth too," I said, rolling my eyes.

"The lady isn't impressed. Permit me to endeavor harder to awe you," Maldridge said as we both stepped into the room.

It was made entirely of gleaming black stone, which made the room seem endless. Stairs led up to a dais where a throne sat adorned with red and black diamonds.

"When Clarke arrives, we will gather the court to witness your ascension. You will stand with Osiria there, and I shall be by your side," he said.

"This is more like it," I said as I approached the dais. From far away, the it didn't seem tall, but as I got closer, I had to crane my neck to look up at it.

"Come, lovely, I have more to show you," Maldridge directed.

He walked to the left of the dais, leading me through an archway and down another red marble hallway. He pointed out a small door and told me that was where I'd been held in the dungeon.

"Been there, done that," I said as he turned and walked toward a door farther down the hallway.

We entered a tower that housed a large spiral staircase that extended up and down as far as I could see. We descended until we reached the bottom level.

"This is the laboratory," Maldridge said.

The room at the base of the tower had endless shelves full of bottles containing different-colored liquids. One bottle, filled with purple shimmering liquid, caught my eye, and I tapped on it.

"Do not disturb anything in here," Maldridge scolded. "This is Osiria's laboratory, where she conducts all manner of experiments."

"Fine, but it's weird down here," I complained.

"Your delicate sensibilities will need some fine-tuning, lovely," Maldridge said. "This visit does come with a purpose. I wanted to show you something we've been preparing for your friend."

He opened a large drawer, and in it sat a red gemstone collar. The stones were sharp crystals. The glow of the stones seemed to be calling me. I reached out to touch them.

"I wouldn't if I were you, lovely," Maldridge cautioned. "The stones are quite sharp."

"You're going to put that on Clarke?" I asked.

"Your friend is powerful, and this will render her powerless. We can't risk her making any rash decisions once she's here. We need her compliant," he said.

Imagining the collar around Clarke's neck elicited a strange, unhinged feeling. I didn't hate it.

"Enough about Clarke. When do I get my power?" I complained.

"Lovely, your time will come. I believe Osiria means to deliver your reward in front of Clarke. It will be more impactful if she sees how elevated you are." Opening another drawer, he continued, "And this will be for you."

Inside the drawer was a red jewel-encrusted dagger.

"What's that for?" I asked.

"You'll know when the time comes."

Oh, I knew what to do with it, all right. One of the most thrilling things I'd ever done was plunge that dagger into Heather's chest. I couldn't wait to relive that experience.

CHAPTER 41

Clarke

You know how you try to prepare for a night out? It's more than the look—it's carb-loading and anticipating the right mood and energy level you need for a good time.

No warning or preparation could have primed me for what I saw as we entered Altfevis.

Music came from all around, and bodies writhed in time to the beat. The first thing I noticed was a sage-skinned fae who was wearing a cape made of leaves and pleasuring another fae wearing a sheer dress that resembled electric jellyfish tentacles.

A massive fire pit in the center of the crowd illuminated bodies contorted in countless positions. There was no shame in their pleasure, only joy and freedom. Screams, moans, grunts, and squeals nearly rivaled the volume of the music.

I stopped dead in my tracks as I watched the sage-skinned fae sprout vines from their cape and began teasing every orifice of the fae wearing the jellyfish dress.

A gorgeous fae with purple skin was surrounded by four men. I had read reverse harem books, but those were nothing like seeing it in real life. One was thrusting inside her from beneath, another was pounding her from behind, the third was plunging his dick into her mouth, and the fourth was getting a hand job from her. Her body seemed suspended by magic.

A blue fae's butt cheeks flexed in front of me while he fucked a fae who was bent over on his knees, positively devouring a fae with a crown of lilies in their hair.

I tried not to get turned on. We were trying to pass through unnoticed, but even without fae instincts, the scene before me was better than any porn I had ever seen. It seemed like the display was designed to captivate you, encouraging your desire to be part of it.

A memory of a dream I'd had just weeks earlier flashed through my mind: *Strong, callused hands grasped my face, and beautiful jewel-green eyes lit with adoration. Sweet kisses and languid strokes awoke my senses. The head of his thick cock teased my entrance as we both moaned at how ready I was for him. As he entered me with a thrust, my eyes flew open at the shock of the stretch in my body. It was the best feeling I'd ever felt. His face came into full view as his dark hair curled around his eyes and sweat dotted his brow. Lachlan stared back at me in awe.*

I was pulled out of the dream memory when a large fae bumped into me. I couldn't believe I'd replaced a face from a previous erotic dream with Lachlan's. I would be mortified if he knew where my mind had just gone.

I like you more than I should permit myself to do so.

Ugh. The throbbing I had been ignoring between my legs kicked up. Why did he have to say that? It was better when he was ignoring me because I could ignore him and all the things my bitch of a vagina and simpering heart were feeling.

"Ooof." I winced when I heard Lachlan and realized he was the fae who had bumped into me. The others continued walking ahead, and I had forgotten he was behind me.

Fuck!

I spun around to apologize, hoping that nothing happening in my mind was visible on my face.

My eyes swept over Lachlan's hulking form. He was tall, strong, and … hard. Holy big dick energy. I wasn't the only one affected by what we were seeing. And was he looking at my boobs?

Luck had helped me get dressed in a colorful gown made up of gauzy shafts of fabric and some that looked like burlap but were soft. The dress was tied at the waist with a golden rope belt. I felt pretty and feminine in the colorful, deep V-neck dress, and my boobs were extra perky in it.

So much for not ogling the drop-dead gorgeous fae in front of me. It was kind of hard not to when he was blatantly staring at me. I cleared my throat.

"I'm up here, big guy," I teased, trying to sound unaffected by him.

"Huh?" Lachlan questioned. "What did you say?" he asked, blinking his green eyes. They were so bright, and up this close, they looked like fine-cut gemstones, each facet sparkling. Was he that affected by my tits? With the amazing assortment of tits on full display, I seriously doubted it. He probably just couldn't hear me over the loud music.

"Nothing," I said, leaning in so he could hear me better. "Let's catch up with the others."

Lachlan nodded and did something I didn't expect. He took my hand and laced our fingers together. The calluses of his fingers brushed mine. Damn it! Now the faceless man from my dream had the same callused hands as Lachlan. This was getting ridiculous.

"So you won't get lost in the crowd," he explained, his words whispered in my ear, sending a shiver down my spine. Once I recovered from my shock, I allowed him to take the lead.

Despite my distraction, I had to admit that Altfevis was the ideal place to hide in plain sight. Everyone seemed to be drunk on lust, and their attentions were otherwise occupied. I sighed with relief as I spotted the backs of our companions, thankful I had not gotten us too lost.

They turned right, and we followed. The area was peppered with tables and lanterns swaying in the night on shepherd's hooks. At a bustling bar, bartenders were slinging drinks faster than my eyes could keep up. Smaller flying fae were delivering them.

Giant mugs were thrust into our hands by servers who were barely dressed. The liquid in the mugs bubbled and sloshed as the crowd jostled us.

I took a small taste. The bubbles from the drink were so loud in my ears that I could hear them charging across my tongue and leaping down my throat. They sounded like a thousand hands clapping. My newly awakened senses were slowly beginning to present themselves. It didn't happen all at once, just short, violent bursts that kept taking me by surprise.

Once the bracelets were off, I hoped my senses would become a steady rhythm that I would somehow get used to.

I was mid-second-sip when a hand clasped my forearm.

"Drink this one slowly," Lachlan cautioned.

Up ahead, Leora signaled for us to continue following her to an alcove away from the bar.

We gathered in an empty tent at the end of the alcove. I exhaled with gratitude. We were here; we had made it. We were so much closer to reaching Alison, and I could finally relax after the erotic energy outside.

I peeked out the flap of our tent while the others began to discuss our next move. I had been too stunned by the sight of so many fae unabashedly having sex in public to fully appreciate how enchanting everything was.

Giant multicolored tents stretched as far as my eyes could see. Some were the size of circus tents, and some were smaller, camping-sized tents, but none looked like any I had ever seen. I could see a fog rolling through, covering everything and obscuring my view. Maybe the fog was laced with the fae drugs everyone had told me about.

Before we'd reached the edge of Altfevis, I'd tried to steal myself, look unbothered, and mask the nerves that were bubbling up. My hand instinctively reached up and touched my mom's necklace. I had talked a big talk about being able to handle their orgy party, but my mask was slipping. I wasn't judging anyone for what was happening—quite the opposite. I was envious of how free they all were, and just a bit overstimulated and overwhelmed.

As if sensing where my thoughts had strayed, Haywood made his way to my side and grasped my hand, squeezing reassuringly. His hand was warm and soft as it grazed my skin. He and Lachlan were so different in so many ways. Haywood's touch no longer made me shiver.

I pulled my hand away from his and smiled reassuringly.

"Are you okay?" Haywood asked. "We can try to find another path if this is too much for you."

"Haywood, I'm fine. You said it yourself; this is the quickest route to Alison. I won't let her be in that dungeon for a moment longer."

"You touched your necklace. You do that when you're nervous," he said.

"Stop coddling her, Haywood," Luck said, playfully nudging him on the shoulder as she passed. "She'll be fine.

Altfevis is meant to be fun. You know, that emotion you sometimes feel," she joked. "Or have you forgotten how to do that?"

"I know how to have fun, Luck. But do I need to remind you that we aren't here to have fun? We are here to pass through unnoticed. Fun is not the mission here," Haywood replied.

"Yeah, yeah, I know, but we're also meant to blend in; having *fun* is part of that," Luck persisted.

Haywood grumbled something I couldn't hear while Luck rolled her eyes. Those two were so much like brother and sister.

"I'm going to get us some of the food we passed by. Altfevis always lays out the best feast," Leora said.

"I'll join you," Luck said.

"If you must," Leora replied.

I gulped from the mug I was holding. The liquid tasted spicy, and the bubbles tickled my tongue. I swayed slightly.

"Whoa, Clarke, are you all right?" Haywood asked while moving toward me.

"Yeah, I just got a little woozy. I think I took too big a swig. What is this anyway?" I asked.

"Oh, no, Haywood, she's slurring," Lachlan said, his humor telling me there was no cause for alarm.

"I think I just need to—" I said, trying to sit on one of the large, plush cushions in the tent.

"You're all right, Clarke. You're not accustomed to the strength of the drink. It's mead made from the sulfuric pools on the Obscurus side of Teleran and then infused with a secret ingredient," Lachlan explained.

"The room is spinning. Is the room spinning?" I asked with a hiccup.

"Just close your eyes for a minute," Haywood suggested. "The girls will be back soon with food, and you'll feel better once you have something in your stomach."

"Can't you just, I don't know, heal me or something?" I asked. "You all look fine. Was I poisoned?" I asked, feeling panicked.

"That is highly unlikely, Clarke," Haywood said. "We are fine because we aren't wearing the bracelets. It's a combination of the drink's effects and the bracelets dulling your strengths."

"Fucking bracelets," I slurred. My eyelids became painfully heavy, so I had to close them. My body felt as if I were floating on an ocean, wave after wave rocking me into a deep sleep. A warm blanket fell over me as I let the current carry me into a deep slumber.

CHAPTER 42

Alison

I was woken up in the best way possible—a gorgeous man was lapping at my clit like it was his job.

Yesterday, Maldridge took me on a tour and showed me Osiria's creepy-ass laboratory full of weird-ass glowing bottles. At least I got to see the throne room.

A pillow was shoved into my face.

"You know, when you scream like that, it makes me think you want to get caught," Maldridge said while thrusting two fingers into my swollen pussy. I cried out again as the pillow bore down harder. "Ride my hand, lovely; take what you want from me."

"I want you," I pleaded.

"And you have me, lovely," he said, smacking my pussy with his other hand. Then he nibbled on my throbbing bud, and I exploded again. Was it possible to die from having too many orgasms?

"You know," I panted, "I meant your dick."

"I've had to take you quickly before. This time, I want to feast and devour you completely," he said. "Osiria has business elsewhere, so her tower is abandoned."

"If her tower is abandoned, why are you covering my mouth with the pillow?"

"Why indeed," he said, hurling the pillow across the room before replacing it with a passionate kiss. "I want your screams now, my lovely. I want you to rattle this tower with them."

"And I want you to give me something to scream about, *lovely*," I said with a challenge.

He pinned my wrists above my head, and I felt cold metal encasing them.

"What the—" I said, realizing I was now handcuffed to the headboard. A wave of anticipation washed over me. I'd always wanted a little BDSM action in the bedroom but hadn't found a worthy partner yet.

"I'm going to fuck your mouth until your pussy is dripping for me, and then I'm going to fuck your tight cunt until it's overflowing with my cum," Maldridge informed me.

Well, damn, and yes, please.

"Promises, promises," I teased.

Maldridge smacked my pussy again as I squealed. Did he think that was a deterrent? If he kept doing that, I was going to cum again.

He brought his dick to my mouth, already dripping with precum. I licked my lips in anticipation. I couldn't wait to taste his salty skin.

He grabbed my hair and held it in his hands, positioning his cock at my waiting mouth. He barreled inside as far as he could go and started to relentlessly pump his hips to a brutal rhythm.

Tears streamed down my face as I gagged on his cock. I swirled my tongue, and he growled, pulling my hair so hard that I felt some of it break.

Usually, I had a no-hair-touching policy, but he felt so good that I didn't want him to stop.

Just as I could feel his cock pulsing, signaling his release was close, he pulled out of my mouth.

I whimpered in protest.

"I want to fuck these glorious tits and cum all over them," he explained.

Oh, yeah, I so wanted that.

His dick was sandwiched between my breasts, and he slipped through them a few times before hot cum shot over them and the lower part of my face.

I licked my lips and looked up at Maldridge. He looked like a feral beast, and I loved it.

He didn't bother cleaning either of us up. He just grasped the back of my neck and delved his tongue into my mouth. I found it so erotic that he was tasting his own release that coated my face.

I felt his cock tease my pussy as I rocked my hips in invitation.

He slipped inside, and we both cried out.

The soreness I'd felt from the other night was still present, but the pleasure far outweighed the pain.

"Keep your eyes on me, lovely," he commanded.

My eyes flew open, and I saw Maldridge coat two of his fingers with his saliva. Excitement quaked through my body.

"I'm going to stretch your tight hole, lovely, and then I'm going to fuck it," he said.

"Fuck yes," I responded. "You can do whatever you want to me, Maldridge."

He circled my hole with his wet fingers and slowly stretched it open. I felt so full; his dick was still thrusting into my pussy while his fingers pumped into my ass. I was wetter than I had ever been.

When I was a panting mess, Maldridge withdrew his cock from my vagina and repositioned himself. I'd enjoyed a little ass play before but hadn't gone all in. This magic man made me want to try everything that existed. The pleasure he extracted from me was world-shifting.

As he pushed inside me slowly, inch by delicious inch, I was so elated that I'd waited to do this until now. With

Maldridge, it was everything I'd ever imagined it would be. My orgasm started to build again.

When his dick bottomed out, he bellowed loudly. I screamed as he started pounding it in me. His entrance had been slow, almost painfully slow, but now that he was in, the pace was ruthless.

I was writhing around, and my wrists were aching from the handcuffs, but I'd never felt more alive.

Maldridge reached between us and stroked my clit as he thrust into me one last time. We both came. I screamed his name, and he leaned over me and bit my neck, hard.

I let out a sound I didn't think I'd ever made before as my release crested once more.

Maldridge was definitely worth killing Heather over, and with my power still to come, I was finally getting everything I deserved.

PART THREE

Aurantia

CHAPTER 43

Clarke

I woke to a dull thrumming in my left temple. Last night was hazy at best, but the hollowness I felt was a telltale sign that I had overindulged. Flashes of fractured memories stormed through my already-pounding head. It was like watching a movie filled with someone else's words and actions, someone who had my face but nothing else that resembled who I thought I was.

What was that stupid phrase Alison always said after a night of drinking? *A sober man's thoughts are a drunk man's words.* It had seemed like utter bullshit to me. Most of the time, after drinking and "blacking out," the retellings of my shenanigans sounded nothing like me. Too much alcohol always made me feel things I truly didn't feel; I cared about things I genuinely didn't care about, and when she recited that phrase, I often felt offended. I knew my own mind, damn it. Drunk Clarke had memories and notions that were nothing like Sober Clarke.

Another wave of nausea ran through my body, pebbling my arms with chill bumps. My skin was damp with sweat, and I smelled like a distillery. And my anxiety was back, buzzing and harsh.

The bracelets on my wrists burned, and the skin underneath was turning raw. I knew their significance, but I had been training. Wasn't I ready to take those things off?

"Clarke?" Haywood asked. I felt a cool cloth on my forehead.

"What happened?" I asked.

"You drank Obscurus mead on an empty stomach and passed out," Lachlan answered. "It happens to the best of us."

"I can't open my eyes," I groaned. "They feel like they have little weights on them."

"We have time. Keep them closed. Rest if you can. You'll feel better. We will pack up and head out soon, but not until you're ready," Haywood said.

"I'm fine; I can get up," I said as I attempted to sit up. I swayed, and strong arms caught me.

"Clarke, please lay back down," Haywood said. "It's still daylight, and we are waiting until dusk to leave."

"Yes, Leora and Luck are scouting the perimeter to ensure the path is clear," Lachlan agreed.

"Fine, but don't let me sleep too long," I said with a yawn.

CHAPTER 44

Luck

Once Clarke recovered, we traveled north from Altfevis on foot for the two day walk toward the place that forged me into the fae I was today, the Guild of Shadows.

The Guild was located in the center of Teleran, north of Altfevis. The closer we got, the more I could feel the hot Obscurus air, and the trace amount of mist that filtered past the border grew redder than the pink of the Estival side.

A thrill ran through me. Though training had been harsh at times, I couldn't wait to see some of my old instructors. I was proud of that place and who I had become there. I imagined that returning after so long would ground me somehow, reminding me of how far I had come.

I was excited to show Haywood and maybe Leora what many fae rarely saw. The Guild of Shadows was where the Estival and Obscurus became lethal and had become my home.

We approached close to twilight, and I couldn't see any lights illuminating the dormitory that lay to the right of the main building, but maybe they'd implemented an earlier curfew than the last time I had been here. Still, I hastened my steps, alarming thoughts racing through my mind as I took lead of our crew. No one spoke, but tension rippled through my companions. Worry and trepidation built as I approached the large ornamented wooden doors to the Guild of Shadows main hall.

I reached for the handle.

"Wait!" Haywood cautioned, but I opened it anyway.

A metallic scent filled the air, and the room was dark. A faint light appeared behind me, and I could make out a fog that had settled inside. I assumed Leora had conjured her fae light.

The Estival and Obscurus all had specific elemental magic, but some of the most powerful of us had unique skills. She was the only fae I knew who could fashion weapons with her water magic, and she could cast a small ball of light whenever she wished. I was envious of that trick, though I had a plethora of my own courtesy of my training.

As soon as my eyes adjusted, I blinked heavily, not understanding what I was seeing. Deep in my soul, I wished that the drugs from Altfevis were still in my system or that what I was seeing was a morbid new training exercise. But, deep down, I knew neither of those things were true.

Bodies littered the path through the main hallway. Others lay across chairs and desks lining the expansive room's sides. They had varying wounds, but all appeared to have been killed with a sword or dagger. Heads of dark and light hair were crusted with blood, and one body was halfway through one of the stained-glass windows as if they were trying to escape.

They'd been ambushed. The most cunning and alert fae were caught by surprise.

The fog I had seen was red like the mist of the Obscurus.

A growl of rage and fury tore through my throat as I turned and launched myself at Lachlan. My rational mind knew he hadn't done this, but the evidence pointed to Obscurus assassins. My body moved on its own accord, seeking revenge on the nearest person tied to the filth.

I palmed my dagger, ready to throw, but it never left my hand. Instead, a strong force intercepted me and hurled me backward. My back collided with the hard stone of the wall, and pain I didn't feel vibrated through me, causing my rage to explode. I directed my fury toward the fae who'd halted my need for retribution.

I conjured a tornado of water full of icy daggers and directed them toward Leora as hot tears poured from my eyes. Instead of being ripped to shreds by my power, the tornado dissolved into a mist of steam in front of Leora. I turned to see Clarke, her hands raised. She'd evaporated my attack with her fire magic.

When the steam cleared, instead of the anger I expected to see reflected in Leora's amethyst eyes, I saw understanding and concern.

Pain stabbed through my knees, and I realized that I had collapsed onto the floor. I braced myself with my arms and wretched with sobs, heaving through each one, gasping for the air that wouldn't come.

Everyone I had ever cared about, the people who helped me become me, the adolescents that had been here training, the place I had been sent to after my world had been ripped from me, all gone, crumbled, destroyed.

Hands came around my body in an embrace. I expected to smell Haywood's scent of his beloved human weed and floral smell, but instead, I smelled juniper and crisp linen. Leora …

It was the closest she had let herself get near me since everything had gone to shit. I sobbed even harder.

"We must find out who did this and make them pay," Leora said.

"It's obvious who did this," I replied angrily. "The red mist is here. The room is thick with it. The Obscurus did this."

"That much is apparent, Luck, but it could be any one of them," Haywood replied. "I'll look around for more evidence." Ever the investigator. His false role on Earth hadn't been a stretch. His investigative skills were among the reasons Solana had wanted him at her side in the first place. His ability to dissect a scene or situation and see through veils of mystery was unparalleled. His sense of smell for magical signatures or specific scents made him useful in apprehending culprits of varying crimes.

Clarke and Lachlan had remained silent but stood close to where I had collapsed on the floor.

I looked at them both.

"I'm so sorry. I don't know why I attacked you, Lachlan. I just …"

"It's okay," Lachlan said warmly.

I tried to stand, but Leora held me firmly while turning me in her arms to face her. "We need to get you out of here. Can you stand?" she asked, her face still the mask of perfect fae stillness, but her amethyst eyes glinted with unshed tears.

"Yes, I think I can," I said, using her to steady my weight as I rose. My legs were still shaky, so I allowed her to assist me to the door.

I kept my eyes forward. While I was no stranger to death, the images I had seen would haunt me for the rest of my existence. I didn't need to see them a second time.

My training kicked in, sobering the hysteria that had taken over with my anger and grief. My mourning transformed into determination. The Guild deserved justice.

When we left the great hall, I turned toward the dormitories.

"We need to check the dormitories," I said reluctantly.

"We'll go check," Clarke spoke up, gesturing for Lachlan to follow her. "You stay with Leora and catch your breath." Lachlan fell in step beside her without a word.

"Here," Leora said while shoving a flagon of water toward me.

"Do you have anything stronger?" I asked, my voice sounding as hollow as I felt.

"I do, in fact," Leora said with a tilt to her lips. She pulled a flask from her pack.

I took a drink, and the smoky caramel flavor of my favorite whiskey warmed my soul. I blinked at Leora in surprise.

"Why do you have this?" I asked.

"You weren't the only one who loved this stuff," Leora answered.

This was the first time she'd even vaguely acknowledged our time together. Mostly, she acted like it had never happened. It wasn't just that she had the whiskey or even that she liked it, but the memory of what it represented. It had been at the forefront of everything we'd shared. The very first time we'd made love had been after we'd split a bottle of it.

It was only later I realized it'd been to calm our nerves before crossing that line.

We'd crossed and abolished that line, and I had thought we'd done it happily. It wasn't until later that I realized everything between us had been one-sided—that what we had shared had been her passing the time.

But she had the whiskey. She'd held me, and a tiny ember of hope bloomed in my chest before I'd even taken a sip. Perhaps it wasn't all one-sided after all. She hadn't even tried to hide the whiskey from me just now.

Was this her way of telling me she remembered? Did she think about the nights we'd spent tangled in each other's bodies, when we'd tasted and explored for hours on end?

"Felicity, I …" Leora started. And when I immediately didn't stab her in the eye for using my given name, her purple eyes darkened, and she reached for me.

The haze of desire lifted as leaves crunched, signaling the return of Clarke and Lachlan. Haywood had also emerged from the Great Hall. I cleared my throat and faced them.

"What did you find?" I questioned, their grave faces telling me everything their delayed response didn't. "No," I whispered, backing away. If they didn't speak it aloud, then it wouldn't be true.

Heaviness and grief towed my soul down to the deepest and darkest fathoms of despair. Fae of all ages were in those dormitories.

Who could have done this? Hadn't peace reigned for eons in Teleran? We'd had no war to speak of—nothing in the histories that told of anything other than the unrest. There hadn't even been murder or retaliation between the Estival and Obscurus since Solana and Osiria took their positions. They'd declared peace, and that peace had been held. Hadn't it?

Did this have something to do with magic weakening and Teleran slowly merging with Earth? Was this the work of vile humans? Had the barrier been broken down enough for their death machines to make it through?

It wasn't possible, not yet anyway. Teleran was still only accessible through the portals, and there wasn't any portal close to the Guild. That's why it'd been built there in the first place. It was essentially in neutral territory, almost smack-dab in the middle of both fae sides. It wasn't even an Estival-only establishment. All fae were welcome if they possessed certain abilities and raw talents aligning with the Guild.

Clarke and Lachlan were speaking with Haywood, their mouths moving with sounds I couldn't hear. The ringing in my ears had returned, and warm hands gripped my shoulders tightly. I was again stunned by who was seeking to comfort me. Leora.

All of this was too much. My sorrow, my stupid hopeful heart, and my rage. The rage was blinding and all-consuming, giving new strength to my limbs.

My voice sounded like someone else as I spoke through an angry snarl. "We will find those responsible for this, and I vow not to rest until they are ground into dust beneath my boots."

As we left, I looked back at the Guild and pulled my cowl up.

I was the last surviving member of the Guild of Shadows. They had sought to destroy us, but they made one grave mistake: They'd left me alive.

CHAPTER 45

Haywood

Grief and anguish had swallowed up my friend. As we made our way toward the bog on the outskirts of the Obscurus, Luck was a shadow of quiet rage.

In her silence, I could see her mind racing with the promise of retribution and death. I knew she was capable, having trained for years with the Guild. She was now the sole survivor of the order, something I was still struggling with. In truth, we were all grieving. The dead were Estival and Obscurus, and the adolescents were those we'd all sought to protect.

The thought that someone in Teleran was not only capable of murdering the Guild but also had the strength to do so was overwhelming. They were a formidable host.

Other than the *how* there was also the *why*. Why destroy the Guild?

I'd found scraps of black lace around the door of the Great Hall, caught in the scattered wood. I'd taken a sample and placed it securely in my pocket. It wasn't that black lace was rare in Teleran, but it was the only material evidence I had. Even the magical signatures were masked somehow.

The red mist suggested an Obscurus was involved, but I couldn't begin to fathom how or why. Granted, our two kinds didn't get along, but we didn't kill each other. The Obscurus were different from us, rough and rugged, while the Estival were more composed and refined. It caused strife and a few brawls here and there, but murder?

Teleran wasn't just physically crumbling; everything I knew to be true seemed to be withering as well. My magic had diminished further. I felt close to burnout conjuring a small drop of water.

"Are you okay?" Clarke asked, her voice full of kindness and concern, which tore a hole straight through my heart. She was touching me, looking at me with those deep, verdant wells. Even though we had established a friendship, I still loved her.

I moved from her grasp. "As okay as any of us are." That was the only response I gave her as I walked toward the front of our party.

After the gruesome scene we had all witnessed, I felt hollow. I hadn't known any of the victims personally, but an ache had taken up residence, compounding my already present guilt.

Could all of this tragedy have been avoided if I had just been honest? Maybe Osiria wouldn't have taken Alison. Perhaps the cracks in our world would be fewer.

What had happened to the Guild wasn't simply a massacre; it was *erasure*. Someone wanted them wiped out, and I feared that by the time I discovered the culprit, the knife would already be at my throat.

CHAPTER 46

Clarke

An unspoken agreement had settled over our group. My training was over for now. Instead, we walked in silence toward the misty bog.

We were nearing our final destination. Finally, we'd rescue Alison, and I'd get her the hell out of here before Earth and Teleran merged further.

With the quickly approaching Armageddon, we needed this mission to go as smoothly as possible. So much was at stake.

As we got closer to the Obscurus side of Teleran, the ground became dry and brittle, and the air was humid, like August in Charlotte. The rotten egg smell was pungent as we approached the bog. Much to my surprise, the bog was not a marsh but a lava field dotted with sharp obsidian rock jutting out at menacing angles and sulfuric pools that could probably dissolve any living thing that fell into them.

The red mist thickened, and I couldn't conceal my worry. My burning eyes met Haywood's worried gaze. His expression mirrored my own. Where was this path Lachlan spoke of, and did we need chainmail to protect us from the sharp rocks?

The heat was almost unbearable, and the burn from the Vincula bracelets was acute and searing, like they were fighting the power inside me even more here. I felt weak, and my body felt heavy as if gravity were more severe.

"We are going through that?" Luck asked. It was the first time she had spoken since we'd left the Guild. Though it wasn't much, it was good to hear her voice again. I also shared her concern. The terrain in front of us was covered in a menacing, thick red fog.

"We are," Lachlan answered, his voice calm.

Leora stepped ahead, assessing the landscape.

"I know you're used to leading, General, but if you attempt to carve out your own path, the terrain will carve you up instead," Lachlan said. He loved baiting Leora, and their power struggle had become playful.

"In this instance, I will defer to you," she returned. "Now, be a good dog and sniff out the correct route."

"This way," Lachlan said, gently taking my forearm as he led me toward an opening I hadn't seen.

As I passed through the mist for the first time, I was thankful that it didn't alter my mind like the drugs at Altfevis had. The red fog was so thick that you could barely see through it.

The path itself was narrow, and the ground was a mix of dark gray, black, and red lava rock. Our group was cautious and quiet as we squeezed through the dangerous path.

Clarke.

I turned to see who had whispered my name but saw only Haywood's masked face. His mouth was covered from the cowl he wore to protect him from the fumes that could be deadly to the Estival. His eyes creased with a smile, and I grinned back. Weird, I could have sworn I'd heard my name.

About an hour into our trek, Lachlan glanced back at me and said, "We are about halfway through. I suggest we pause here a moment to hydrate and solidify our plan."

"You want to stop here?" I questioned, gesturing to the boiling sulfur springs surrounding us.

"Only for a moment," Lachlan said, handing me a flagon of water. I gulped it down. Through my fear of being impaled on one of the sharp rocks or burned alive by lava, I hadn't realized how parched I was.

"I know you said that Haywood was to accompany you to Osiria's chambers, but I will say again, I am more suited to this task," Luck said.

Haywood stepped up. "I think she may be right, Lachlan. You know the way, but she can conceal you both with her shadows if needed."

"Then it's settled," Leora said. "Haywood and I will take Clarke through the dungeons to find her friend."

"Agreed. I would be honored to have the shadow at my back," Lachlan said. "The path splits ahead. Luck, you and I will take the right path to the servant's entrance of Osiria's tower, where her chambers are. Leora, Haywood, and Clarke will take the left path. It will lead you to stairs that descend underground. There, you will find a concealed door to the cells. It is commonly unguarded, but be wary. Do not assume safety in this place; keep your guard up. Past this point, try not to speak, as our voices could carry on the fog, and we will be found out before we have any chance at success."

"Be safe," I whispered to Lachlan.

"Always," he whispered back.

. . .

I gasped despite myself as the hulking palace came into view. After we'd split off from the others, Leora had taken the lead as Haywood, and I trailed after her.

Aurantia was jarringly beautiful, like a giant dragon come to life. Its walls were a red scaly stone, likely as indestructible as dragon scales. Spires jutted up toward the swirling black sky like talons. The walls were high and winding like a barbed tail, and the lava flows were like fire from the dragon's jaws. The gates protected it like menacing wings.

Haywood took my hand, and I blinked as he leaned closer. "The stairs are just ahead," he whispered. My hand was clammy from nerves and the heat, but I was thankful for how stable his touch made me feel.

I was about to enter an underground dungeon. I should've been scared, but I wasn't. I was going to save Alison. We were so close now; I almost couldn't believe it.

The relief I felt when I saw the door Lachlan had described was immense. We were here.

Grunts sounded ahead from Leora as she attempted to open the door.

"I tried using a strong wind to open it, but it won't budge," she explained.

"What about water?" I asked, not sure what it could do against the lock or the wood.

"I tried that too, but it's so hot here, it keeps turning to steam," Leora said.

"Clarke, could you try melting the lock?" Haywood asked, still holding my hand.

"I can try," I said.

I carefully maneuvered in front of Leora and placed my hands on the doorknob. It was hot to the touch, but it didn't burn me. I closed my eyes and imagined the lock melting from where it was secured.

When the lock fell away, I pushed the door with my other hand. It creaked and groaned but gave away as it opened to reveal a vast cavern. The three of us entered, and dread was a weight in my stomach. We were finally here, but I hadn't considered the size of the dungeon until now.

How were we going to find Alison in here without getting caught ourselves?

I clutched my mother's necklace, wishing it could somehow guide me to the correct floor.

Clarke.

The melodic voice from earlier whispered to me again. This time, it was clearer, and I didn't mistake it for one of my friends. The magic in that place was cruel, for it had conjured the gentle caress of my mother's voice. It was a prison, though, and likely inflicted mental torture on anyone unfortunate enough to end up there.

I just hoped we weren't too late. Alison had to be okay; I couldn't accept another option.

Phantom screams and moans filled my ears, the ghosts of people who'd suffered and died in this place. The hair on my arms stood up. It was almost too much to imagine Alison in a place like this.

The smell of sulfur worsened. Mildew and mold hung heavy in the air as we moved farther inside the cavern.

Cell after cell was empty. I don't know what I imagined, but to not see anyone else imprisoned here was peculiar.

We were going off instinct, making sure to remain quiet. Any word we muttered to one another would've echoed off the spiraling chamber, and we'd immediately be caught.

Just as I was beginning to feel defeated, we turned right, and a flash of blonde hair pierced the corner of my eye. I motioned to Leora and Haywood, and they followed me.

I shuffled toward the golden beacon; it had to be her. Leora and Haywood were on my heels as we reached the cell.

She was curled up in a ball, facing away from the cell door. She looked so small and dirty.

I crouched down to be level with her, reached through the bars, and touched her shoulder gently.

"Alison?" I called softly as I rocked her.

Her body stirred awake, and she turned toward me.

But the face that came into view wasn't Alison, but a woman smiling cruelly at me. I could see she didn't have a tongue through her gnashed teeth. *What the fuck?* I thought as she grabbed my wrist and dug her nails into my skin hard enough to draw blood.

"We've been expecting you, Clarke," drawled a honeyed voice from behind me, one that I didn't recognize.

I stood slowly and turned, then horror seized my body. Haywood and Leora were being held by black-veiled women, daggers pressed against their throats. The fear I saw in Leora's eyes made my legs quake. If she was afraid … Haywood's eyes begged me to run.

I can't leave you, I told him with mine.

Sorrow lit his eyes when he realized I wouldn't.

The stranger who'd spoken stepped into the light. He was beautiful, like the rest of the fae, and dark skinned. He extended his hand to me. His gesture was friendly, his eyes giving nothing away, but I knew whoever he was, he was the most dangerous person I had ever met.

I did the only thing I could. I let him take my hand. I couldn't let them hurt my friends. I hoped my compliance would buy us time. Lachlan and Luck had to be successful.

"As I said, my lady," he said, bowing slightly, "we have been expecting you. I would caution you not to delay the inevitable. My sovereign does not treat kindly with those who keep her waiting."

I was going to meet the sovereign of the Obscurus. After everything I'd heard about her, I would've been an idiot not to be afraid.

After the veiled women shoved Haywood and Leora into cells, I was led out of the dungeon into what I assumed was the bottom of one of the large spires.

Haywood screaming my name over and over rang in my ears.

As we climbed, I felt dizzy from the spiral staircase. I wanted it to end to regain my equilibrium, but I was terrified of what waited at the top.

When the stairs ended, I saw an enormous hallway that seemed endless.

"Who are you?" I risked asking.

"I am Maldridge, my lady," he said as he opened the door to our left and held it open for me.

Inside was a huge, ornate room.

"What is this?" I asked.

"You stink," he answered, wrinkling his nose. "A shower awaits you. Then these lovely ladies will help you dress. We've picked out something special for you to wear," he said.

"What the fuck do I care if I stink? I'm not getting dressed up for your sovereign. I'm not doing anything until I know my friends are safe," I said, resisting.

The fae smiled, but it didn't reach his amber-colored eyes.

"If your concern lies with your friends, I suggest you do as I say. What you do next will determine their fates. And I don't just mean the friends in the cells below."

I ground my teeth so hard I felt something pop. Did he mean Alison or Lachlan and Luck? I had to do this for all of them.

"Fine."

"I'll be back to collect you in an hour. And as I said—"

"Your sovereign doesn't like to wait. Got it."

"My lady," he said, bowing his head again and exiting the room.

CHAPTER 47

Lachlan

"It's this way," I directed Luck as we made our way through the labyrinth of the tower that housed Osiria's chambers.

It was eerily quiet, but I wasn't normally here when Osiria was not. My office and apartments were in another part of the palace.

"There are no guards," Luck pointed out, sounding suspicious.

"I did say there was a chance there wouldn't be, didn't I?" I replied. "But you're right. Something is off."

As we approached the library, dread settled in my gut.

"We're here," I said, gesturing to the library's double doors.

As the doors opened, I felt it. Osiria's power signature pulsed through the room.

"Luck, run," I said as I turned to her, but she was … gone. She'd retreated to the shadows.

I left the doors open as I entered, just in case Luck was outside. She'd either witness whatever was about to happen, or she'd witness my death.

In any case, she could warn the others. I had known it; I had known Osiria would be ten steps ahead of us, but I had foolishly let myself hope. I took a breath and squared my shoulders, ready to face my fate.

"Hello, Lachlan," my sovereign cooed. I lifted my eyes to Osiria. Next to her was a stunning blonde.

CHAPTER 48

Clarke

I felt numb as the tongueless woman dressed me. I didn't care. It didn't matter what I looked like. We had failed. Lachlan had warned us, but we didn't listen. I had been blinded by my need to save Alison and help my new friends save their world and mine.

Maybe it would be okay? Lachlan had been sent to retrieve me, not murder me. Maybe his sovereign needed me? If she did, I could try to barter for their lives. I could promise to help her as long as she let them go.

It was an objectively lousy plan, but it was all I had.

When Maldridge knocked on the door, I tried to stand up straight and will bravery into my aura. I was a badass fae now—I could fight, I knew how to use my powers (sort of), and if I could get these bracelets off, I could wield some serious damage if I had to. Well, maybe. No one knew for sure how powerful I'd be without the bracelets.

We walked down a red marble hallway toward a set of the most enormous doors I had ever seen. Horns blared, and the doors in front of us opened on their own.

The tall dais crowned with a giant throne told me where we were. Fae lined the sides of the room, creating an aisle that Maldridge led us through. All the fae were clad in black and red. Some gnashed their razor-sharp teeth at me, and others reached out to claw at my clothes. They all oozed with power, but their forms were gaunt and grim as they sneered their disgust.

I averted my eyes. I felt like I was being marched to my death.

When the crowd parted, I gasped.

"Alison!" I said, running to her, but Maldridge grabbed my arms and held me back.

Alison stood tall in a red velvet floor-length gown with a neckline so low I could almost see her belly button. She looked incredible. To her right, Lachlan stood in chains. His ashen face was bruised and bloody. I didn't see Luck and wasn't sure if that was good or bad. Fear was like a vice around my heart.

"Clarke, you're finally here," Alison said, her voice sounding cold, nothing like herself. What had they done to her?

"I came for you like I promised," I said, my voice shaky.

As a hush fell over the room, my voice echoed loudly. The clicking of heels reverberated like the ringing of a death bell. Something or someone ominous was coming, and the fear in the room was palpable.

From behind the enormous diamond-encrusted throne, a tall figure cloaked in a baroque, hooded cape emerged clutching a glass jar full of a shimmering purple substance.

As the hood fell back, I felt like my heart stopped and exploded all at once—like I was seeing a ghost. Somehow, I knew it was really her. Alive. Right here.

Osiria was my Mom.

CHAPTER 49

Clarke

The woman standing in front of me was more beautiful than I had ever seen her. Or perhaps more *refined* was the word. Her hair and eyes were ebony black instead of the warm brown my mother had in my memories. Her lips were a shade of crimson that matched the room's decor. Her gaze was indifferent as she looked out at the crowd. I shivered as her eyes reached me.

So many times, I had begged, wished on every birthday candle, and pled with whatever entity was listening that I could somehow see her again. But this was a cold and callous representation of the mother I knew.

My mother was here, in Teleran, *alive*. I started shaking with fear or excitement—I wasn't sure which.

"Alison, can't you see your friend missed you? Why don't you explain to her why you're here?" my mother said in a cold and unfeeling voice.

Alison's friend? Did my mother not remember me?

"What's going on?" I asked, hoping for a viable explanation. The pit in my stomach grew deeper as my body started realizing the truth my mind and heart refused to accept.

"Just look at you," Alison said with a smile. "You're in the presence of Osiria, and you look like that?"

Just as I was about to respond, Maldridge threw me to the ground. My knees erupted in pain, and I cried out. He left me there and walked up the steps to stand beside my mother, who still hadn't acknowledged me.

"You're pathetic, Clarke. The way you begged me to be your friend," Alison continued. Her words hit the center of my chest, which still held my mother's necklace. "Gosh, you are so naive. You could never see what was right under your nose, could you?" She looked down on my kneeling form from her position on the raised dais. Still, she must have seen the hurt and confusion in my eyes.

"Didn't you wonder how your shoes were discovered with blood on them?" she asked. I hadn't. In the chaos after Heather's death, I hadn't even stopped to think of the why, only that I needed to prove my innocence and get out of prison. "You never stopped to think about the bloody shoe prints or how the shoes mysteriously ended up in your closet? It was almost too easy. You sleep like the dead. I walked right into your closet and got your shoes, wore them after I killed Heather, and threw them back in your closet, so they'd be easily spotted when the police searched your place."

Each reveal was a shot to my heart. I was fractured and bleeding out, though no wounds were visible. I held my hand to my chest and brushed the jewel of my necklace. Instead of the comfort it usually brought me, the gesture only splintered me further.

"I can see you are still processing, so let me spell it out for you," Alison said. "I. Killed. Heather."

As if it could feel my agony and was responding, the power inside me felt like a caged animal banging at the barriers of my skin. I could hardly bring myself to speak. Grief was a downward spiral of inky black and sharp claws.

"Why?" I croaked. My friend, whom I had loved so deeply and risked everything and everyone to save, only held hate for me in her eyes.

"Why?" she laughed, throwing her head back. "Why? Um, because I could. Because you tried to take what was mine. Because Heather tried to take what was mine."

"What are you talking about?" I asked, rising to my feet, the movement taking my remaining strength.

"Quit playing the innocent card, Clarke. Cody is mine—or he was." Emotion, vitriol, and rage swam in her eyes. She *knew*. She knew Cody was dead. "You tried to take him from me, and now he's dead because of you," she spat.

"Alison, I'm so sorry. I never meant—" I couldn't deny my fault in his death.

"You didn't mean for him to die? Well, I don't forgive you. I won't forgive you, and now, I don't need you. I don't need you to save me. I'm strong, and when you're finally gone, I'll be powerful too, and you'll be nothing. I won't even remember you," Alison said, ripping the last bit of hope I had.

Maldridge retrieved a small, tufted pillow where a dagger rested from behind the throne and walked it over to Alison.

I couldn't take it anymore. My mom wouldn't even look at me.

"Mother!" I cried out. "Look at me!" I yelled.

The crowd gasped at my outburst. She barely turned her head toward me.

Lachlan looked at me, confused and shocked, while something clicked into place.

Realization lit Alison's eyes, and a knowing grin split her full lips. She reached out to take something from the pillow.

But fast as the wind, Maldridge took the dagger from the pillow and dragged it across Alison's throat.

My eyes flashed to Alison. She clutched her throat, her eyes wide, as blood leaked down her body. She attempted to say something as she hemorrhaged her life force onto the black floor.

As I reached for her, the bracelets on my wrists warmed, glowing bright reddish orange. I didn't even feel the molten metal slip from my flesh.

I felt like I had swallowed battery acid. It curdled and ate through my stomach, leaving an empty well, an endless chasm of cold sorrow, vile and deteriorating. Just as quickly, the well filled with ugly desires: retribution, violence, and destruction.

Power sizzled violently through me, itching to be released. I was barely containing it, and apathy was growing. Why not just burn it all to the ground? Nothing mattered anymore.

"Control yourself," I heard my mother say. "Obey me," she boomed as she descended the stairs toward me. Her words only fueled my anger.

Debris from the ground floated up, along with the blood pooling on the floor. It looked like it was raining upside down, raining red.

I closed my eyes as power erupted from me like an atomic bomb. A blinding white light filled the throne room, and a deafening boom rang out. When I opened my eyes, a red mist barrier surrounded my mother, Alison's body, Maldridge, and Lachlan. Everyone else had been reduced to dust. There had been no warning, no screaming, just an explosion, and they were gone. I'd killed all those fae.

I collapsed to the ground. The well of power inside me retreated. Was this what burning out felt like? My friends had warned me, but I had forgotten.

"Clarke!" Lachlan yelled as he tried to move toward me. Maldridge slugged him in the face, and he fell backward, unconscious.

I looked up to see my mother peering down at me, still holding the bottle with the swirling purple substance. A sinister gleam lit her eyes, and she looked pleased. She motioned to Maldridge, commanding him to do something, but her words were muffled. Had the blast damaged my hearing?

My mother reached down toward me. Would she acknowledge me at last?

Instead, she wrapped her hand around my necklace and ripped it from my neck, along with the last shred of who I was.

Maldridge sped toward me, locking a spiked red collar around my neck.

The last ember of my power was extinguished, and I fell to the floor. The pain from the collar barely registered as the spikes pierced my skin. As everything went black, I no longer cared if I ever woke up.

CHAPTER 50

Clarke

When I woke, I sensed I was in the dreary dungeon, but I lacked the strength or will to open my eyes. My neck ached painfully from the collar Maldridge had put on me.

I had never felt smaller or more alone in my life. I had felt helpless many times, but this was so different, and so much worse. How had this happened? How could I feel so close to someone, know and love them so well, and feel so known and loved by them, and then in one action, one dismissal, one look into their empty, pitiless eyes see that none of that had ever been true? How could it happen twofold? Both my mother and Alison?

Was I so starved for love and attention that I willfully chose not to see what was right in front of me? Was Alison right? Had my mother only seemed kind and loving next to my father's wrath? Had I been drawn to Alison because I sensed the same kind of cruelty that, apparently, my mother was capable of? And how was my mother Osiria, the sovereign of the Obscurus, the very woman who'd sent Lachlan to bring me to her? How had she gotten here? When had she gotten here? If she was in Teleran, could my dad be here too?

My desire to fight back was gone—had been obliterated. What had happened to her—to them both?

I knew no words would fix this. Even if they could, I didn't know the right ones and wasn't equipped to use them.

It didn't help that my anger, resentment, and pain were nearly blinding.

I knew for sure only a handful of things now: Alison killed Heather and was now also dead; my mother had ordered it; and my mother was evil.

It was like losing my mom all over again.

My life had been painful enough. There was no reason to add to it. Alison had been the one to help pull me out of that deep depression I had been in.

What was the point? To show me love and joy and then rip it away, all because she held me responsible for Cody's death and had thought I was trying to take him from her? How could any of this be real? What the fuck was happening? I couldn't focus enough to rationalize anything.

I once thought that there was a limit to the amount of pain one could feel in one's life.

When I'd moved to Charlotte, I truly believed that the worst was behind me, that all the pain and abuse I had endured as a child was all I would have to face, and that true happiness was on the horizon.

I realized how foolish that thought had been. Was it my mind's way of helping me cope, ensuring that I moved on and survived?

Alison was right. I *was* such a stupid, naive girl.

Perhaps I would rebuild all the walls around my heart that I had ripped down in an attempt to seize the life I had so longed for. Maybe I would become as hard as a stone like my mother obviously had. As I lay my head on the floor, I willed my body to merge with the stone.

The scent of cedar and cinnamon cut through the stench of the fluids littering the cell floor, and I knew it was *him*.

I didn't turn around as the cell door opened and clanged shut.

When I heard retreating steps, I rolled over and gasped. Lachlan was lying on his side facing toward me, his body beaten, and his face so swollen that even if his eyes were open, I wouldn't be able to tell. He was still in chains.

"Lachlan? Lachlan, can you hear me? Where's Luck?" I asked, my heart racing as tears clouded my vision. He grumbled his response. "Why aren't you healing yourself?" I asked, confused.

His hand twitched slightly, allowing me to notice the silver gleaming bracelets on his wrists. They'd put Vincula bracelets on him, and now he wasn't healing.

After I had melted the Vincula bracelets and exploded, they'd put a collar around my throat before throwing me in here. Whatever it was made of or spelled with worked better than the bracelets had. I'd attempted to heal him myself, but I'd felt nothing, not even a glimmer of power.

I moved to comfort him, but he recoiled from me. Distrust rippled from him.

"I didn't know your sovereign was my mother, Lachlan, I swear," I said.

He only grunted and rolled toward the wall.

Silly me. I didn't think anything was left of my heart to break.

My mother was alive but clearly didn't care if I was. Alison had hated me too, but now she was dead.

Was I any better? In my rage, I had killed every fae in the throne room that my mother hadn't protected with her mist.

My friends had been right to fear me; I was a killer.

EPILOGUE

Heather

When Death dragged me down to the depths of hell and imprisoned my soul in a bottle of shimmering purple liquid, I discovered that Death had a name, and her name was Osiria. I'd heard it first when she'd come down here with her lover, Maldridge. They were crafting something spiky and red.

Her appearance seemed to be ever-changing, easily slipping from one form to another. No longer was she a hooded figure wrapped in shadows. She was now beautiful, terrifyingly so, with black eyes and hair.

Before meeting Osiria, I would've said magic didn't exist. Now, I knew it did. And it pulsed like a heartbeat under this palace in this warped realm full of lies. Sometimes, it would rattle the bottles on the shelf where Osiria kept me. I imagined it was a sleeping giant and that Osiria created mayhem and atrocities to placate it.

No one else seemed to know that I was alive—or whatever the suspended state I was in was called. I was aware of my surroundings and could see. How long had I been down here? A week? Eternity? Time only existed outside of this bottle.

I'd seen Alison once; she'd clinked a pink nail against my glass prison but didn't seem to know I was inside it. Until I saw her in the throne room, I'd thought she'd been an apparition, something Osiria or my own incorporeal mind had sent to torment me. Then I thought Alison was the worst part of this scenario, until they brought Clarke into the throne room.

I had seen Osiria carry a red-jeweled dagger on a pillow and place it behind her throne. Someone was about to die at her hands, and I hoped it was Alison, who stood tall and glorious on the dais with Osiria. I wasn't an evil person. I had never wished for someone's death before and never thought I could take a life, even in self-defense. But seeing Alison gloating and baiting and tearing Clarke to shreds with her words … I can't say I was that upset about Alison's death, especially not after everything I had endured because of Alison.

First, I lost the love of my life. Then she murdered me. Then whatever she was mixed up in had me stuck in a fucking bottle waiting to be bait or leverage against Clarke. Clarke, who was the kindest person I knew, didn't deserve this.

Before Osiria's lover cut Alison's throat, I could've sworn I heard Clarke cry out "Mother" to Osiria, but I had to be mistaken. Clarke's mother was dead.

As Alison lay there bleeding out on the floor, I saw Clarke explode with a deadly force.

Now that Alison was gone, I had a sinking suspicion about Osiria's plan for me. She'd told me she needed me for leverage.

Even though we hadn't been close, I knew Clarke would do whatever she could to help me. I vowed then that I wouldn't do it—whatever Osiria was planning. I wouldn't be used against Clarke if I had any choice left. Clarke was innocent in all this, and if I was ever whole again, I had to help defend her against whatever Osiria had planned for her.

As they carried Clarke away with the beaten man in chains, whom I didn't recognize, Osiria exited the throne room with me in tow. She returned me and my bottle to the shelf, the prison I would reside in for eternity, a penance for every bad deed I'd committed while being alive.

Glowing eyes, warped through the glass, peered at me in my bottle. I wondered how sight was still possible when I didn't have eyes. Osiria had retaken her true form. The beautiful facade was a mask for the rest of the world, but I knew what she really was.

"You've been patient, my dear," she said, addressing me directly for the first time since she'd put me in the bottle. "Of course, you cannot answer me in this state," she continued. "I made you a promise. I trust you remember it. Unfortunately, one pawn had to meet her end, so I am in need of another."

When she stepped out of the way, I saw a body draped in red fabric on the once-empty table in the center of the laboratory. Blonde hair peeked out from the shroud, and there was no mistaking who lay in front of me. I wished on everything I could that Alison's soul would not rest with mine for all eternity.

"You see, my dear, to restore you, I require a body to put you in. As yours was quite ruined and already decaying, I'm sorry to say that I couldn't procure it in time," she said. Dread unfurled in my mind. "As luck would have it, we now have a perfect specimen available for you," she said, touching Alison's dead body. "This one is still warm, so this process should be seamless."

I thrashed in my bottle in protest. *No! No! No!* She couldn't mean to put me in Alison's body. I couldn't fathom living in the skin of someone so evil, who had ruined my life and then murdered me. *I hated her.* I refused to become her.

"You're excited? As am I, my dear. She's nearly perfect, just a small cut at the throat, but I'll repair that. It'll be a small scar, barely noticeable."

Osiria then spoke words I didn't understand, and agony ripped through my soul. Briefly, I felt a release, a sense of freedom to finally pass on and find peace. Then I was violently pulled down, like gravity was trying to suffocate me.

The feeling of falling persisted for a moment, and I heard ringing in my ears. I also felt squeezed, like I'd been forced into clothes two sizes too small. I felt the weight of my eyelids lift as I opened my eyes.

"Take a look, dear Heather," Osiria commanded as she held a gilded mirror above me.

I reached up and touched Alison's face, moving the skin around to try to make sense of what I saw. This was worse than dying, worse than the bottle. This was hell. Perhaps Osiria wasn't death, but the devil.

I clawed at Alison's face and throat. I tore at the flesh, attempting to remove the skin from the bone.

I sobbed and gagged and wretched. My thrashing caused me to roll off the table. I tried to stand, but the unfamiliar legs buckled, and I crashed onto the cold stone ground. As the pain registered, the link between Alison's body solidified.

Vomit that tasted like acidic wine surged as I emptied the contents of Alison's stomach. I choked and sputtered as hot tears ran down Alison's face. I screamed and screamed until Alison's throat was raw and gave out.

I stood again and stumbled into one of the bottled-filled shelves. I whirled around; rage and tears warped my vision, bottles flew across the room, glass shattered, and shards cut my feet. I was crazed, pulling out Alison's hair while I yelped in pain, dragging her long nails down her face as blood dripped.

I wanted to crawl out of this body, and I tried until I had nothing left.

I bent at my waist, breathing labored as I looked up at Osiria with pleading eyes.

Instead of pity, Osiria forced me to look in the mirror again. Alison looked back at me—scared, broken, and destroyed. Hair was missing along her hairline, and blood dripped into her eyes—my eyes.

Osiria waved her hand slowly in front of me, and I watched in horror as Alison's face stitched back together. The face in the mirror was more beautiful than ever—it was perfect and appeared to glow. The hair grew back shinier and fuller than before. Everything was flawless except a faint pale pink line across the throat.

"You can attempt to destroy this body, Heather, but I will continue to mend it. This is where you'll remain, imprisoned in this body until I deem it otherwise."

A Note From Carter

Hey there. How ya' doing? Sorry, not sorry. I had to do it. I really did. A small part of you has to love it, too, right? It had to happen this way, but don't worry. We have time. Maybe Clarke and Heather will get their happily ever after's. To be honest, I really don't know. Or maybe I do. You won't know until the next two books come out. Yes, two. But, Carter, isn't this a trilogy? Strictly speaking, yes. There will be three full-length novels in the Death Book Series and two prequel novellas. Up next is Osiria's back story. Don't you want to know how Clarke's sweet Mommy became the evilest fae in Teleran? You do; you really do. Following that novella, the next and final book of the Death Book Series will tie up loose ends, wreck your heart, and hopefully stitch everything up in a pretty little bow. Only time will tell. Thank you for sticking with me through all the twists and turns. It's been a fun and wild ride, and it's just going to get more fast—more furious. I digress. You guys are the absolute best. Thank you for taking the time to read my book babies.

Acknowledgments

There are so many of you to thank this year. I started writing in 2023, and almost two years later, I have published three books. In less than two years, people. I almost can't believe it. Each and every one of you has contributed to this. Every word of encouragement, every time you invited me to your bookstore or to your event, showed up to said event, took a chance on my book, or told someone about my book—all of this gave me fuel to keep going. You are my inspiration. You guys know who I'm going to thank first. Mr. Carter Pugh. Prior to 2023, he was not a reader, and as soon as I told him what I planned on doing and told him that I would need his help if I had any hopes of being successful, he started reading. He read all of Mother's books, Sarah J. Maas, for those who also worship at her altar. His design talents have always been glorious, but what he's done for my cover art and branding has made the Death Book Series come to life. It jumps out at you, makes people stop and look and ask questions, and compliments the cohesiveness of our brand. He has also become my writing partner—involved in the shaping of this series just as much as I am. He understands how my brain works and helps me bring these stories to fruition. My gratefulness is endless. Secondly, my sister. She is my biggest cheerleader and loves these books. It means the world to me that she is part of this. Next, Melisa Graham. My editor is the best, you guys. I never had to go through any of the nightmare things I hear about editors because I had her from day one. She is simply brilliant, and I'm so thankful to have found her. To Jax Hendrickson for hosting woman's self defense classes in Charlotte and inspiring the scene where Leora trains Clarke. To my indie bookstore friends, I love you all so much. Thank you for bringing me and my books into your space and making us feel at home. Thank you for inviting us to do such cool things and creating a space where indies can thrive. To my author friends, you guys and this community mean more to me than I can tell you. The encouragement you provide is beyond anything I ever hoped for. I can't wait to share success with you all as we realize our dreams together. To my Death Rattlers, your stories, posts, dm, texts…I have no words to accurately describe what they have meant to me. I started this journey with so many wishes, but one of those was that you would see yourself in my stories. I was a lot like Clarke growing up—I was an outcast, a little too weird for my small southern town. Seeing you all relate to Clarke makes me feel like we are not alone in this world. There are more of us who came from struggle that still hope and, yes, still believe that magic exists. Thank you from the bottom of my heart for reading and loving my stories. Your love is while I'll never stop doing this. So much more is coming, and I'm so thankful you are all here, in this space, with me.

Glossary of Terms

Obscurus- dark fae with the power of fire and earth.
Alternae- the elders of the fae.
Estival- light fae with the power of air and water.
Teleran- the realm of the fae
Lesult- earth
Alfmam- fire magic wielder; Nerites
Cielgas- ice magic wielder; Estival
Enstompian- all powerful
Impestuses- power to regenerate after death
Anet Vireo- magic of both light and dark fae
Mae Obires- mate
Mae- love
Fates muciparous- open up
Incataovitia- prophecy
Rafunto- fate
Lifia- daughter
Tamer- mother
Erpta- father
Alstrum- husband/wife/spouse
Rubiroam, Borurami, Amiburro- fuck, various expletives
Cremtnux- shit
Lucamor- oracle
Furrem Mirots- death by iron and darkness
Juanamira- marijuana
Nivos-wine
Enterna-language of the fae

About the Author

Carter Pugh lives in North Carolina with her husband and her puppy son, Cheese. She loves reading fantasy, romance, and sci-fi. Writing has been a love and passion for her most of her life, but she didn't start her writing career until 2023 when she published her debut novel, Death Rattle.

When she isn't reading or writing in her spare time, she loves watching British TV shows such as Escape to the Country and Absolutely Fabulous. Carter's family is from England, and she has always shared a deep love for the country and its culture as a result.

To learn more about Carter and to follow along for more details on future releases, please follow on Instagram (@carterpughwrites) or visit her website (carterpughwrites.com).